# SCIMIDAR

AIRSHIP 27 PRODUCTIONS

Scimidar
© 2017 R.A. Jones

Published by Airship 27 Productions
www.airship27.com
www.airship27hangar.com

Interior illustrations © 2017 Rob Davis
Cover illustration © 2017 Ted Hammond

Editor: Ron Fortier
Associate Editor: Peg Livingston
Marketing and Promotions Manager: Michael Vance
Production and design by Rob Davis

ISBN-10: 1-946183-11-3
ISBN-13: 978-1-946183-11-8


Printed in the United States of America

10 9 8 7 6 5 4 3 2 1

# SCIMIDAR

## BY R.A. JONES

OTHER AIRSHIP 27 TITLES BY R.A. JONES

*DEATHWALKER*

THE JASON MANKILLER SERIES:

(1)  *GUN GLORY*
(2)  *COMANCHE BLOOD*

WITH MICHAEL VANCE

*MOTOR CITY MANHUNT*

# PROLOGUE

When the time nearly everyone feared finally came...the world ended with a bang.

And with a whimper.

The beleaguered planet and the life that crawled upon it didn't actually end, of course. It continued to limp along, though man and nature had consorted to wound it most grievously.

It was no single event that wrought such damage to the globe, but rather an entire series of catastrophic occurrences that brought the Earth and its inhabitants to their knees.

Some mark the beginning of the end as being the day that would come to be called *Red Tuesday.*

That was the day when a relatively small thermonuclear device was detonated in the center of Tel Aviv, Israel. The force of the initial blast, and the buildings it brought tumbling down, accounted for more than 20,000 deaths within a matter of moments of the detonation.

Those closest to Ground Zero were mercifully incinerated before the sound of the blast reached their ears. Those farther out died more horribly; painfully aware if only for a second of limbs tearing away, of gaping holes being torn through their bodies by hurtling debris.

Many died writhing in agony: their ears bleeding from the shock waves even as their insides turned to jelly.

Mortal injuries and raging radiation burns and sickness would continue to raise the death toll by thousands.

The identity of the extremist organization or rogue nation responsible for this carnage was never definitively established. Many tried to claim credit for the atrocity: the Army of Allah, the Christian Soldiers for Armageddon, the Righteous Sons of Zion, splinter groups in nearly every Middle Eastern nation.

It didn't really matter. Enraged and bent on retribution and retaliation, Israel launched virtually its entire nuclear arsenal at *all* of its many enemies. Several of the Muslim countries of the region had already been locked in debilitating armed conflict one against the other for decades, and lacked both the will and resources to continue a cycle of retaliation. As they and their Israeli adversaries were compelled to turn inward and devote themselves to recovery, peace of a sort finally settled over this troubled part of the world.

The peace of the dead.

At nearly the same time, but independent of these events, Muslim extremists finally succeeded in achieving one of their long-sought goals: seizing the reins of power in the country of Pakistan. Doing so placed that nation's nuclear missiles at their disposal.

Fearful of what this development would mean for it, India hastily decided to launch a preemptive nuclear strike against its longtime neighboring enemy. Its strikes were not so rapid, though, as to prevent Pakistan from hurling its own nuclear thunder bolts.

As a result of these two searing, ground-fusing thermonuclear exchanges, the entire Middle East and much of the Indian sub-continent was now grimly referred to as the world's largest mirror.

As if to put a pitiful cap on this nuclear cataclysm, the painfully inept North Korean regime somehow managed to accidentally trigger an atomic warhead in the center of its own capital city of Pyongyang, during a state-sponsored "victory parade." As every one of its ruling members was on hand for the triumphal march, the entire ruling hierarchy of the government disappeared in a blazing instant.

Finally freed from generations of tyranny, poverty and hunger—yet now faced with anarchy and the horrors of a nuclear winter—that country's long-suffering people became a massive wave of refugees that threatened to flood both South Korea and China.

Similar swarms of refugees fleeing from the ravages of two nuclear wars were poised to sink both Europe and Russia under their weight. Such desperate refugees were often met with armed force intended to hurl them back into the radioactive wilderness they had fled.

When central authority in Russia cracked and then broke in the face of multiple crises—both internal and external—that enormous country splintered into half a dozen separate and autonomous nation/states.

The economic impact of these and other catastrophes led to a period of unparalleled hyperinflation; one nation saw loaves of bread selling for the equivalent of a thousand dollars. The entire world economy was brought down in a crash that made the so-called Great Depression of the early 20th Century pale in comparison: dwarfing it by a factor of ten.

This new Depression began with the utter collapse of one of the most robust economies on the planet—that of China—and spread outward like the shock waves from one of the devastating nuclear explosions.

Even before the Crash, a class war had been brewing inside that Asian juggernaut, sparked by the continually growing chasm between its elite handful of billionaires and the tens of millions struggling to survive in soul-crushing poverty. The armed, virulent conflict between the haves and the have-nots that erupted there quickly found sympathizers in Russia, Europe and the Americas.

One early leader of the militantly deprived masses took to calling himself and his followers "*the cake-eaters.*" Their creed and their goal were darkly and terrifyingly simple: kill the rich and take what they own.

These class rebels were instrumental in fomenting a series of food riots all over the globe.

Especially violent were the clashes within what remained of India. A "Caste War" had been brewing there for decades already, and the horrible aftermath of the nuclear war sparked a wave of slaughter virtually unprecedented. The few wealthy who survived both the nuclear holocaust and the widespread murders fled the country, which now resided in a state of egalitarian anarchy.

Further, China's once proud capital city of Beijing now sat nearly empty, a virtual ghost town. All but the poorest and the weakest of its inhabitants had fled from the cloud of life-threatening pollution that had been ignored for far too long. With the addition of fresh and increasing amounts of pollutants and radioactive particulates, a dense black cloud perpetually hung over the city, periodically spilling down showers of acid rain that ravaged structures and melted human flesh.

In Central and South America, drug cartels that had previously been content simply to ignore governments now seized active control of them. National names and borders became meaningless as individual warlords established personal fiefdoms they ruled with bloody iron fists.

These drug traffickers continued to thrive in a world where those without money begged for a cup of rice while those with wealth, even if only a little of it, indulged in the escape from reality that illicit drugs could provide them.

As if in response to all this social turmoil, Nature itself seemed to rebel against mankind. As political and economic chaos roiled, all efforts to slow, control or stop global warming had been abandoned.

In Africa, the already massive Sahara Desert had grown exponentially larger, now encompassing nearly a third of that continent. In South Africa, the Kalahari had similarly expanded its bounds.

In Equatorial Africa, multiple paramilitary "armies" waged war. Most of them were composed of soldiers who had been mere children when initially pressed into service forcibly by various guerilla units.

Eventually, these unwilling, man-made little monsters, upon reaching adulthood, turned on their creators: killing their masters and assuming control of their armies.

These new military forces, varying greatly in size, resources and leadership, waged nearly constant war against the thinly stretched regiments of local governments—and against each other.

The expanding deserts of the African continent resulted in severe shortages of potable water, leading inevitably to a series of regional "water wars."

Around the world, the many natural disasters, and even more so the numerous wars, rebellions and riots had exacted a horrendous death toll unprecedented in all of human history. One contemporary commentator grimly wrote that it was as if the Black Plague, the Holocaust, the purges of Stalin and Mao, the eruptions of Krakatoa and Vesuvius and the asteroid extinction event that wiped out the dinosaurs had all happened almost simultaneously.

In the many places where human corpses in the tens of thousands lay unburied where they fell, disease had become rampant: primarily cholera, but other scourges as well. The enormous number of cases of water and food-borne illnesses became pandemic.

Afflictions that had been virtually eradicated by medical science now experienced a vengeful resurgence. Somewhere in the midst of one of the many armed conflicts, the few remaining vials containing living samples of the smallpox virus were shattered, and that ages-old scourge again plagued the planet.

Medical supplies and those trained in treatment became extremely scarce and wildly expensive, and again the wealthy kept the lion's share of both for themselves. Doctors and nurses in some parts of the world were often kidnapped and pressed into the service of municipalities and even of individuals. What had once been standard vaccinations became luxury items, adding to the numbers of the sick.

Hounded by the apocalyptic horsemen of war, famine and plague, large portions of the Earth's population saw their average life expectancy drop to below forty years of age.

Weather patterns continued to be extreme. Tornadoes, hurricanes, blizzards: all were more widespread, all occurred with increasing frequency and intensity. As if the planet were shivering in fear and fatigue—or trying to shake off the dominant and pestilent life form infecting it—earthquakes wracked the globe.

In America, much of the state of California was nothing but a wildfire-ravaged desert. Coastlines planet wide continued to recede beneath rising ocean tides, radically changing the map of the world. Great expanses of Florida, Scandinavia, Malaysia and Italy simply disappeared. Most of the Netherlands and may island nations were now but waterlogged memories.

A newly militant Japan, emboldened by the domestic turmoil that had compelled China to focus all its attention on domestic problems, and in desperate need of replacing parts of its own land now submerged under water, had again imposed its will on large portions of Southeast Asia, Indonesia and the surviving island nations of the Pacific Rim.

Their expansionist moves went virtually unopposed, save for a notable ongoing and costly resistance to their dominance by rebellious Muslim armies in Indonesia. Accusations of atrocities were leveled against both sides with equal fervor and credence.

Partially in response to this Japanese adventurism, Australia had isolated itself almost entirely from the rest of the world; little news from it had reached the outside in years. Any unauthorized foreign ships or planes approaching the limits of its territorial waters and air space were attacked and destroyed.

The nuclear decimation of the Middle East had eliminated several of the world's principal sources of oil, driving the price of that dark commodity to astronomical heights. Civil wars and natural disasters curtailed other supplies.

Countries that continued to produce crude and refined oil products found themselves exerting enormous influence on the world stage. None begrudged the fraction of their petroleum revenues required to pay for the armies assigned the task of protecting wells and refineries from the many who sought to seize them for their own personal or national interests.

Coal had enjoyed a resurgence in popularity as a source of power and heat, regardless of the harmful impact its use had on the environment. Neither time nor money was wasted on efforts to filter its noxious clouds as they rose above industrialized cities.

In many rural areas in the developing countries, peasants who had no other option for fuel and heat had denuded the forested land. Stripped of the protection of the trees and the grip of their roots, the land turned to dust that every careless breeze hurled into the polluting mix obscuring large parts of the globe. The bare and barren rocky ground left behind was unfit for agriculture.

Many poorer cities were forced by shortages of oil or coal to shut down their power grids completely for as long as half of each day. Even in more prosperous regions, rolling blackouts were not uncommon.

The famines that had become rampant across the face of the globe fueled what was hoped to be no more than rumors or urban legends regarding acts of cannibalism. Even in America, where relative normalcy largely prevailed, stories were whispered of serial killers who feasted upon the corpses of their victims.

At all times in human history there have been instances of humans being treated as no more than another commodity to be bought, sold, traded or stolen. In the face of such widespread deprivation, this activity appeared in the form of sex trafficking and the physical selling of men, women and children into the bondage of slavery. Both trades were widely practiced in this horrible new world order, and largely ignored by what passed for authority.

A mankind that had increasingly turned to technology as its source of salvation, almost developing a form of worship for it, now found itself betrayed by its digital deity.

The various and widely spaced detonations of thermonuclear weapons had unleashed massive electromagnetic pulses that played havoc with electrical devices of all sorts, proving to be especially devastating to those controlled by computers.

Seizing upon this window of opportunity, a loosely knit network of "cyber terrorists" worked en masse to further corrupt all such operating systems by infecting them with debilitating worms and viruses.

Why did they do this? Because they could.

The systems-wide cyber crashes brought on by their insidious efforts caused more widely spread damage than had the actual bombs.

So dependent had most of mankind become upon its tiny god, the computer chip, that it was totally unprepared for what followed.

Power plant grids went offline. Air traffic control failed catastrophically. Police and fire services were heavily impacted. Navigation and flight systems, hospitals, traffic lights: all became unreliable at best.

Cell and broadcast towers went silent. Satellites grew dark. No longer receiving computer facilitated commands from below, they lost power, failed to make course corrections and began to plummet back to earth with sickening frequency.

The worst of the power outages caused by the EMPs and the computer hackers lasted a full year. One nearly immediate result of this was food shortages brought on due to both the lack of transportation and refrigeration: becoming in turn yet another catalyst for food riots.

People were killed for as little as a can of tuna.

A desperate back-to-the-earth movement saw millions flee the fruitless concrete and steel canyons of the cities to return to an agrarian lifestyle they hoped would at least stave off starvation.

The massive, pervasive loss of computer connectivity gave rise to a sub-culture known as "wire-heads." So addicted had they become to being constantly plugged into the worldwide web that when most such services were disrupted or destroyed altogether, they went into the same form of shocking withdrawal common to drug abusers, forced to quit cold turkey.

Some actually withered and died from the shock, while many others found they were no longer able to function at anything approaching a normal level.

Wire-heads were easy to spot. They often would unconsciously be tapping their thumbs against the tips of their index fingers, typing at an imaginary keyboard, writing texts that no one would ever read. Some would be seen to do this even in their sleep.

Remnants of the computer net still existed, mostly in the hands of governments and the ultra-wealthy.

The wire-head appellation applied to the hopelessly cyber addicted derived from a phenomenon whereby in extreme cases these people literally had cybernetic ports installed in their skulls, with links directly into the brain. Cables or flash drives could be inserted into these ports, in essence making that person a human computer, capable of viewing digital images on the surfaces of his or her eyes.

With byte peddlers demanding as much as a hundred dollars per half-hour for such service, those so addicted would beg, borrow, steal, prostitute themselves and in extreme cases even kill for a few minutes spent blissfully swimming in the cyber-sea.

Around the world, even with poverty and deprivation so all encompassing, there did still exist the wealthy few, especially those able and willing to exploit and capitalize on the elements of chaos and death.

The richest 1% of the global population controlled nearly 80% of all its wealth.

Knowing that this wealth made them tempting and succulent targets for the envious, the cake eaters, the criminals and the despondent, most members of the upper class lived in virtual fortresses, usually protected by small or not-so-small private armies.

Equally unsurprising in such devastating times, religious fervor had increased dramatically.

Many new apocalyptic cults, both Christian and otherwise, were attempting to prepare their followers for the End Time. Some did so from genuine conviction; some were merely exploiting fear to fill their own coffers.

Others found a return to various forms of neo-paganism better suited their fears and hopes, their view of a world now vastly changed from the one they had previously known.

Convinced that this epic wave of pain and suffering had been visited upon the earth by one angry, vengeful god or another, those espousing differing faiths engaged in even more frequent, hateful warfare one against the other.

Conversely, atheism had also seen a large increase in its number of adherents, as disillusioned people decided that no merciful god, if one existed, could possibly stand idly by in the face of such global afflictions of body and soul without offering tangible relief and comfort. Absent any sign of a supernatural healing hand, their belief in such vanished in the wind. Collectively, these non-believers came to call themselves "the Godless."

People of faith derisively called them "the Hopeless."

Even the richest and most powerful nation on the planet, the United States of America, had been greatly humbled by the tumult; and was embattled on both its long borders.

To the south, minefields and barricades manned by heavily armed soldiers fought a continuous battle to turn back the tide of refugees attempting to flee the havoc of their Latin homelands and to stave off the flood of illicit drugs entering the States. Neither battle was going well.

In an odd turn of events, to the north the army of Canada was engaged in similar armed conflict to block those seeking to leave the more densely populated U.S. and take up squatters' rights on the relatively empty expanses of Canadian grassland.

When the cyber crash and other disasters caused shipments of food to be sorely curtailed, millions of Americans fled from the sterile streets of their cities. To these unprepared and unqualified would-be new agrarians, fertile open land became more precious and beguiling in their eyes than gold, silver or jewels.

With more hungry people than there seemed to be arable land to support and feed them, many were not particular about whose land they seized and settled.

In the face of so many desperate Americans, hawkish members

of Canada's government had done the formerly unthinkable: begun a campaign urging greater and more aggressive use of military might, so as not to just stave off unwelcome migrants but to actually invade their once invincible neighbor and extend Canada's territorial border farther to the south.

Feelings ran high on both sides of the present border, and occurrences of armed conflict became increasingly common.

So all-pervasive were the disasters raging against mankind that the concept of the "Super Power" had been rendered practically meaningless. Some nations were still wealthier and more secure than others were, but not so much so as to make it viable to spread a wide net of influence. It had become very much an every-man-for-himself world, with isolationism becoming the dominant foreign policy philosophy of many. Even the American giant was but a pale shadow of its former self.

New York City, previously the biggest and brightest of America's metropoles, had been in large part abandoned by those frantically fleeing toward the perceived haven of the country. Two million citizens still called it home; but that was less than a quarter of its pre-crisis population.

Most of America's once-great cities were now virtually if not literally bankrupt; the services once routinely provided by them enormously diminished if not absent all together.

One of the hardest hit areas of public service was law enforcement, which was now financed and administered entirely by the federal government—and not well. The *National Police Force* allocated officers to the various cities and municipalities of the country as best its sorely limited resources would allow.

New York, whose finest once boasted of a force composed of 35,000 officers, now had only 200 men and women charged with maintaining law and order in the city: a number that would be inadequate to served the needs of a community one-tenth its size.

In such a world as now existed, where mere survival was all to which most could aspire, there were very few individuals who by their deeds could succeed in rising to near mythical levels: either of heroism or villainy. Few whose names were widely known, who were spoken of with any degree of awe.

One of those few was an extraordinary woman who called New York City her home. Her exploits, her lifestyle, her dark and light achievements, would all become the stuff of legend. The facts of her life were often more incredible than were the fictions.

She was a poet.  A lover.  A dreamer.
She was also a ruthless and deadly efficient killer.
Her name was *Scimidar*.

# CHAPTER 1

*M*ama Farush was dying.

Everyone inside the small, cramped apartment on East 6th Street in New York's Ukrainian Village knew this. They still held out hope for her immortal soul, but not for its tiny shell of a body that age and infirmity had reduced to little more than a fragile, hollow vessel.

More than a dozen family members kept silent vigil around the bed occupied by the 88-year-old woman. They were her children, the spouses of those children, grandchildren and great-grandchildren. The only noise was the whisper of devout prayers; Mama Farush herself had not uttered a sound for nearly three days, save for the faint, dry rattling that sometimes accompanied her labored breathing.

Her son Tabor's head cocked to one side as he thought he heard another faint sound trying meekly to intrude upon their vigil. A moment later, the sound came again and he now recognized it as being a light tapping on the apartment's front door.

As discreetly as possible he withdrew from the bedroom. He'd gone only a few steps when he realized his wife Annika was softly following behind him. He glanced back at her, shrugging his ignorance as to the source of the tapping.

Nor was his ignorance dispelled when he pulled the door open. Standing alone out in the hallway was a young girl, probably no older than twelve. Tabor did not know her from the neighborhood, but was struck by her almost angelic appearance.

She was a beautiful child, with long blonde hair and crystal blue eyes that sparkled with the gleam of wisdom no one so young should yet have attained. Her dress was snow white: simple yet elegant in design and obviously expensive. She said nothing, but merely stared at Tabor and Annika with her soulful eyes.

"What do you want, little girl?" the ever practical Annika asked, presuming the child was there in an effort to sell them something.

"I've come to see the dying woman."

To hear such an utterance from the mouth of one so young was startling. The girl's voice was like her eyes: soft and sparkling yet carrying the weight of age and experience.

Annika stared back at her, not knowing how to reply. When she finally glanced over at her husband, she found Tabor was similarly gazing at the girl, his mouth hanging slightly agape.

His head then swiveled to look at his wife. Neither knew what to say, so without a word they stepped aside and motioned for the child to enter. Even as they did so, they could not have explained their actions; they did not know this odd girl, had never laid eyes on her before.

The child turned her head toward each of the adults, gracing them with a wistful smile before stepping over the threshold. She strode confidently, with the two slightly dumbfounded adults falling into step behind her. Though she had never been in this building before, had never even been in this part of the city, she walked without pause directly toward the bedroom where Mama Farush lay.

Only when she reached its open doorway did she hesitate, perhaps inwardly struggling with herself before taking the first slow steps toward the bed.

The old woman had been unresponsive, essentially comatose. But now, as if sensing the presence of her strangely beautiful little visitor, Mama Farush's eyes snapped open. Those nearest to her let out involuntary gasps. Slowly, and with great effort, the fragile woman turned her head to one side.

Seeming to recognize this girl she had never seen before, Mama Farush smiled weakly. Her right arm fell as much as lifted off the bed, and she extended a bony, trembling hand toward the little girl who had come to a halt a few feet away and was nervously wringing her hands and shifting on her feet from side to side.

But whatever trepidation she felt vanished at this silent and desperate invitation. As she resumed walking toward the bed, her own right arm rose and her small hand reached out toward that of the old woman. Everyone else in the room stood as if frozen, looking on with silent fascination.

The young girl's fingers slipped between those of Mama Farush, intertwining with them. The old woman's hand almost convulsed, clutching at that of the girl. As it did, the child's eyes widened.

"Aaah!" she cried out, clearly in pain. Not relaxing her grip on the old woman's hand, she dropped to her knees.

Horrified, Tabor stepped toward the child, only to be held back by his wife's hand on his arm. He looked with despair at Annika, but she merely shook her head knowingly.

Panting heavily, the child finally rose back up on rubbery legs. She maintained her grip on Mama Farush's hand: indeed, now clutching it with both of her own.

Stepping close to the bed, clutching the woman's hand to her tiny bosom, this ethereal child leaned forward. With her lips close to Mama Farush's ear, she began to whisper words no one else in the room could hear.

When the words ended, Mama Farush gave out one last, long, loud exhalation of breath...and then expired.

The girl, amazingly calm and still holding her hand, gently laid the old woman's arm down by her side on the bed. Still leaning over the dead woman, the girl stroked her white hair and tenderly kissed her on her thin, still warm lips.

When the girl at last turned away from the bed to face the awed and wide-eyed members of the assembled family, they saw that tears were rolling down her cheeks. Blinking them back, she shifted her gaze so as to focus on Tabor.

"Your poor momma," she said in emotion-choked tones. "She suffered so much. Her pain was more terrible than you can imagine. Almost unbearable."

Tabor's breath sucked in as he fought a wave of grief, regret and guilt. Annika squeezed his arm tightly. Similar choking sounds came from various other family members.

"But it's all right now," the blonde girl hastened to assure them all. "There's no more pain now." She smiled slightly. "There'll never be any more pain. Not for her."

Her eyes swiveled back and forth over those gathered. "And even before she died, there was one thing she was feeling that was even stronger than the pain. Much stronger.

"It was love. She knew you were here, and that you loved her. And she loved you all in return. Very...very much."

Several members of the family, men as well as women, began to weep openly and loudly at these words, their emotions bursting from them like water through a broken dam.

Tabor, unashamed, laid his head on Annika's shoulder and wept deeply. Her own sobs matched his as she patted his graying head.

Both jerked nervously as another knock, louder than the first, again sounded at the front portal.

Wiping at his eyes with the back of his left hand, Tabor rumbled down the hallway and impatiently flung open the door.

He blinked in mild confusion. It was an adult woman he now found himself facing: albeit one small in stature, not much taller than the strange blonde girl he had left in the back bedroom. From the look of her, this new arrival was in early middle age, and of Eurasian ethnicity. At her side, holding her hand tightly, was a ten-year-old girl who looked rather like a miniature version of the woman. Both had slightly careworn expressions on their round faces.

"Please excuse me, sir," the woman said in a soft and lilting voice. "I am Dominique Fontaine, and this is my daughter, Marie Celeste."

Tabor nodded with inborn courtesy. "How do you do."

Dominique sighed. "We've come to retrieve our girl."

"Ah." Tabor turned to the side and motioned for them to enter.

"I hope she hasn't caused you any trouble, sir," Dominique said.

"Not at all," Tabor said with no hesitance. "Quite the opposite, in fact. I've never seen anything like it. She's really quite the remarkable little girl."

As he led the way toward the bedroom, Tabor told Dominique what had happened just minutes earlier.

"I'm really very grateful to her," Tabor said when he saw what he took to be a troubled look cloud Dominique's face. "The gift she gave me and my family is too wonderful to describe."

"That's a good thing, I suppose," Dominique replied; but her inflection showed she was uncertain of that.

Dominique inhaled her breath sharply as she was ushered into the room and saw her sometimes exasperating ward slumped on the floor next to a bed upon which lay the body of what seemed clearly to be a dead woman.

Any thoughts of scolding the child for running off on her own and intruding on strangers fled from Dominique's mind in a heartbeat as she knelt down beside her ward and gently enfolded her in her arms.

"Oh!" the girl gasped fearfully. Dominique's eyes followed hers down and saw the child's beautiful white dress was now stained with a small patch of blood, near the girl's groin.

"Am I dying, Dominique?" she cried, clutching frantically and tightly at the woman as she began to grow almost hysterical. Little Marie Celeste, now frightened too by seeing her nearest and dearest friend in such a state, began to cry.

"No, Scimidar, no," Dominique crooned, stroking the girl's luxurious hair. "Your time has come, that's all. I've told you about this, remember? The blood just means you've changed, crossed over." She kissed the girl softly on the cheek.

"You're a woman now."

# CHAPTER 2

*Asia: three years later.*

**T**he Shaolin temple was nearly a thousand years old, but Scimidar felt at home the moment she followed Dominique and Celeste into its cool confines.

The teenaged girl was physically very much beginning to look like a fully-grown woman. She already stood several inches taller than Dominique did: both her breasts and her hips had begun to swell. Her lithesome figure was starkly displayed within the confines of a clinging black unitard that was all she wore today, in defiance of Dominique's cajoling efforts to get her into something the older woman felt would be more appropriate.

As the three women boldly entered through the front doors of the temple, saffron-robed priests hurriedly averted their eyes, so as not to look upon these females who had dared breach a sanctum normally denied to those of their gender.

Dominique paid them no mind, for she knew they were expected. Celeste did likewise. Scimidar giggled, taking delight in the discomfort she wrought amongst these celibate and cloistered clerics.

Unable to repress her mischievous nature, she skipped over to one of the priests, grabbing him by the sides of his head and planting a loud kiss atop his shaven pate. He cried out in horror and fell to his knees. His nearest brethren scampered away.

"Scimidar!" Dominique hissed, snapping her fingers and motioning for the girl to fall back in behind her. "Behave yourself!"

At least pretending to be suitably chastened, the teen fell into step behind her elder, hanging her head and holding her hands behind her back. But she could not help glancing over at Celeste, who was shaking her head wearily, and giving her friend a wink.

The only sound as they penetrated to the heart of the temple was that of their own footsteps. Passing at length through an ornate archway etched with bas-relief images of creatures both earthly and alien, they found themselves entering a long corridor that ended in a small and dimly lit round chamber.

"Wait here," Dominique ordered the two girls, before continuing on alone down the corridor.

Flaming braziers set in sconces buried in the stone walls provided a bright if flickering light. By their glow, Scimidar could see that Dominique's path took her between two rows of pedestals, totaling half a dozen in number.

Each pedestal rose about three feet above the level of the floor. Atop each pedestal stood a man. Each was barefooted and wore bright red clothing that reminded the girl of pajamas. Each also seemed to be holding what Scimidar assumed were weapons, though oddly shaped ones she did not recognize.

These guardians all stood at stiff attention, making not the slightest move as Dominique passed quickly between them. Clearly, unlike the priests, they were not frightened or shocked by the appearance of a woman, but neither did they make any move to impede her progress down the corridor.

Dominique's destination was the chamber that rested at the far end of the corridor, just beyond where the silent sentries stood on their perches. There, atop a small raised platform, an older man sat crosslegged atop a large and plush velvet cushion.

He wore a simple robe of cotton, light blue in color. His arms were folded over his chest and in his hands he held a pair of *tonfas*. Made of cedar wood, these implements resembled the batons employed by many Western police officers: they looked like cylindrical sticks, but with a vertical handle rising up near one end by which they were held.

Dominique stopped a few feet in front of the old man, who studied her dispassionately. She in turn scanned his face. The only hair on his head was a white moustache that hung down well below the line of his jaw. His eyes were little more than narrow slits. The many wrinkles lacing his skin spoke of advanced age. After nearly a minute of this mutual scrutiny, Dominique bowed respectfully at the waist before him.

"Thank you for granting a humble servant this audience, sensei," she said to him.

"You have always been a friend to this temple," he replied, in a voice that didn't require great volume to convey great authority. "And to me."

"And you to me."

"But it's been a long time since you've graced us with your company, Dominique."

"Too long. I ask your forgiveness."

"Asked for and given, always. What brings you here now?"

"I've come to ask a favor."

"Ah."

"Not for myself," she hastened to add, straightening now. "It's for another: a girl who's been left in my charge."

"Not your daughter?"

"No. One who's like a daughter."

The sensei sighed softly. "What kind of service can an old monk provide to a young woman?"

"My hope is that you'll accept her as a pupil."

The sensei's eyes opened wider at these words, and Dominique plunged ahead before he could speak.

"I think you'll find she's a most extraordinary girl, sensei. She's extremely bright and clever: artistic and inquisitive.

"But she lacks discipline and self-control and is prone to putting herself in situations that are potentially dangerous."

"And you've failed to teach her to control such inclinations." The monk's words were merely a statement of fact, not a question or a judgement.

"I have," Dominique admitted, "though I've tried my very best."

"I have no doubt of that," the sensei declared by way of compliment.

"But my best isn't good enough; not with her. She's a good girl, truly she is. But a willful one who can't seem to stop herself from plunging into dark waters."

"And you think I can teach her not to take that plunge?" the sensei asked.

"That may be beyond even *your* capabilities, good sir. But you might at least be able to teach her how to swim."

The old man chuckled softly. "A clever analogy, daughter."

"My greatest hope," Dominique continued, "is that you can curb the child's impetuous nature while giving her the tools and the skills that would help her survive in a world swarming with all sorts of dangers.

"I love her, sensei. She desperately needs the kind of training you can provide. Without them, I'm afraid that one day she'll be consumed by her own inner demons."

Again almost a full minute passed in silence before the aged monk replied.

"This is a most unprecedented request you have made. No monk of this temple has ever accepted a female student."

"I know that, sensei," Dominique said with urgency in her voice. "But I also know this is the best place for her to learn what she needs to know in order to survive. You may be my best and last hope."

The monk sighed again, more deeply.

"Does this child have a name?"

"She's called Scimidar."

"That's an unusual name."

"She's an unusual girl, master. As you'll see."

Though he held great affection for the supplicant standing before him, the sensei was still inclined to deny her request; bringing a young woman into this cloistered environment did not feel right to him. Not proper. Then he raised his eyes to take a closer look at the girl standing across the long corridor.

His breath caught slightly in his throat as he did so. Even from this considerable distance and with his age-diminished capabilities, he could see blue fire dancing in her eyes and sense a spirit such as he had never encountered. Nothing in his multitudinous and varied experiences had prepared him for such a one as this.

He found himself to be simultaneously intrigued and discomfited by her—for she seemed to have more than *one* spirit residing inside her.

"I make no promises," he said, returning his gaze to Dominique, "but I'll talk with the child."

"Thank you, master," Dominique said with relief. "I couldn't ask for more." Turning, she motioned with one hand for the two girls to approach.

Celeste had been standing alongside the older girl, but the thought of entering deeper into this strange place filled her with fear and she pulled back away.

"Don't worry," Scimidar said soothingly, herself feeling no such trepidation as she patted her dear friend on the arm. "You can wait here for me."

Throwing back her shoulders, the blonde girl boldly stepped into the corridor.

The instant she strode between the first two silent guards on their pedestals, however, she cried out in sharp pain.

Eyes squeezed tightly shut, she clutched at her head with both hands, reacting as though twin swords were being plunged into her brain.

Moaning loudly, she dropped to her knees, then swiveled and pitched to the floor on her back.

Seeing this, Celeste's personal fear disappeared and she raced forward to the side of her fallen, beloved friend.

"Stop!" a commanding voice rang out.

The panicked girl froze in her tracks, terrified to see that the old sensei had risen to his feet and was pointing one of his tonfas at her.

"Leave her be," he said sternly. "Back away."

With a defiance she had never shown to any elder, Celeste stood her ground, clutching her tiny fists at her side.

"It's...all right, Celeste," Scimidar whispered through gritted teeth. "Stay away from me."

She then cried out more loudly, her back arching off the floor as a fresh spasm of sharper pain ripped through her.

Celeste fell to her knees to embrace her friend's convulsing body. She lacked the strength to stop the gyrations, and feared that Scimidar in her agony might bite through her own tongue.

"Go away!" Scimidar moaned, her eyes fluttering uncontrollably. "Please..."

Celeste wiped beads of sweat away from the blonde's forehead before kissing it. She then reluctantly stood, stepped away from her and walked back out of the corridor. She stood there with her back turned, unwilling and unable to watch her sister's misery.

At the other end of the chamber, Dominique turned frantic and questioning eyes on the sensei. He failed to acknowledge her concern; his own gaze remaining firmly focused on Scimidar.

In truth, he had no idea what was happening to the girl, or why. He had never in his long and eventful life witnessed such an occurrence. He was frankly curious to see how it would play out.

The six sentries gave no sign that they were even aware of the girl writhing on the floor below them. As was their training and their way, they remained standing at silent, unflinching attention.

As though possessed by a demon (the sensei momentarily entertained this as a possibility before dismissing the notion), Scimidar rolled back and forth on the cold stone floor. Unintelligible syllables gurgled up from her throat.

Slowly then, her uncontrolled thrashing began to quiet down. One last time her back arched, its thrusting impulse nearly lifting her into the air. Then she fell still, her heavy breathing gradually returning to normal.

As her senses cleared, she rolled over, pushed herself back up onto her feet and again proceeded forward.

She moved slowly, her body trembling and twitching as it continued to adjust to whatever forces were assailing her.

The subsequent sentries remained still as Scimidar passed between them, though a tiny voice within told her that her presence was causing a great unease within them.

"GO AWAY!  PLEASE!"

Every time she came to the point between two of these highly disciplined martial artists, she would pause briefly before moving on. She never deigned to look at them, preferring to keep her vision locked on the sensei awaiting her at the end of the corridor.

He had now stepped down from his platform and taken a step or two in her direction before stopping. Closing the gap that remained between them would now be entirely her task to perform.

Scimidar's confidence and physical coordination grew stronger with each step. By the time she passed beyond the final two sentries, she seemed to be in complete control of her faculties once more. Her stride became smooth and firm.

Dominique was beside herself with worry, but didn't know what else to do save watch and let this strange ballet play on.

Scimidar came to a halt when she was no more than two feet away from the aged sensei. Their eyes locked and the old man licked his lips unconsciously; he was unnerved by a hitherto unknown sensation, a feeling that some part of himself was being torn away from him.

The girl closed her eyes and bowed at the waist. With contact between them thus broken, the sensei shivered slightly before regaining his composure.

"Welcome to my home, child," he said benignly. "You should be pleased to know that, at the request of your guardian, I have decided to accept you here as a pupil."

Scimidar's response was not at all what he had expected in reply to his generous offer and it puzzled him greatly. She raised her head, and the smile she bestowed on him was decidedly wicked.

"Thank you for your kind offer, sensei," she said smoothly.

"But there's nothing more you can teach me."

# CHAPTER 3

"**O**h?" the sensei replied, simultaneously annoyed and amused by the girl's presumptuous declaration that there was nothing he could teach her.

"May I?" was all Scimidar said in return; but without waiting for an answer, her hands whipped out and, before the master could react, snatched the tonfas from his hands.

Bending at the knees, she then sprang upwards. Her back arched as she executed a perfect back flip. Then another and another: each carrying her farther away from the old monk.

His head snapped around to glare at Dominique, and the anger almost shooting from his eyes caused her to cringe before him.

"She's already been trained?" he accused.

"No, master," Dominique declared firmly. "I swear it: not one lesson. I don't know how she's able to do that!"

Scimidar's final back flip landed her between the last two pedestals upon which stood the sensei's sentries. Coming back to earth with catlike grace, the girl whirled into a classic fighting posture.

For the first time, the two sentries acknowledged her presence: looking down at her and then up at each other.

With overlapping screeches, they leaped toward her, weapons at the ready as they accepted her unspoken challenge. The first of them wielded a pair of *kamas*: weapons with short wooden shafts topped by sickle shaped blades. The other carried a long *stick ax*: more like a spear, but with the point at one end and an ax head at the other.

The first warrior came at Scimidar with both kamas whirling like propellers. She retreated before his assault, but at the same time was expertly deflecting his weapons with her own.

Seemingly possessed now with eyes in the back of her head, she arched backwards just as the sentry behind her thrust with the pointed end of his weapon.

Scimidar watched, enthralled, as the deadly weapon appeared to pass before her eyes in slow motion. She sprang back fully erect, slapping at the shaft of the weapon with one tonfa. The other tonfa arced to the right.

The warrior to that side of her had been forced to use his kamas to protect himself from the spear point that had missed the girl, but this left him vulnerable to her attack. The hard shaft of her tonfa smacked against his face, crushing his nose in a spray of blood and dropping him to the floor.

Scimidar forgot him in the instant, as he would no longer pose a threat. The warrior with the stick ax twirled his weapon, swinging down at her with the ax blade.

Her crossed tonfas stopped the blow, but the force behind it nearly drove her to her knees. With a loud grunt, she pushed back and shoved him away. He expertly maneuvered his weapon, going rapidly back and forth, between thrusting it like a spear and swinging it like a staff or ax.

Scimidar grew momentarily overconfident when she thought she had discerned a pattern to his attacks. She believed he was about to swing the weapon overhead, but he surprised her by thrusting it instead.

Having been moving forward to launch her own attack, she found herself unable to fully turn aside from the thrust. Again as if in slowed motion, she saw the spear point of his weapon slide between her left arm and her torso. As it did so, it raked along her side, slicing both cloth and flesh.

The resulting pain registered on her brain, but did not deter her. She stood her ground, letting the spear thrust pull its wielder closer to her. Faster than his eyes could register, she swung the tonfa in her right hand.

Its cedar shaft slapped against the sentry's throat, crushing his larynx. He dropped his weapon, clutching at his neck with both hands as blood filled his gorge and spewed out of his mouth.

Pressing her advantage, Scimidar struck him in first one side of his head, then the other. She raised a foot to press it against his stomach, then shoved. He was hurled back, flying over the pedestal upon which he had been standing moments earlier. Unlike his comrade, he would never rise again.

Scimidar knew he was dead before he did. In the same way, she had felt the pain she had inflicted upon him and the other fallen sentry with nearly equal intensity to the pain she felt from her own wound.

If it disturbed her in any great way that she rather enjoyed this sensation, she gave no indication of it as she stalked toward the next two sentries waiting on their pedestals.

Nor did she give a second thought to the inexplicable expertise she was demonstrating with the tonfas (weapons she had never seen or handled before today) or the superior fighting skills that now came naturally to her. Only later would it occur to her that she had somehow absorbed those abilities from the very men against whom she was now employing them.

She was barely thinking at all, but merely acting and reacting; reveling in the wave of emotional turmoil sweeping her along. She leaped forward eagerly as the next two martial artists bounded down from their pedestals to confront her.

One of them carried a long length of chain; at one end of it was a large ring by which he gripped it, while at the other end was a metal blade to which was attached at one side a sharp hook. The second sentry wore metal gauntlets on his hands; from each of which extended two sharpened steel "claws."

He attacked first. Having seen the way this disturbingly queer girl had so brutally dispatched his two brothers, he carried no thought of pulling his punches in deference to her age and gender; nor did he intend to give her any quarter.

Again she employed her tonfas masterfully in parrying his blows. He was equally skilled and she could find no opening through his defenses. In a rare and potentially fatal lapse, she forgot about the second sentry—until she felt his chain wrap around her ankles and pull her feet sharply out from under her.

She hit the floor so hard that her teeth rattled, yet still she had the presence of mind to roll in time to avoid a downward blow from the clawed hand of the first sentry. Sparks flew from the impact of his steel hooks striking the stone.

While he was momentarily off balance, Scimidar sat up and dropped her tonfas, freeing her hands to grab at the chain around her ankles. She yanked fiercely, pulling the chain out of the hands of its wielder. Now slackened, the chain was easily untangled from her legs and cast aside.

She retrieved the tonfas and sprang to her feet in time to meet a lunging attack from the clawed warrior. Her weapons locked with his, but his weight and momentum drove her back until she slammed into the nearest wall.

They stood toe-to-toe as the sentry brought his greater strength to bear. Scimidar saw light flicker off his razored claws as they inched closer to her flawless face.

Then she unexpectedly thrust her head forward and bit off the tip of his nose.

Yowling in pain and clutching at his mangled nose, the sentry staggered back. Angered nearly more than hurt, he swiped at the blood gushing from his mangled nostrils and whipped his arms about, yowling in a high-pitched call as he prepared to launch a fresh attack.

Breath hissed between his teeth as he gazed at the girl. She appeared to be calmly chewing on the stub of his nose, as if it was no more than a stick of gum!

Turning her head to one side, she spit the piece of chewed flesh out, used the back of one hand to wipe away his blood from her lips and assumed a fighting pose of her own.

She let out a fierce scream as she launched herself toward him. Only, he was not her target; she took only two steps toward him before then pivoting and lashing out with one foot.

Nearby, the second sentry was bent over to retrieve his blade hook and chain. He was the focus of her attack, and her foot caught him alongside his jaw. He was lifted off the floor and sent spinning away.

Scimidar twisted and went after the clawed sentry. Now it was he who was forced to give way before her assault. He parried almost every thrust and blow she sent his way, but at length she plunged the blunt end of one tonfa into his midsection.

The force of the blow doubled him over. As he folded, Scimidar brought her right knee up sharply. It connected with his chin, breaking his jaw and filling his mouth with blood.

He bounded back, banging against a wall and slumping. Howling triumphantly, Scimidar slapped her tonfas one after the other against the sides of his head. Consciousness fled and he fell limply to the floor.

As his mind went blank, the flood of anger, fear and pain coming from him also ceased. Unable to bathe in it further, Scimidar lost all interest in him; instead wheeling to face the second sentry.

What she saw when she spun around was that he had regained his footing and retrieved his chained weapon.

And its steel blade was flying straight toward her face.

# CHAPTER 4

In that crawl of time that was but one of the new sensations now possessing her senses, Scimidar clearly saw the point of the blade flying directly at her.

She swung one tonfa in an arc. So close was she to death that she actually felt the tip of the bladed hook prick her chin before her own weapon clacked against it and sent it flying away to one side.

The sentry had shifted his grip on the chained weapon, now clutching it in the middle of its links. Seeing that his blade had been deflected from striking home, he swiftly twirled the ringed end toward the girl's head.

Incredibly, she thrust upward with her second tonfa, so that it passed through the center of the ring and stopped it in mid-flight. Twisting her weapon so that the chain looped around it, she yanked hard. Caught flat-footed, the sentry was jerked forward toward her.

As she turned sideways while jerking the chain, Scimidar dropped her right tonfa and grabbed at the blade hook on the other end. She thrust it forward; impaling the sentry as his body flew forward. He made sick choking sounds as she twisted the blade.

She then pulled it free from his innards and pirouetted, driving the hook part of the weapon into the warrior's neck, just below his right ear. His eyes bulged before rolling up into their sockets.

As the lifeless man dropped to the floor, Scimidar dropped the chain, bending to scoop up her second tonfa.

She had barely straightened back up when the final two martial artists were upon her. Having seen how callously efficient the girl had been in dispatching their brethren, they had no intention of waiting for her to come to them.

Scimidar leaped back from their initial assault, as weapons seemed to fly at her from multitudinous directions. This was because one of her attackers was employing a three-sectioned staff—composed of three wooden shafts connected loosely by two short lengths of chain—and the other flashed a double-ball mace. This weapon consisted of a short, leather-wrapped shaft, from the end of which sprang two short lengths of chain attached to a pair of spiked steel balls.

Scimidar moaned as one section of the staff clipped the side of her head. From the wetness she felt sliding down her temple she knew it had drawn blood.

She was forced to ignore it by the more immediate need to defend herself from the sentry with the mace. The two fighters engaged in a beautiful if deadly dance, their hands whipping back and forth nearly faster than the eye could follow.

One ball of the mace struck Scimidar's left forearm, forcing her to drop her tonfa. Thin bubbles of blood oozed from the places where the ball's spikes had penetrated her skin.

She dropped to one knee, seemingly from the pain of the blow; but this was merely a ruse. As the sentry moved forward, raising his mace for another blow, she surprised him by leaping toward him.

Her empty hand grabbed one of the steel balls. Ignoring the pain as its spikes dug into her palm, she gripped it and plunged it down into the sentry's right eye.

He screamed in agony as blood sprayed, staggering backward with the metal ball embedded in his skull. He fell to the stone floor, arms and legs twitching.

Scimidar landed in a crouch and began to rise just as the last sentry's sectional staff struck her again. The blow caught her in the side, just below the ribcage.

She rolled with the blow to put some distance between herself and her attacker and to give herself time to regain the breath the blow had expelled from her lungs.

Screeching like a catamount, the warrior pressed his advantage, advancing on her with his staff flailing.

With only one tonfa still in her grip, and her left arm beginning to grow numb, Scimidar was hardpressed to defend herself. She found she was growing angry at the prospect of impending defeat. The fact that she had already brought low five expert martial artists was meaningless to her: she wanted all or nothing.

She whipped her lone tonfa from side to side, deflecting blows from right and left. Then, in a desperate move that would leave her virtually defenseless, she reared back her right arm and threw the tonfa at the sentry's head.

With a flick of both wrists, he sent the middle section of his weapon snapping up, successfully deflecting the projectile. Scimidar anticipated he would be able to do so, but hoped the movement would impair his sight of her for the second she hoped was all she would need.

She had left her feet as her arm had snapped forward, leaping ahead in the wake of the thrown tonfa.

With his hands on the two outer sections of the chain staff, the sentry had popped both tightly, causing the center section to lance upward and deflect the hurtling tonfa. As that center section of staff did its job, it obscured his vision for just a fraction of a second.

On such can life or death hang.

As the center length of the staff began to descend, the warrior saw Scimidar coming toward him. Grabbing hold of the shaft before her, the girl thrust it forward. It struck the sentry in the mouth, snapping his head back.

Scimidar then slammed into him, her weight carrying him to a bone-jarring fall that slammed him to the floor with her astraddle him. Reeling from the blow the back of his head had thus received, he was unable to stop her from snatching his weapon from his hands.

Too fast for him to defend against, she looped the two lengths of the chain around his neck and yanked both ends tightly.

With a snap so loud it filled the nearly silent corridor, the sentry's neck broke like a stick of dry and brittle kindling. Scimidar felt him buck a time or two beneath her: heard and smelled his bowels as they involuntarily voided.

She continued to pull on the taut chain for several seconds after it was obvious the man was dead.

Tumbling off his body, Scimidar snatched up both her fallen tonfas as she rolled. Bounding to her feet, she again executed a pair of high, vaulting somersaults. With the last one she twisted her body so that she landed and went down on one knee a short distance before and facing Marie Celeste.

The younger girl was transfixed in amazement and fear that became sheer terror at the sight of her most beloved friend in the world kneeling before her drenched in blood.

When Scimidar raised her head to look at Celeste, the child became even more horrified.

Scimidar was smiling, and the expression on her face could best be described as one of pure ecstasy.

Averting her eyes, Celeste pulled a kerchief from one pocket of her jacket and took a knee beside her friend. As she began wiping at the blood covering Scimidar, she quickly realized that most of it belonged to the wounded and slain sentries.

Scimidar was breathing heavily as Celeste tenderly put one arm around her neck and used her other hand to brush away blood-encrusted strands of blonde hair from Scimidar's face. It bothered Celeste greatly, knowing the panting could be attributed to excitement rather than to fear or exertion. Scimidar's eyes were wide and the only sound other than the breathing that issued from her lips was one that was akin to joyful laughter.

"It's awesome!" she told Celeste, bubbling with exuberance. "It's like there's another world—and I can fly in and out of it, whenever I want.

"It's dark—but bright. It's like it's the end of it all…but the beginning of everything.

"I don't think anyone's ever been there but me. Death and life are twined together; and both of them speak to me.

"I never want to give it up!"

She was obviously thrilled by what had just transpired, even as Celeste was being shaken to her roots. She didn't really understand a thing her friend was saying to her, nor did she want to. To do so, she thought, one would first have to go mad.

She wondered helplessly how she might stop Scimidar from embarking on a journey down that road—without having to tread it herself.

At the other end of the corridor, Dominique appeared stricken by what she had just witnessed. At the touch of a hand on her arm, she willed herself to turn away from the carnage and switch her gaze to the sensei.

The old master bore a grave look on his face she had never seen before. Tugging at her arm, silently urging her to join him, he started the long walk to where the two girls knelt.

The heel of Dominique's right foot slid out from under her, nearly causing her to fall. Her face blanched as she looked down and realized it was a small puddle of blood that was responsible.

Much as she wanted not to, she kept looking back and forth at the bodies littering the floor; most of them were no longer breathing. Heads and limbs were twisted at unnatural angles: blood spattered floor and walls.

The horrible realization that this slaughter was the work of one who was little more than a child, who to Dominique's knowledge had never before raised a hand in anger, was nearly more than the woman's heart could bear.

"What is it you brought me?" the sensei hissed quietly.

"I don't know, master," Dominique gasped. "God help us all…I don't know!"

Hearing the light sound of their footfalls behind her, Scimidar swiveled around but remained on one knee. The move unbalanced Celeste, who unceremoniously fell over on her bottom.

As the sensei and Dominique drew near, Scimidar rather theatrically pulled her arms straight back behind her and bowed her head.

The aged monk stared down fiercely at her with his slitted eyes for a very long time before at last he spoke.

"You were right," he said in a strained voice. "There is nothing more you can learn here."

Scimidar's head snapped up sharply and she smiled broadly.

"But you were right as well," the sensei said to Dominique. "A great gift—or a great curse—has been visited on this child.

"There is still so very much she has to learn. If she can't or won't gain control over this awful power…I'm afraid she's doomed."

Scimidar seemed not to hear his words, or to not care if she did; the smile remained on her lips. She lifted up the tonfas she had purloined from the sensei earlier.

"Would it be all right if I keep these?" she said cheerfully, lightly tapping the two batons together.

"I rather like them!"

# CHAPTER 5

*I*n the luxurious East Village apartment in New York that she shared with her real and adoptive daughters, Dominique Fontaine stood and stared out the patio doors. What lay beyond them didn't really matter; at the moment, the woman saw nothing.

Four months had passed since their return from the Orient, and Dominique had yet to come to a decision regarding Scimidar. Almost every night, visions of the angelic child's smiling face streaked with blood haunted the woman's dreams. She was close to despondency.

A firm, loud knock on the apartment's front door pulled her back from the edge of gloom. Suspecting she knew who awaited, she hurried to answer the summons.

Pulling the door open, she stepped back to take in the full view of the man waiting without. He was large, tall and broad, with skin the shade of black that borders on purple. He appeared to be in his late twenties; his head was shaved and he had a handsome but almost cruel looking face. He was dressed impeccably in an expensive, hand-tailored white suit. His right hand rested on the handle of a heavy and ornate walking stick.

He too was a person who preferred to go by a single name: *Shadrak*. And he was there at Dominique's invitation.

Though he was still quite young, Dominique knew Shadrak to be a man of great means: having already amassed a large fortune.and the amount of influence that came with it. It was Dominique's hope that he might be able to provide the guidance her dear Scimidar so needed.

"Ms. Fontaine?" he said, in a voice that, while cultured, also carried a deep undercurrent. "I was told you wished to meet with me."

He extended a large hand in greeting, which she accepted. While it gripped with a feathery lightness, she had no doubt it possessed the strength to easily crush her own.

"Won't you come in?" she said, and he smiled slightly as he accepted the invitation.

"I've not made your acquaintance before, have I?" he inquired.

"No. I was given your name by a friend."

"After which, you had me thoroughly investigated," he said casually, casting his gaze about the room. When he looked back at Dominique, he saw her eyebrows arch slightly.

"I've found it pays to be aware of such things," he told her, smiling tightly. "I trust I passed inspection?"

"Well enough," she replied rather cryptically.

"Meaning you need help badly enough to overlook any danger flags your inquiries may have raised."

"Meaning I care enough to take risks, even with a man with some shadows over his life."

"Risks about what?"

"Let me show you."

She headed toward the back of the apartment. She'd offered none of the usual social amenities: refreshments, introductory chitchat. Shadrak appreciated that fact; he was a busy man who didn't lightly suffer what he considered to be wastes of his time.

Momentarily, he and Dominique came to a closed door, into which was set a small window (Whoever was beyond the door, he surmised, was allowed a degree of but not total privacy). At a wave of his hostess's hand, he stepped closer to peer through the window.

He was surprised and a little disappointed to see within the room what seemed to be two perfectly ordinary girls: sitting on the floor of a shared bedroom, playing with a small kitten. Shadrak cast a quizzical eye back at Dominique.

"The younger of the girls is my daughter Marie Celeste," she explained. "She's growing into being a kind and gentle, loving woman. Overly sensitive, I fear, but such is her nature."

"And the other girl?"

"She's the reason I asked you here. Her name is Scimidar."

"What an odd name." When Shadrak saw Dominique smile, he shrugged. "My mother liked Biblical names."

"At least yours is your real name," Dominique said. "Hers is not the one she was given at birth."

"Oh?"

"No. One day, when she was about four, I think it was, she simply refused to respond when I called her by her given name.

"She informed me that from then on she now wanted to be called 'Scimidar.' She in fact adamantly insisted upon it; and so it's been ever since.

"Today, no one but I remembers or knows her true name."

"What does her new name mean?" Dominique could tell from Shadrak's tone of voice and the expression on his face that the man was becoming intrigued, as she had felt sure he would.

"I couldn't say. Where it came from, what it means; I just don't know. She refuses to say."

"What of her parents?" The question was posed to Dominique, but Shadrak's eyes were turned back to watch the girls at play.

"Both dead, so far as I know," Dominique replied, bringing his puzzled gaze back to her.

"Scimidar was brought to me as an infant and left in my care. She had apparently been conceived in the course of their first impulsive and no doubt tempestuously animalistic roll in the hay."

Shadrak suppressed a smile. He found the woman's obvious, unconcealed disapproval of such things to be provincial but amusing.

"The two of them never married—at least not each other," she continued, oblivious to the entertainment she was providing her guest. "They were both too busy adventuring around the world, I suppose.

"But they possessed tremendous wealth; primarily from stockpiles of gold of dubious origin. More than enough to leave the child comfortably set for life.

"For reasons known only to them, they chose me to be her guardian."

"Do you regret that?" Shadrak asked, and noted the woman reacted as if he had physically slapped her.

"Of course not! It was probably the wisest thing the two of them ever did. And for me, one of the best." The love behind her words was clear and genuine.

"But now there's a problem with her," he prompted.

"Yes." Her voice and her gaze drifted away for just a moment. "An... affliction, you might call it. It's blossomed within her and sets her apart from everyone else."

"She's ill?"

"Not in the way you mean, no. She is an *empath*."

Shadrak cocked his head to one side. "Enlighten me, dear lady. What is that, exactly?"

"She has the ability to not only sense what those around her are feeling— but to experience those feelings herself. Like an emotional mirror.

"She's not telepathic; she can't actually read minds. But her ability does give her great insight into whether or not a person is being truthful."

"Sounds quite useful."

"Perhaps it would be, if that was as far as it went. But she has virtually no control over this power, and she suffers greatly because of it. When she's caught up in a crowd, for example, she can be subjected to spells of both despair and euphoria: sometimes going back and forth so rapidly between the two extremes as to have them occurring virtually simultaneously within her own psyche."

"Manic-depression to the nth degree," Shadrak observed.

"Yes. But just as disconcerting to me is the fact that she seems to enjoy experiencing and absorbing into herself all the negative emotions as much as she does the positive ones.

"And she seems to be especially and rather morbidly fascinated with *death*."

"Are you afraid she's suicidal?"

"Not overtly so, no. She realizes her own death would mean the end of the emotional pool in which she loves to bathe.

"But lately she's begun to secretly sneak out of the apartment at night. Going to rough parts of the city. Deliberately putting herself in potentially dangerous situations."

"So you fear for her life."

"I fear for her *soul*."

"And you think I can help you? Help her?"

Dominique exhaled a deep breath. "Yes. I don't know. A friend suggested that with your far-flung interests you might be able to at least guide me toward someone who can."

Shadrak didn't reply immediately. He stood watching the girls at play, rolling the situation over in his mind. The possibilities that Scimidar's unique abilities might present tempted him greatly.

"Could I speak with her?"

"Of course," Dominique replied quickly, relieved and grateful. She opened the bedroom door and ushered the large man inside.

He saw that Scimidar was smiling as she teased the kitten with a strand of woolen yarn, delighting in the simple pleasure of dangling it before the feline's slapping paws.

But when she glanced up and saw Shadrak for the first time—the smile disappeared in an instant.

She emitted a shrill, fearful shriek. Falling over backwards, she rapidly crab-walked away from the man until she was backed into one corner of the room. She began to whimper as she huddled there with her arms thrown protectively over her head.

After casting a short, shocked glance at the equally stunned and uncomprehending Shadrak, Dominique rushed over and knelt beside the terrified girl. She circled Scimidar's shoulders with an arm and stroked her cheek with one hand.

"It's all right," she crooned to the girl in a soothing voice. "Everything's all right. Mr. Shadrak's only here to help you."

"No, mother," Scimidar sobbed, large tears welling up in her eyes. "Not him. Not him."

"Why not, darling?"

"Because some day he'll kill me," the girl declared grimly, almost angrily. "Or I'll kill him!"

Dominique looked up questioningly at Shadrak, who stood motionless as he watched the drama being played out before him. With one finger motioning for the woman to join him, he turned and left the room.

When Dominique rose to her feet and followed, Celeste rushed over to take her place in comforting Scimidar.

"I'm so sorry," Dominique said as she closed the bedroom door behind her. "I've never seen such an outburst from her before. I can't explain it."

"Don't give it another thought, dear lady," Shadrak said, apparently unfazed by what had just happened.

"But it's obvious I can be of no direct aid to her; she wouldn't stand for it."

"But I have to do something!" Desperation fairly dripped from Dominique's trembling lips.

"I agree. She definitely needs more training than you alone can provide." He took Dominique's diminutive hand in his and patted it reassuringly.

"I'll tell you what I'll do. As soon as possible, I'll send you a list of prospective people and places that might be able to tame the beast within her. Ones with no direct link to me."

"I'd be most grateful," Dominique replied. "I just need some hope."

"You'll have it," Shadrak said firmly. "And now, I'll show myself out."

Hearing the front door click closed behind the man, Dominique sagged weakly against the wall. Her own eyes now moistened.

And as with every waking minute of every day, she wondered if there truly was any hope for the troubled child who was as precious to her as was her own daughter.

# CHAPTER 6

*Five years later.*

**T**hough she was part Asian herself, the petite and pretty young woman slowly making her way up the narrow and winding mountain path on the southern coast of China seemed completely out of place.

And she was.

The locale was unfamiliar to her, though not the type of terrain. Marie Celeste Fontaine had spent a great deal of time in the mountains; but hers were half a world away and usually covered in snow. And the atmosphere was totally different.

When she reached the spot on the trail where she could finally see her destination, Celeste paused to catch her breath. Though dressed in sturdy hiking clothes rather than her preferred satin or silk, she still wanted to look her best; and so used her hands to smooth out any real or perceived wrinkles, patted her short but thick black hair into place, even bent and wiped the dust from her boots with a kerchief.

Extending forward from the rocky face of the mountain from which it had been carved was a monastery. Its origins were lost in time, but legend had it that the edifice had been chiseled in a single piece sometime in the Second Century. So the story went, an early sect of Christians, shunned by both their fellow followers of The Way and the Jews and displaced by ravaging Roman armies during the height of the Bar Kochba Rebellion, had somehow made their way here: thousands of miles from their homeland.

Directed by their god, they had built this Holy Place and had set as their mission to show their love for the divinity by devoting themselves to prayer and teaching. Such was still their calling.

As gray and forbidding in appearance as was the very stone from which it sprang, still did the monastery fill young Celeste with joy and excitement at the mere sight of it.

For all these long last few years, this was where Scimidar had resided.

How their mother had even come to know of this obscure site was unknown; but apparently it was spoken of reverently in rarified circles as a place where some of the great minds of their time had undergone schooling and training. Other than drawing comparisons to the breaking of wild horses, no one spoke of the methods the monastic school employed; but its results were said to be quite remarkable and undeniable.

Celeste had passionately wanted to accompany her life-long friend when she was sent here, but her mother had insisted that the two girls go separate ways for a time.

The girls had not seen each other in person in all that time, though they did manage to maintain a fairly steady stream of mutual correspondence via long letters and, when they were able, by sporadically reliable electronic means.

Actually, Celeste now recalled warmly, there had been one occasion, now nearly two years gone, when they had been physically reunited briefly. As if by magic, Scimidar had simply shown up unannounced and unexpected in Switzerland, intent on celebrating Christmas with her dearest friend.

It had a brief yet magical and cherished time, one of discovery for Celeste. But it was also strange, in that Scimidar had sworn her to secrecy about the visit, and that Celeste had awakened the morning after Christmas to find that Scimidar was simply no longer there.

During these years of maturation, Celeste had attended private boarding schools in Paris as well as Zurich and had recounted her experiences in those places in great detail during the times of her contacts with Scimidar.

The older girl, on the other hand, spoke seldom and little of her life in the monastery: a life she did however frequently refer to as her "exile" or her "time in the wilderness."

But now the two of them were to be fully reunited at last; Dominique had sent her daughter to fetch Scimidar back to New York. Celeste could hardly contain her joy at being able to again see the beloved companion she had taken to calling "angel."

Yet wait she must, at least for a short while longer. One did not simply waltz into the revered monastery of St. Nicodemus and sweep unannounced into the cell of the head priest, Father Deimos.

When at last she was called into the office of the schoolmaster, Celeste was disappointed to see no sign of Scimidar there. The abbot, dressed all in black from his high-peaked hat to his worn but polished shoes, was seated behind a small, unassuming desk. Celeste studied his face as she took the seat offered her on the opposite side of the desk. His long beard was more gray than black, though he looked more weary than old.

"May I offer you some tea, Miss Fontaine?" he asked. His English was laced with a not unpleasant accent she couldn't quite place.

"That would be nice, thank you."

The priest personally poured her a cup of dark, nearly black tea. As the brew passed her lips, she thought it was like the man's voice: unusual but not unpleasant in its flavor. He took a sip from his own cup before setting it aside.

"I wanted to directly give you a report on Scimidar," he said, folding his hands together on the desk top, "that you in turn could relay to your mother. Dominique is doing well, I hope?"

"I only saw her briefly before catching my flight here," Celeste replied. "To be honest, she looked a bit tired to me. But when I asked about it, she insisted she was fine."

Father Deimos smiled. "She would. Tell her we all pray for her, every day."

"I will, Father. I'm sure she'll appreciate your thoughtfulness."

The priest stared down at his clasped hands for a brief moment before resuming talking.

"I've live a good, long life," he began. "But I don't mind confessing that in all of it I have never encountered a more difficult or aggravating pupil than our Miss Scimidar."

Now it was Celeste who smiled. "That's her, all right. I don't think she can help herself."

"I don't think she tries," Deimos said sternly. "Oh, she's intelligent: so very intelligent. But she's also high-spirited and has no respect at all for authority."

Celeste sat quietly; she had no doubt these last two were not attributes the priest admired.

"In subjects that she enjoyed," he expanded, "or that she believed had some relevance to her life—art, literature, music, history—she excelled.

"At all others—math, the sciences and technology—she failed miserably. Not for lack of intelligence: no, no, no, no. Simply for lack of trying, which in turn came from lack of interest.

"Any attempt to immerse her in the philosophical or religious proved to be an exercise in futility: an utter waste of time.

"She dismissed all such as being nothing more then the pronouncements of men she felt no inclination to follow. She told us she preferred to forge her own path to and through the spiritual.

"Did I mention before that she was arrogant?"

"No, Father," Celeste said meekly.

"Well, she is. And the only 'path' she seemed interested in following was one that mostly led her through the carnal world!"

"Oh, dear," Celeste said, feeling genuinely concerned.

"At least some of our failure to get through that thick skull of hers," the priest continued, "came, quite frankly, from our inability to keep the girl in one place!

"She ran away from here more than once. Our security team was forced to track her down and fetch her back from Hong Kong, Shanghai, Bangkok—once, from as far away as Switzerland!"

Celeste lowered her head, to hide both a blush and a smile.

"But there were small victories to be cherished as well," Deimos declared with unconcealed if faint pride.

"At least now she merely absorbs the feelings of others, and not every ability they possess." At a quizzical look from Celeste, he nodded his head.

"Yes, your mother told me all about the horrible affair at the Shaolin temple. Apparently, she has retained all the fighting skills she somehow absorbed that day and even built on them, or so I've been informed. She remains a remarkably gifted physical specimen: as capable as any martial arts master. And she still loves to exercise those skills whenever possible. I think everyone here is either secretly, or not so secretly, afraid of her.

"We couldn't tame her heart, but we did at last manage to get through to her mind.

"It took the efforts of every brother here to do it, but we were at least partially successful in training the poor child in the mental disciplines required to keep that unholy empathic ability of hers in check enough to save her from being overwhelmed and driven mad by it."

The priest sat back in his chair, a pensive look on his face as he slowly shook his head from side to side.

"But *only* partially successful," he admitted. "I fear life will never be easy for her."

"But much better because of your guidance, I'm sure," Celeste said earnestly.

"I pray you're right."

Celeste drew herself up slightly straighter in her chair and smiled. "And I thank you, Father Deimos, both for the report and for your efforts on behalf of my friend. I know mother will feel the same way."

The priest smiled slightly in acknowledgment of the compliment.

"May I see Scimidar now?"

The smile evaporated.

Heaving a sigh, Deimos leaned forward. "Honesty compels me to confess that the girl is not actually within the confines of the monastery at the moment."

"WE COULDN'T TAME HER HEART..."

"What? But why not?"

Deimos threw his hands up in a gesture of resignation and defeat. "She went out three days ago, to celebrate what she called her 'graduation'."

He shook his head again.

"We haven't seen her back here since."

"Oh, no," Celeste gasped. "What if something's happened to her?"

"There's no need for alarm, young lady," the abbot declared in a voice as weary as his face. "My agents know where she is."

"And where might that be?" Celeste was losing patience with the man.

"No more than a mile from the base of this mountain: to the west and on the beach. There's a compound there that serves as what is laughingly called an artist colony. A flophouse for aimless drifters from all over the world would be a more apt characterization.

"That's where you'll find our Scimidar." In a moment of unplanned honesty he added, "And you're welcome to her."

Celeste rose to her feet and reached across the desk to shake Deimos' hand. "Thank you again, Father. I guess I'd best be at it."

"Bless you, girl. We'll be sure to add you to our nightly prayers."

At the slight twinkle she detected in the priest's eye, Celeste chuckled.

"From what you said—I expect I'll need them."

Celeste briskly walked from the monastery and descended the mountain. From there she had no difficulty at all in finding the compound of which Father Deimos had spoken; though she felt it barely qualified for that term.

It seemed to consist of nothing but a large and sprawling single-storied building that appeared far too ramshackle to qualify as a house: maintenance and repair were clearly not high on the list of priorities for its occupants.

The place didn't even have a door in its front entryway, which Celeste took as an open invitation to step inside unannounced.

Unprepared by knowledge and her nature for the sight that greeted her eyes, Celeste found herself shocked, appalled and also a little saddened as she entered upon what was clearly the aftermath of some demented and orgiastic bacchanal.

As cautiously as if she feared she might catch some disease (as well she might), Celeste picked her way over and around scores of naked bodies sprawled all over the floor and furniture. None of the revelers appeared conscious at the moment; it would not have surprised her to discover some of them were dead.

Her foot sent an empty bourbon bottle spinning and skittering across the floor; there were many such lying haphazardly about. She also spied several water pipes and discarded syringes. Atop one table, a line of powdery cocaine had somehow miraculously managed to survive.

Mixed with the lingering smell of marijuana was an even stronger and more palpable odor. Celeste was neither so innocent nor so sheltered that she did not recognize it as well.

Sex.

After several minutes of, by necessity, viewing enough human genitalia to last her a lifetime and beyond, she at last came upon Scimidar, lying as naked and exposed as the other partyers.

She had at least succeeded in laying claim to one of the compound's few beds, though she was not its sole occupant. A young and somewhat filthy looking man lay curled in a ball beside her. An almost skinny, small-busted black woman was to her other side, lying with an arm and a leg atop Scimidar. All three were deeply asleep enough to be considered dead to the world.

Celeste remembered back to that brief clandestine rendezvous in Switzerland. At one point, Scimidar had conspiratorially shown her a tiny scar on her upper left arm. She revealed to her friend that this was a subdermal capsule that she had had implanted under her skin.

The chemical cocktail it contained was slowly dispensed by the capsule and served a dual purpose, Scimidar had explained. It simultaneously acted as birth control and protection against a wide range of sexually transmitted diseases.

At the time, Celeste had been shocked by this admission, much to Scimidar's amusement.

Now, she was thankful for it.

Only after a small hand gently shook her and a familiar voice softly called her name several times did Scimidar finally rouse partially. She opened her eyes, blinking several times in an attempt to bring blurry vision into focus.

"Is that you, Celeste?" she said at last in a slurred voice.

"Yes."

Celeste was taken by surprise when Scimidar reached up and grabbed her by either side of her head. Pulling her down so she nearly fell atop the naked man, Scimidar planted a deep and soulful kiss on Celeste's mouth.

Her tongue slid between her friend's lips, carrying several tastes along with it, but also a pleasing warmth.

"I love you too, Celeste," she whispered after breaking the kiss, smiling sleepily.

"Come on, angel," Celeste said, stroking the blonde's hair and smiling back at her.

"It's time to go home."

# CHAPTER 7

*Florence, Italy.*
*Three years later.*

*A* strikingly handsome, one could almost say pretty, young man of twenty years lightly tapped the bristles of his brush to the red paint daubed on the palette he held in his left hand.

Alone in his tiny loft apartment, Tyler Sinclair found his attention had wavered slightly from the canvas upon which he worked. He set down the brush for a moment, blowing hotly on the fingers of his right hand.

Winter was drawing near, having sneaked in like the thief of light and warmth it was. Unlike in southern Italy, this town some one hundred and fifty miles northwest of Rome actually did experience cold. Sinclair hoped he would be able to make sufficient money to keep his humble dwelling place adequately heated.

Before picking up the brush to resume his work, the young artist paused to gaze out the nearest window. Below him ran the winding Arno River; in the near distance rose the Apennine Mountains.

Sinclair truly liked this ancient city, which the natives lovingly called *Firenza la Bella*.

Florence the Beautiful.

Every day since he had first arrived, the young artist felt he was continually communing with the spirits of the many famous figures that had also called it home at one time or another: da Vinci; Michelangelo; Dante; Filippo Lippi; Bocaccio; Donatello; Cellini; Machiavelli; Galileo and the brilliantly devious de Medicis.

An inner dialogue he was conducting with Bocaccio was interrupted by the sound of knuckles lightly rapping on his door.

Sinclair liked receiving callers, so long as they were not landlords or bill collectors; they enabled the inherent laziness that possessed most artists to come to the fore and provided an excuse for putting off work. And occasionally it was someone interested in buying one of his paintings, or an acquaintance who would have the means and largesse to lend him a few lire.

He could not have expected to open the door on such a vision of loveliness.

The blonde and blue-eyed woman there stood as tall as he did. She had a figure that could best be described as voluptuous, and her full lips curled in a sensuous smile.

The slender Eurasian girl who stood behind her and to one side was not so riveting in her appearance, but possessed beauty of her own.

"Won't you come in?" Sinclair invited without hesitation. The blonde woman thought his voice carried at least the trace of a British accent. Her smile broadened as she accepted his invitation.

"Would you like some wine?" he asked as he closed the door.

"That would be divine, Mr. Sinclair," the blonde responded in a voice that fairly dripped with sexuality.

"Have we met before?" he asked, mildly puzzled that she knew his name.

"Not until today."

"Before we go on," he said, "I have to ask: you *are* Scimidar, aren't you?"

"You recognized me?"

"Almost immediately. How could I not?"

Indeed, though still quite young herself, no more than a few years older than the artist, this woman had already achieved a certain degree of fame: both for her eccentric and exorbitant lifestyle (which included several alleged high profile love affairs: among them ones with a head of state and another with a highly placed clergyman of the Catholic Church) and increasingly for whispered rumors about a darker life she led in the shadows.

"I'm delighted to meet you," Sinclair gushed, gallantly taking her offered hand and lightly kissing the fingertips.

"Your renown as a patron of the arts is exceeded only by your acclaim as the face that launched a thousand male fantasies."

"Not just male," she replied airily, retrieving her hand and casting her eyes around what to her was the relative squalor of his loft dwelling.

Her eyes then returned to him, and he found himself feeling slightly exposed as she examined him. She tilted her head slightly, looking him up and down. He was slender in build: probably as much by the necessity of eating on a limited budget as by design. His hair was black and hung in waves down to his shoulders. His eyes were the green of the Mediterranean, and his lips were nearly as full and sensuous as her own were.

At first glance, the style in which he dressed seemed to be of complete indifference to the artist. The high-necked sweater he wore was unraveling at the wrists and stained with both old and new splotches of paint. His trousers, on the other hand, were nearly new and of a size she suspected was deliberately intended to boldly outline the shape of his genitals. She smiled, equally boldly and openly examining what he displayed.

"I already know all I need to know about myself, Tyler," she said at last, easily slipping into the familiarity of addressing him by his first name.

"Tell me more about you."

He shrugged but said nothing, merely gesturing for the two women to takes seats on his threadbare sofa before hustling off to the kitchen and returning shortly with three glasses and a bottle of red wine. After pouring a glass for each of the ladies, he poured one for himself and took a seat in a chair facing the sofa.

"You spend more on your wine than you do on your clothes," Scimidar observed after taking a shallow sip. Sinclair smiled, sensing this was not meant as a criticism.

"Why wouldn't I?" he replied. "One merely shelters us from the elements and the wrath of the bourgeois blue-noses…while the other nourishes our souls."

"Spoken like a true artist," she said. "Or an alcoholic."

He laughed, and she found she liked the sound of it.

"Now, tell me about yourself," she repeated. "Your life story, if you will."

He blinked, surprised that she really did want to know his story. Why, he had no idea. Nor was he normally inclined to speak of his past; but something in this woman's eyes made him want to open up to her.

"It's not exactly a fairy tale, my life's story," he told her. "I never knew my parents. Apparently, within days of my birth, I was found on the front steps of a convent in Ireland.

"I was raised, or at least I grew older, in a series of foster homes; all of them so bad they've pretty much blended together into a single, ugly gray memory.

"My last and longest stay was with a family named Sinclair. The mother there at least tried to be good to me.

"But the father was an animal. He hurt me: physically…and otherwise."

Sinclair paused, staring quizzically at Scimidar. This woman who had known him for only a few minutes appeared to be on the verge of crying. It was almost as though she could feel his emotional pain herself.

He was even more puzzled when this stranger reached out and squeezed his hand, and he drew comfort from the contact.

Sniffing rather wetly, Scimidar made a slight circling motion with her other hand, silently urging him to continue on with his narrative.

"I left the Sinclairs and their home behind me the day I turned sixteen, taking nothing with me but the clothes on my back and their name; which I figured to be as good as any other.

"I've just been knocking around ever since. Along the way, I taught myself to paint."

"You've had no formal training at all?" It was the other woman; the quiet one named Celeste who asked this question of him. She was clearly amazed at such a prospect.

"Only if you call spending hours on end inside the Louvre to keep warm and stay out of the rain formal training. And that lasted only as long as it took for them to finally kick me out.

"And I pestered a lot of street artists as well; asking them endless questions about how they did what they did. Then I just imitated all of them—a bit from this one, a dab from that one—until I developed a style that's more or less my own."

Both women were struck by how casually he relayed the details of a life that had clearly been filled with more than its share of hardships.

"I moved here to Florence about six months ago, with a girl I'd met in Spain. I think she was mostly slumming, using me to thumb her nose at her rich papa.

"About six weeks ago, though, I awoke to find her and all her belongings gone."

"And she didn't tell you why?" Scimidar asked.

"Not so much as a farewell note." Sinclair shrugged. "I suspect she went off to find an even sharper stick to poke in papa's eye."

Given the artist's philosophical and even cavalier manner, it was plan to Scimidar that this had been no ardent affair of the heart. The girl had had her fun, and Sinclair had gotten a roof over his head.

"How have you been getting by since?" she asked him.

"Oh, I've been scraping by; selling the occasional painting from the sidewalk at the Piazza Duomo, drawing funny caricatures for tourists along the Ponte Vecchio."

Sinclair leaned forward, chewing his lower lip.

"Can I ask you a question now?"

"Of course." Scimidar graced him with a warm smile before taking another sip of her wine.

"How does someone like you even know about a little nobody like me? And to what do I owe the honor of your visit?"

Rather than replying immediately, Scimidar rose from the sofa and began to walk around Sinclair's loft, pausing at each painting on display and gazing at it reflectively.

"You really are very talented," she said at last. "Gifted."

"Kind words for such meager offerings," he replied, downplaying the quality of his efforts.

Nor was he being coy or displaying false modesty. Scimidar could sense he truly believed this of his work. That he did so troubled her.

"I think maybe my preferred style is simply too old-fashioned for most modern tastes."

"That's nonsense," she snapped almost harshly. "You have a wonderful vision and it deserves to be on display at some major art galleries."

She turned from the painting she had been examining, and Sinclair felt the gaze of her pale blue eyes burrow all the way into his soul.

"I can make that happen," she told him firmly.

"I especially like this piece," she continued in the next breath, stepping in front of the canvas upon which he had been working moments earlier. "It's...provocative."

The painting she was studying was clearly a representation of the Crucifixion of Christ: but from a somewhat different perspective.

All that could be seen of the cross of execution, coming down from the top of the canvas, was the lower portion of its central, upright beam. The legs of Jesus, only shown from the shins down, were splayed to either side of that beam and held in place there by large spikes driven sideways through his anklebones and into the wood of the upright.

The bulk of the painting's surface was dedicated to the image of a young woman with auburn hair. She was partially reclined on the ground at the foot of the cross, and her hands were drenched in blood as she clutched at the crucified savior's pierced limbs. Tears flowed freely down a face whose features were twisted by horrible anguish.

"I call it 'The Sorrow of Magdalene'," Sinclair told Scimidar as he rose and came to stand beside her.

"I must have it when it's finished," Scimidar said breathlessly. "Money is no object."

"It is when you don't have enough of it," the artist joked.

"The emotion of it," she said, ignoring his jest. "It speaks to me more than you can know."

"Then consider it yours," he replied.

"At what price?"

"No one's ever offered me the moon for my work before," he said. "Or fallen in love with it so passionately."

"So it's yours for nothing: a gift from me. When it's finished."

Sinclair surprised the woman (and himself, a little) with the generous offer.

"I couldn't" she protested strongly.

"You must. It speaks to you, remember? I'm sure it wouldn't speak to anyone else."

"Thank you, Tyler," she said softly. "It'll have the best home possible."

"I'm sure it will."

She reached toward the painting with one hand, but pulled it back before she could disturb the paint by touching it.

"I've always had a great love for all forms of art," she said, tilting her head and smiling at Sinclair. "I dabble in poetry a little, myself."

"'The blood's the life'," Sinclair quoted.

"'But what is life? A dream viewed but vaguely, in endless night'."

"You know my work?" she gasped, clearly amazed. All she had ever produced were two, slender volumes she had self-published.

"Very well," he replied. "I bought both your books."

"So you were the one," she said, smiling thinly at her own self-deprecating comment.

"Purchased second hand, as you might expect. But I've read them both several times."

"I'm not very good," she declared, returning her gaze to Sinclair's painting. "But fortunately I can afford to write poetry purely for the love of it."

"Now you're the one talking nonsense," Sinclair said adamantly. "Your poems have the power to transport the reader to a place out of space and time."

He chuckled softly. "I'll admit, they *are* a bit dark: even the ones that deal with love. But at the same time you have the uncanny ability to instill beauty into even the darkest subject of them all: death."

"It's amazing. I mean that."

"Artistic inclinations must run in our family," Scimidar said rather cryptically and to Sinclair's puzzlement.

Without elaborating, Scimidar turned and returned to the sofa. Resuming her place, she took Celeste's right hand, squeezing it and placing it in her lap.

"I was raised by someone other than my parents, too," she told the artist. "But I was luckier than you. I was placed in the hands of Celeste's mother, Dominique. A more wonderful mother I could never have hoped for.

"But we lost her just a few months ago."

"I'm sorry," Sinclair replied sincerely.

"Thank you." Scimidar exhaled deeply before continuing on.

"Just before she died, Dominique gave me a small box containing certain...delicate information. That's why I'm here."

"I don't understand."

"You will. The box contained reports Dominique had received from a private investigator she had hired in response to a rumor that had reached her ears."

"What sort of rumor?"

"One regarding the possible existence of a *half-brother* of mine." She smiled warmly.

"*You're* that brother, Tyler."

His reaction to this revelation was a non-reaction; he just stared at her in stunned silence and disbelief.

"Is this a joke?" he said at last in an accusatory tone. "Some kind of trick?"

"Neither; I swear." Scimidar had a somewhat sheepish look on her face as she made an admission.

"Please don't be cross with me; but before coming to you in person I hired an agent of my own to clandestinely retrieve a sample of your DNA."

The artist blinked, even more stunned than before.

"I had the material tested. Twice, by separate laboratories," she hurried on. "The results of both showed conclusively that you and I are closely related.

"Apparently," she said, shrugging and speaking almost apologetically, "our father got around quite a bit in his life.

"It's really a marvel, I suppose, that there are only the two of us—that I know of."

"I still can't believe it," Sinclair mumbled.

"But it's true," Scimidar insisted. "Why would I be so cruel as to torment someone I'd never even met? What would be the point?"

"None that I can think of," he conceded. He sank back farther in his secondhand chair. Covering his mouth with one hand, he turned his head and stared silently out the window. Scimidar and Celeste exchanged worried glances.

They began to relax and breathe again when his head turned back in their direction and he removed his hand to reveal a smile.

"This is still a lot for me to absorb," he said. "But if it really is true…"

"It is."

His smile broadened. "Then I'd be delighted and proud to have someone like you as family."

"And *me!*" Celeste chimed in hopefully.

"And you."

Smiling through tears welling up in her eyes and still clutching Celeste's hand, Scimidar reached out to take Tyler's hand and pull him over to take a seat on the other side of her.

"Family should be together," she told her new brother. "So I want you to come live with us in New York. If you're willing."

"And leave all this?" the artist replied jokingly, making an exaggerated and sweeping motion with his free hand.

"How soon can we go?"

# CHAPTER 8

*A* thick and oppressive fog had descended upon New York City, casting a pall that made National Police Force Captain Jefferson Cooke feel even more uneasy than usual as he approached the imposing two-story Victorian mansion on Park Avenue.

But then, the campaign-hardened cop *always* dreaded coming here.

Only forty-five but looking nearly a decade older, Cooke was stooped with the invisible weight shouldered by most men of authority. As he ran a hand over the black skin of his weathered face, he felt every crevice of every wrinkle he thought he had justly earned in his life and career.

There was no denying that the dwelling he was about to breach was a beautiful home: possessed of grace and elegance.

But all Cooke really saw when his eyes lit upon it was the enormous and impassibly wide gulf that existed between those who lived in houses such as this and the rest of the teeming, struggling masses.

People like him.

But even more than the house, it was the individual who dwelt within it who generated such bilious distaste within his belly.

It was Scimidar for whom he felt such near-hate.

Unlike most such manors, this one did not have armed guards blocking the entrance or patrolling its grounds and perimeter. The deserved reputation of its owner was enough to deter most would-be intruders.

As protection from the foolish few, a fifteen-foot tall iron fence surrounded the estate: powerfully electrified and strung with rolls of concertina along its top. The grounds surrounding the mansion were also rumored to be booby-trapped, with small explosives and other, more insidious devices. The house itself contained yet other security measures.

Working against its antique appearance were rows of solar panels lining its peaked roof. Tall towers projected upward from each corner of the front of the house. Atop one of these sat a bladed windmill that generated additional power. Like most upscale houses, and as if its owner feared the dark, this one also had its own backup generator in the basement, to insure continuous electrical power through any disaster: natural or man-made.

Resigned to the inevitable, Captain Cooke pressed the button of the buzzer set in one side of the estate's heavy front gate.

"Yes?" a tinny voice that issued from a speaker challenged.

"Captain Jefferson Cooke, NPF," the lawman replied, holding up his badge for the camera lens near the speaker. He then stood perfectly still as sensors began to scan him from head to toe.

Damned foolishness, as far as he was concerned. They knew damn good and well who he was and were expecting him. Just another way for them to flout their fucking superiority in his face, was his opinion.

The sensors detected the 9mm semiautomatic service pistol in the shoulder holster worn under his jacket, as he knew they would. In his left hand was carried a small and badly abused brown leather case; its contents were also laid bare to the X-ray eyes of the sensors and found to be harmless. But these intrusive security devices' retinal and DNA scans also showed the man was indeed who he claimed to be.

Only then did the front gate swing open to allow him entry.

The finely crushed gravel of the driveway crunched under Cooke's heels as he resolutely strode toward the entryway of the manor.

In a ritual that never failed to irritate him, the oaken front door swung open while his finger was still inches away from ringing the bell.

"Good evening, Captain," Tyler Sinclair said, smiling by way of greeting.

Cooke simply grunted in response as he stepped across the threshold.

The Sinclair kid seemed like a nice enough boy, the police officer allowed, though a bit too effete in both looks and manner for Cooke's taste.

And whatever virtues he might have possessed at one time, they were bound to have been corrupted by extended exposure to and the influence of his incorrigibly decadent sister.

Cooke had by now been inside the mansion on several occasions, but still never failed to be somewhat awestruck by its sheer size and the opulence that was evident even to his unsophisticated eye.

It reminded him of a museum, so filled was it with various artifacts and works of art. Some of them, Sinclair had informed him, dated back to the time of ancient Greece.

All the furnishings were lush and expensive, and a small army of servants kept everything looking shiny and new. Even the antiquities.

The place fairly dripped with the trappings of conspicuous consumption.

The walls of the manor were resplendent with paintings: both those of the old masters and ones by relative unknowns Scimidar delighted in "discovering."

Cooke knew that Scimidar's brother had produced a fair number of the paintings adorning the walls. They included in their number several portraits of the mistress of the manor herself, usually portraying her in some stage of undress.

Cooke had no doubt she had personally posed for these, and his distaste at the thought made him again shake his large head.

Yet, grudgingly, he had to admit, at least to himself, that these were no less true works of art for all their foul, incestuous undertones.

Once he began to benefit from the patronage of his famous, long-lost sister, Tyler Sinclair had seen his stock and career as a fine artist skyrocket.

His works now hung in the finest galleries around the world and fetched astronomically high prices when put up for sale or auction.

He was widely hailed as being the leader and the finest executioner of a neo-Renaissance art movement that in its style and subject matter harkened back to the work of the masters of the 15th and 16th centuries.

And behind it all was the sister.

"She's in here," Sinclair said now, opening a mirrored door and motioning for Captain Cooke to enter.

"Jesus-fuckin'-Christ!" the cop growled as he stepped into the chamber beyond the door.

The scent of lavender washed thickly over Cooke as, to his surprise, he saw he had been ushered into a bathing room: one that was nearly as large as his entire apartment. In the center of the room was an enormous sunken tub, almost big enough to be considered a small swimming pool.

At the moment, at least half a dozen nubile young women of various shapes, sizes and colors were in it: luxuriating in thick bubbles and bathing each other.

It was not the tendrils of steam arising from the warm water alone that caused beads of sweat to erupt on Cooke's forehead.

His eyes eventually settled on the lady of the house herself. Scimidar was pressed up against one side of the tub, only partially submerged in its cleansing waters.

Her right arm rested on the marbled edge of the pool; her left arm was circled around the shoulders of the petite girl Cooke recognized as being her closest friend.

Celeste was fondling Scimidar's right breast, lightly tweaking its distended nipple. Her lips encircled the nipple of the blonde's left breast, suckling as if a babe in arms.

Scimidar's eyes were closed contentedly, and as Captain Cooke drew near to her he heard her suddenly moan and saw her arch her back, as if experiencing a mild orgasm.

Which, the veteran officer realized to his dismay and disgust, was exactly what had happened. From underneath the frothy water, yet another woman bobbed to the surface from between Scimidar's splayed legs, smiling and wiping suds from her eyes. Scimidar reached out and put a hand around the woman's neck, pulling her in for a deep and sensuous kiss.

"Captain Cooke is here to see you, darling," Tyler said, apparently inured to such sordid displays. Cooke grimaced.

"Captain!" Scimidar exclaimed, rolling over and placing both arms on the edge of the pool. "A pleasure to see you, as always."

The feeling was not mutual.

Totally unselfconscious, the woman thrust herself up out of the pool and to her feet. Standing directly in front of him as she was, Cooke's eyes were compelled to take in the sight of all of her.

She was a tall woman: six feet if not slightly more. Except for her eyebrows and the thick, long blonde tresses atop her head, her body was totally absent of hair. The muscles of her body were finely developed and defined. Her legs were long and shapely; her tummy flat until it descended to the first swells of the mound between her legs. Her breasts were large and firm: slightly conical in shape and tipped by large pink nipples and aureoles.

Captain Cooke tried his best, as he always did, not to show how shocked and appalled he was by her blatant exhibitionism; even though he knew full well that as an empath she was not only aware of his true feelings but was experiencing them herself to a degree.

He also knew she enjoyed this.

As Scimidar stood still with arms akimbo, smiling at the peace officer, Celeste took up a thick and fluffy towel and began gently drying her. Celeste dried the back of her dear friend's body first, before moving around to the front. As Celeste ran the towel up her torso and caressed both breasts, Scimidar bowed her head and playfully kissed her companion lightly on the tip of her tiny nose.

Celeste then knelt and began to briskly dry Scimidar's legs. As she worked her way up, the dark-haired girl reached around and lovingly cupped the full and swelling cheeks of Scimidar's ass.

Clutching at the blonde's bottom, the petite Eurasian softly kissed the mount of Scimidar's pussy. Moving her head lower, she snaked her tongue out and slid it between her beloved's nether lips. Almost eagerly, she lapped up the dewy juices oozing from between Scimidar's thighs.

Without conscious thought, Scimidar spread her legs to accommodate Celeste's flicking tongue. She gasped softly as Celeste began to lick in slow circles around the aroused and growing bud of her clitoris.

Celeste's head dipped, her tongue again pushed its way between the swollen lips of Scimidar's pussy. Pressed as tightly to the shaved mound as possible, she snaked her tongue inside the moist opening as far as she was able, laving the inner walls.

Scimidar sighed deeply and began to thrust her hips forward as if she were being fucked by a soft yet probing cock. Celeste let her tongue slide out of the fiery cavern and continued running it upward until it again swirled around the bud of her lover's clitoris.

Feeling her devoted lover take all her clit in her mouth, Scimidar bucked harder against her. As Celeste sucked ravenously on the nubbin, Scimidar grabbed her tiny lover's head and pressed it more firmly against her mound.

Celeste began to alternate between flicking at the love button with her tongue and sucking on it. Her hands clenched tighter on Scimidar's ass and pulled her forward so as to facilitate increasing the pressure she was applying to the tiny organ.

Captain Cooke, more repelled than aroused by what he was watching, saw Scimidar's entire body shudder multiple times as she rose up on her toes and moaned loudly.

A similar moan rolled up from Celeste's throat, and only then did the lawman notice that while she had been orally ministering to Scimidar, Celeste had dropped one hand between her own legs and was now rapidly plunging two fingers in and out of her likewise slick and hairless pussy.

As the breathing and body movements of both women slowed to normal, Celeste pulled her head back, tilting it to smile up at Scimidar. She then once more kissed the blonde's swollen vaginal lips and patted them dry with the towel.

As she did, Scimidar shuddered lightly once again.

Only then, from behind her, did her brother approach. Tyler was holding up a diaphanous dressing gown into which Scimidar slipped her arms.

Tyler pulled the gown around her to the front, hugging her around the waist as he did. Looking lovingly at him over her left shoulder, Scimidar reached up and caressed the flawless skin of his beautiful face.

Her fingers laced into his thick hair and pulled his head down closer to hers. The two of them exchanged a deep, lingering and passionate kiss. When their mouths at last parted, his then traveled a path down the outer swell of her neck: while she whispered words meant only for him in his ear.

When she at last broke contact and pulled away from her brother, Captain Cooke couldn't help but notice the unmistakable bulge of an erection straining against the tight material of Sinclair's trousers.

The staid police officer nearly felt physically ill to his stomach.

# CHAPTER 9

*A*s he had done so often before, Captain Cooke silently cursed the fact that Scimidar insisted upon having him alone act as the principal liaison between her and the NPF; she would talk to no other.

He was convinced the reason for her adamant stance on the matter was plain: the crazy bitch took some sort of perverse pleasure in seeing him squirm uncomfortably when she inflicted such twisted scenes upon him. His anger, discomfort and disgust fed some sick hunger within her empty soul, and she went out of her way to provoke such reactions from him.

"Are you on your way to some sort of emergency situation?" she asked him, catching him slightly off guard.

"No. Why?"

"Oh, that simply seemed like the most likely explanation for why a gentleman would not remove his hat in the presence of ladies."

Cooke's cheeks burned hotly as he snatched his battered fedora from his head, nearly crushing it in his beefy, clutching hand. Scimidar smiled at him coolly.

"We'll all be more comfortable in the drawing room," she then said, laying one hand lightly atop Tyler's offered arm. "Won't you join us, Captain?"

She didn't wait for his reply before walking away. Behind her and Tyler came Celeste, now dressed in a shimmering blue and gold silk kimono.

Before following, Captain Cooke looked skyward, praying for the strength to resist the temptation and urge to pull out his gun and shoot the crazy cunt.

The tiny entourage marched into a nearby room nearly twice the size of the bathing chamber. (And what of all the women they had left behind there? If anyone besides Cooke gave this a second thought, he saw no indication of it. Apparently, like all the inhabitants of this wildlife preserve, they were free to come and go as they saw fit.)

The drawing room was darkly cool and dimly lit, with elegant furniture sprinkled about. The walls were paneled in mahogany.

On an end table next to a velvet sofa, chilling on ice and always kept handy, was a bottle of Scimidar's favorite beverage: champagne.

"We always find refreshment to be a welcomed treat after bathing," she said, accepting a glass of bubbly from Tyler before he poured libations for himself and Celeste.

"Won't you join us, Captain?" she asked as she took a seat on the sofa. "It's Dom Perignon, shipped to us directly from the Marne Valley."

"Not while I'm on duty," Cooke replied, though truth be told, he probably would have indulged had the offering been something a little stouter, like beer or bourbon.

"Ah, yes," Scimidar said, drawing her legs up and languidly reclining on the divan.

"Duty. Which brings us to the nature of your visit, my dear Captain."

About damn time, he thought. But before the lawman could voice his aggravation, a low rumbling sound that rose into a high-pitched yowl caused Cooke to jump and his hand to instinctively flash toward his shoulder holster.

Slightly abashed by this unthinking reaction, he lowered his hand as Scimidar laughed lightly. The sound of her mirth caused the nerves of Cooke's spine to twist painfully.

As Cooke had known intellectually, and as he realized too late to be spared her galling laughter, the growling noise had come from the twisted branches of a faux "tree" displayed in one corner of the drawing room. Rising to a height of ten feet from floor level, it had been carved from the preserved trunk and branches of an actual cedar tree; thus, after a fashion, turning it into a work of art.

The primal growl that had sparked Cooke's reaction had issued from deep inside the throat of a fully-grown *leopard*.

Cooke's eyes had now fully adjusted to the faint lighting in the room, and he could clearly make out the beast lying on its belly astride one of the tree's lower limbs; its paws dangling down on either side of the branch.

It was an Arabian leopard, the smallest sub-species of that branch of the feline family: weighing no more than fifty pounds.

It was no less potentially dangerous for that, Cooke knew. This creepy creature was yet another of the many reasons he had for hating to set foot in this madhouse.

Yet Scimidar insisted on keeping it as a pet, as others might an ordinary house cat. She had named this big she-cat *Belladonna*, and gave it free rein to prowl the house and grounds as it pleased.

That, at least, Captain Cooke could see some practical point to. A leopard on the prowl served as yet another deterrent to would-be home invaders.

The cop shifted uncomfortably from one foot to the other as the big cat chose this moment to hop down from its perch and pad across the room.

As it passed near Cooke, the leopard chuffed its dislike for the man. A rumbling sound came out as the cat curled its upper lip back in a sneer that revealed inch-long fangs

"Belladonna," Scimidar scolded. "We mustn't mistreat guests."

The cat swung her head away from the man to fix its baleful yellow eyes on Scimidar. As she then approached her mistress, her growls became more like purrs. Drawing nigh, she rubbed her head against the woman, seeking attention.

Scimidar gladly and lovingly obliged. She took the leopard's head in her hands and began to gently scratch behind the cat's ears. The woman lowered her head and kissed the animal with the same passion she had shared with Tyler and Celeste minutes earlier.

A cough from Captain Cooke killed the moment. Belladonna drew away from her mistress and loped back to her tree.

"If you're through havin' inter-species sex...?" Cooke said in a growl that was deeper than that of the leopard.

"THERE IS NO BEAUTY WITHOUT THE BEAST."

"There is no beauty without the beast," was all Scimidar replied enigmatically before draining her wineglass and holding it out for Tyler to refill.

"Right," Cooke said, not even attempting to understand. "But I'd like to get down to business."

It was the "business" of which he spoke that made a traditionalist such as Cooke bristle the most.

In these unprecedented and depressed times, conventional methods of law enforcement were sorely lacking: not just manpower, but also supplies, equipment and other resources. The results were inevitable: a more dangerous and crime-ridden society.

To counter the increasing levels of lawlessness, the wealthy few in New York (as in most major cities of America) had formed their own *Citizens Crime Committee*. To men such as Captain Cooke, their activities smacked of vigilantism such as had been rampant in the days of the American Old West; but with no other viable solutions presenting themselves at the current moment in time, such was a bitter pill he was forced to swallow.

The controlling members of the CCC had pooled a portion of their considerable financial reserves into an enormous endowment fund devoted to whatever they deemed essential and best for public safety: "public" primarily meaning themselves.

They had overseers installed within the halls of Police Headquarters and City Hall; and whenever a potential problem arose that they decided was beyond the level of the threats the tiny and beleaguered police force could handle, they turned elsewhere.

Not to their own security forces, of course, those being needed to provide them with their own personal protection; but rather to individuals such as Scimidar whom they had come to trust to deal effectively with such menaces.

Scimidar was valued because she was one of their own; but more especially because of her unique ability to hunt down fugitives and suspected troublemakers. Her empathic powers essentially made her a sort of "psychic bloodhound."

The board of directors of the CCC was both able and willing to pay her large sums of money to keep said difficulties from their own front doors. Their wealth (often used to pay for what the government subsidies alone could not provide to the local police) granted them enormous influence with both city government and law enforcement. They used that to dictate when their private agents were to be used and to guarantee that those agents received both full cooperation and great latitude in the means they used to achieve their ends.

As a long-time veteran who proudly proclaimed he bled NYPD blue, Jefferson Cooke deeply, bitterly resented having to submit to the dictates of civilians. Rubbing salt in this wound of the ego was the fact that he knew Scimidar was often fed official information that was above his pay grade, to aid her in her efforts on behalf of the authorities. This and the favoritism shown to her and others of her kind galled Cooke greatly.

He also knew that Scimidar was already tremendously wealthy in her own right, and most certainly had no real need for the extra income derived from her paralegal activities.

In fact, though her life code seemed to be that money serves no real purpose save to make one feel better, Cooke believed this crazed female relished the danger and the license to kill her position bestowed upon her to such an extreme extent that she would probably perform these dark duties for free.

What Cooke didn't know, and would never learn from her or the members of what she considered to be her family, was that in essence this was precisely what Scimidar did.

She had secretly set up a dummy non-profit, philanthropic foundation, administered by Celeste, that funneled most of the money she earned from the CCC into food banks, shelters for the homeless and for abused women and children, refugee camps and scores of other charitable causes around the world.

Even if he had been informed of this, so deeply was the loathing for this woman beyond his comprehension ingrained in Cooke's heart that he would probably not have believed it.

And it was true that Scimidar freely used her personal fortune to fuel a life of excess, decadence, debauchery and self-indulgence. She couldn't and wouldn't deny this.

Cooke knew this much about her for certain. It was this almost schizophrenically dualistic aspect of her psyche that resulted in few people who knew her having neutral feelings toward the woman. They either loved her or they hated her.

Cooke was firmly in the latter camp, holding nothing but contempt for her and all her ilk. Just a few minutes in her presence, he had confessed to some of his fellow officers, and he was almost ready to become a card-carrying cake-eater. Kill the rich bitch and be done with it.

But above all he was a good cop, and an honest one. So he followed orders and did as he was told.

"Now, what was this business you wanted to discuss, Captain?" the woman now asked, intruding on his dark and brooding thoughts.

By way of responding, Cooke reached into an inner pocket of his cheap suit coat and pulled out a well-used smart phone. Tapping a few commands on its clouded, cracked surface, he then set it down atop a coffee table in front of Scimidar's sofa.

Accompanied by a rather anemic humming sound, a faint cone of light sprang up from the phone. Moments later, the flickering, holographic image of a man appeared inside the cone.

Even though only able to view it dimly, Scimidar knew in the instant that she was looking at the face of a killer.

# CHAPTER 10

Scimidar swung her legs off the divan so she could lean in closer to the image being projected upward by the smart phone; so faint was it that she could not otherwise have made out any details. The 3-D picture was of a brutish-looking man: his hair was dark and unkempt, his eyes small and nearly touching above a broad nose. His mouth was crooked and no razor had met his square jaws in several days.

The image began to sputter and spark; then disappeared altogether.

"Fuckin' piece o' shit!" Cooke cursed. "Just like every other mechanical device nowadays." He picked up the defunct phone and slapped it a time or two in the vain hope that such abuse would fix it.

"Not that it would matter if it was brand new," he declared, slipping the dead device back into his pocket. "We only get reliable signal half the time—if we're lucky." He tilted his head and squinted as if trying to peer through the roof of the mansion and into the night sky.

"The FCC informed us that yet another old communications satellite's orbit has begun to decay.

"It's expected to come crashing back to Earth somewhere here on the Atlantic Seaboard any day now."

"Are you here to ask us to repair your phone, Captain?" Scimidar said archly.

The cop's eyes burned daggers into the woman, but he clamped his lips tightly and bitterly swallowed the words he wanted to hurl at her.

"The guy you saw in the hologram," he said instead, "is a foreign national named Stavros Bolgarus. About this time yesterday, security guards on duty at the Port Authority believed they caught sight of him entering the city."

"And I take it that's a bad thing."

"Maybe the worst thing, sister, though there's not a whole lot we know about him with certainty. We don't even know if that's his real name.

"He's thought to be originally from somewhere in the Balkans. He has ties to several different terrorist networks worldwide. All of them have made good use of his particular expertise."

"Which is what?"

"Explosives. He's made bombs small enough to fit inside an ink pen—and big enough to take out half a city block."

"You said he's plied his trade around the world, and for different groups," Scimidar probed. "Is there any other connection between these various terror cells?"

"None that I know of," Cooke replied, his eyes narrowing. He recognized the look on the strange woman's face; he should, as he'd now seen it on numerous occasions.

It was the look of growing excitement.

"As near as we can determine, Bolgarus is totally devoid of any specific national, ethnic, religious, political or ideological loyalty.

"He's purely mercenary, willing to hire himself out to whoever will pay him the most. He's strictly in it for the money."

"And the thrill," Scimidar speculated. Her lips curled in a near smile.

"Maybe. You'd know more about that than I would," the lawman groused. "Clearly he has no conscience. Men, women, children: he kills without hesitation or discrimination."

"And you're sure he's here."

"Sure enough not to take chances. The security guards who thought they recognized him told us he bolted when they tried to confront him. They gave chase, but he managed to give them the slip."

Cooke now held up the small case that he'd been carrying this entire time, extending it out toward Scimidar.

"He left this behind. Near as we can tell, there's nothing in it but a change of clothes. I figured that would be enough for you."

"It will be," Scimidar said confidently. She accepted the case into her hands; as she did so, Cooke noted her head and shoulders shake slightly.

"And what specifically is it you want me to do, Captain?"

"Officially, we want you to track down Bolgarus, capture him and place him into our custody." His features hardened.

"*Un*-officially...no one at the NPF would shed a tear if you just killed the murdering bastard."

"That option doesn't sound very prudent," the blonde hunter commented, frowning slightly.

"It seems almost certain that a man like this Bolgarus is only here in response to a job offer."

"Yeah."

"So if I simply kill him...there will be no way of learning who made him the offer or what their plan for him was."

"What you say is true," Cooke conceded. "But at the very least his death would probably delay whatever scheme is being hatched; might even cause it to be scrapped.

"But as always," he concluded grudgingly, "you have total autonomy and can pursue this matter in any way you see fit."

"I will, Captain," she said coolly. "Tyler, would you be kind enough to show our guest out?" The dismissive tone of her voice was not lost on the police officer.

"Don't bother," Cooke snapped, slamming his fedora back on his head. "I can find my own way out. Contact me as soon as you learn anything." His left eye twitched as he struggled to voice the next words.

"Or if I can be of any help to you."

"Don't I always?" Scimidar replied.

Cooke's eye was twitching faster as he spun and left the room. As the lawman stomped away, eager to be gone, Tyler knelt down before his sister.

"Would it do any good to ask you to be careful?" he said solicitously. She smiled and reached out to stroke his hair with one hand.

"I'm always careful, darling," she said sweetly. And though they both knew this to be a lie, her brother returned her smile.

"Now, I have to get ready," she told him. "And if I'm not mistaken, you have work to do, too; and a model waiting upstairs for you." Leaning forward, she tenderly kissed him, her tongue flicking out to dance along his own.

"Try not to break her heart."

# CHAPTER 11

*F*inishing her second glass of champagne, Scimidar rose from her sofa and stretched languorously.

"Will you assist me, Celeste?" she said.

"Don't I always?" her diminutive companion replied, imitating both the wording and the inflection of the reply Scimidar had made to Captain Cooke.

Scimidar laughed heartily, then spun in a swirl of chiffon and headed out of the room. Passing breezily through two adjoining chambers, she came to the only door inside the mansion that normally remained locked.

She raised her right hand and pressed its palm against a keypad embedded in the wall. Seconds later, the door slid open; so smooth was the mechanism that it made virtually no noise.

Beyond the door was a room no larger than one of her walk-in closets. This chamber seemed more like a religious shrine; it had no electric lights but was rather illuminated by large candles that ignited with the opening of the door. Their soft glow did not dispel all the shadows from the room, adding to its air of mystery.

With Celeste's practiced assistance, the tall woman began to prepare herself, as might a professional athlete: first dropping her gown to stand naked. Her porcelain skin fairly glowed in the reflected light from the candles.

Celeste taped her wrists and ankles with copper-infused wrappings that offered extra support. Specially designed elastic bracings went over her knees and elbows.

Scimidar next donned a unique undergarment that began at her thighs, then covered her torso to the base of her throat. It was composed of thin, gel-like padding under a state of the art, lightweight Kevlar weave.

This garment served multiple purposes: squeezing and protecting her hamstrings; softening the impact of blows to the body and to an extent deflecting knife blades and small caliber bullets. All without impeding her freedom of movement.

After a few moves crafted to test that flexibility, she was ready to don her final garment: one she called her "*night suit.*"

This was a sort of form fitting unitard that covered her entire body from its soft yet firmly soled booties to just under her chin. The suit was almost entirely black in color, but its torso, arms and legs were marked by slashing stripes of white: the suit thus provided her with a degree of camouflage protection in the dark world where her work usually took her.

Facing some of the candles with her arms raised, the hunter swiveled slowly back and forth from side to side. As she did so, the white stripes in her suit would change shape slightly; sometimes, one stripe would disappear and elsewhere on the suit another would take its place, thus enhancing its cloaking capabilities.

All that remained was for her to take up the only type of armament she chose to carry. She stepped close to the chamber's far wall, upon which hung—framed and above a small pedestal—the pair of tonfas she had received (taken) from the old Shaolin martial arts sensei the day she had first fully tapped into her unusual abilities.

Atop the pedestal rested two small objects she now took in hand. At first glance they appeared to be another set of tonfas, but these consisted of nothing more than the short butt end and the vertical grips by which they could be held.

They were actually special metal housings of her own design, forged by Swiss craftsmen under her personal supervision.

Holding them tightly, Scimidar flexed her hands on the grips in a specific way. When she did, telescoping titanium tubes shot out from the fronts of the grips. Each was fifteen inches long, making them formidable weapons: ones far stronger than was a pair of traditional wooden tonfas.

But this was not the limit of their capabilities, for she had added yet another modification to the design of these lethal tools of her trade.

She flexed her fingers yet again, in a subtly different way, and the titanium tubes collapsed back into their handle housings. Remaining behind in their place was that which otherwise rested inside the tubes: two glistening blades. Forged from Damascus steel, one edge of each pointed blade was honed to razor sharpness.

The blonde hunter took several minutes to execute a series of ritualized moves, rather like those native to tai chi: flexing and loosening her muscles, reacquainting herself with the balance and feel of the tonfas.

As always in such times, Celeste looked on with trepidation, unhappy about the dangerous journey her angel was about to embark upon yet again. Yet, also as always, she gave no voice to those concerns.

There was no need, and no purpose to be served.

Finishing her warm-up exercises, Scimidar flexed her fingers to trigger the mechanism that retracted the steel blades back into the butts of the tonfas. She then slapped them against the outer thighs of her night suit, where special materials sewn into the fabric held them firmly in place but easily retrievable.

In another familiar part of the ritual, Scimidar circled Celeste in her arms and kissed her softly.

"I'll be all right," she promised, before turning to leave the room.

Celeste remained behind. In times like this, she used the small, candle-lit chamber as a chapel of sorts, wherein she always fervently prayed for her dearest friend's safe return.

And for her soul.

With eyes closed, Scimidar listened to the soothing humming sound made by the private elevator she now rode to descend to the mansion's basement garage.

There she kept a small collection of automobiles, both vintage and new. Front and center was the vehicle she preferred on such operations: a customized and armored black limousine.

Her personal driver, dressed in a black, somewhat militarized version of a chauffeur's uniform that she had also taken a hand in designing, stood at attention next to the auto. In a shoulder holster worn on the outside of his uniform nestled a blue steel .45 caliber semi-automatic pistol.

Ray Crawford was a large man—6'3" of rock hard muscle—as well as being a former Army Ranger. In his mid-30s, he had features that could have been chiseled from weathered granite. He held one of the back doors open for his boss, nodding curtly and silently to the woman as she entered the vehicle.

Her relationship with this highly capable man was strictly business, and she took comfort in seeing that he was on full alert even though they were still in the safe confines of her home.

There were four different exit tunnels that led out of the basement garage. Only Scimidar ever knew which one they would take in departing and she tried to make her choice as randomly as possible. Each tunnel led to a different concealed exit, all of which were located several blocks away from the mansion. She conveyed tonight's choice of exit to Crawford and the limo quietly raced forward as he fed it the gas.

Once out on the street, she directed the driver to take her to the approximate location where the bomber Bolgarus was last seen. There were some limits of both time and distance to the effectiveness of her empathic abilities, so she wanted to waste not a minute.

Their passage through the city was not constrained at this time of night. With fewer people living within its bounds, and fewer still that could afford the luxury of owning and maintaining an automobile, traffic was relatively light at all times. This was even truer after sundown, when the lawless element made even the shortest commute a potentially dangerous adventure. As they proceeded toward their destination, Scimidar read and memorized the sparse contents of a file on Bolgarus that Cooke had given her along with the bomber's case.

Crawford pulled the limo to the curb upon reaching the spot a short distance from the Port Authority where Bolgarus had succeeded in eluding the rather inept security guards who worked at that facility. The place was on 8th Avenue, about midway between the Port and Penn Station.

Only now did Scimidar open the small leather case she had been given by Captain Cooke. He had not exaggerated; there was nothing inside it save a pale blue shirt, dark trousers, underpants and a pair of socks. She removed the shirt, lifting it up close to her face.

At the sound of a gasp coming from the back seat of the car, Ray Crawford tensed. His eyes darted to the rearview mirror.

His muscles immediately relaxed and his hand fell away from his pistol as he realized his boss was simply reacting to the empathic "scent" she was absorbing from the shirt.

The blonde hunter moaned gutturally and her eyes clenched shut as her brain was assaulted by horrible, violent images.

Images of fire and smoke that blotted out the sun. Of destruction. Of blood by the gallons; and body parts too small to identify as male or female, adult or child.

Most disconcerting was the simultaneous sense of *glee* that accompanied those images. This was a man who delighted in his terrible, bloody handiwork.

Finally, and more importantly to the task at hand, Scimidar flashed on a visual image, as if she was looking through the killer's own eyes, of Bolgarus ducking down into a subway entrance she recognized as being nearby.

She returned the rumpled shirt to the case, closed the lid and threw the bag out the window.

"I'll be leaving you now, Ray," she told her driver. "Return to the mansion—but remain on call."

Crawford never questioned her orders, nor did he now; knowing that she preferred to hunt alone but also that she would not hesitate to summon him if and when she felt the need for further service from him.

So he simply said, "Yes, ma'am," as she exited the limo and moved off into the night.

She was now in her own element.

# CHAPTER 12

**S**cimidar's soft footpads made no noise as she descended the concrete steps into the bowels of the subway station.

As she expected, the station was largely deserted at this time of night. Because of the Depression and the enormous loss of population New York had experienced, the trains only ran twice a day now: for brief periods in the morning and again in the evening, to accommodate those few who did still work in the city.

There was no longer a great flow of traffic between the several parts of town. The lack of jobs, depressed economy and difficulty in travel had necessitated each section of the city becoming more self-sustaining than had been the case for several generations. The five boroughs of New York had again become like separate, individual cities.

This did not mean that the vast subway system was totally empty during the long off-hours: quite the contrary. To a greater extent than ever before, an entire sub-culture, consisting mainly of the extremely poor, the criminal, the mentally impaired and those simply malcontent with society had made the myriad of tunnels and stations their country, their home.

Collectively, these lost souls were known both to others and to themselves as *Downsiders*.

Within them all festered a violent, unquenchable hatred for all *Toppers*: those who dwelt above ground.

That didn't stop them from roaming around the above world at night, on foraging missions: digging through trash or robbing those foolish enough to be caught out in the open at certain times of night and in certain parts of town.

Such victims of the Downsiders seldom lived to regret or repeat their mistakes.

The Toppers nursed a similar hatred for these dregs of society, thinking of them as no more than wild animals.

Some of these dwellers in darkness more than fit that description.

Downsiders usually avoided the stations during those periods when the trains ran, for there were always armed police patrolling them in those times. But in the off hours, like roaches when the lights go dark, they would scurry out of the tunnels and congregate on the loading platforms to scour through garbage receptacles and to "socialize."

A cluster of perhaps a dozen such Downsiders was gathered on the platform of the station as Scimidar made her way from the stairwell. At first they took no note of her, so engrossed were they in the contents of a large trash can they had tipped over so they might more easily pick through the treasures thus revealed.

Then one of them glanced up from her work: a woman whose age was near impossible to determine due to her lack of teeth, possibly prematurely gray hair and the layer of filth that concealed the contours of her face. She ducked back down and began to frantically whisper a warning to the others in her clan.

All eyes then turned toward Scimidar. They all recognized her instantly: all Downsiders were familiar with this blonde angel of pain and death. Most of them feared her with near superstitious dread.

Others felt no such fear. To them, she was just another Topper to be despised and disposed of.

As several others of the cluster quickly backed away and melted into the concealing darkness of the subway tunnel, those brave souls who remained began to shuffle toward the interloper.

Most of them wielded the Downsiders' weapon of choice: lead pipes. At least two of them flashed knives.

"Don't come any closer," Scimidar warned them, in a voice that was calm yet firm.

"You're safe from me—tonight," she said. "I haven't come for any of you, nor for your kith nor kin."

"Don't matter," a large, knife-carrying man replied, his brown teeth revealed by lips attempting a dangerous smile. "Don't care. You're here… and we aim ta gut ya."

As the derelicts moved toward her, their murderous urges swept over Scimidar's psyche. In response, she snatched loose her tonfas and raised them up before her, with arms crossed. She then snapped her arms down and to the sides.

*ZZHHNNGG!*

The metallic whirring sound made by the titanium tubes telescoping out of the tonfas filled the station. If landed in a blow to the proper spot on the body and with sufficient force, the glistening tubes could be just as lethal as the bladed attachments they concealed, but were much less certain to be so.

The blonde hunter seldom killed *solely* for the fun of it.

A few more of the clustered Downsiders, clearer of mind and less driven by rage, upon seeing Scimidar deploy these givers of pain turned face to flee and join their brethren who had already departed for the sanctuary of the tunnels.

The man with brown teeth called after them to come back, but his command was ignored. In the Downside, there were no recognized leaders; it was every man for himself.

Casting a jaundiced eye back at Scimidar, who had now assumed a defensive pose that almost dared attack, Brown Teeth let out a loud and primal scream. This was echoed by a collective yell from the others as they charged at the woman en masse.

They were immediately thrown on the defensive themselves when Scimidar, rather than waiting for them to come to her, instead pounced forward into their midst.

As they stumbled back, Scimidar whipped her tonfas from side to side. One slapped against the side of a man's head, dropping him as if he had been poleaxed. Another caught a scrawny woman under the chin, lifting her off her feet and hurling her over the edge of the loading platform to land on the rails below with a sickening thud.

The untrained derelicts could not match Scimidar's dexterity as she bobbed and weaved amongst them. With a sharp jerk of her head, she dodged the swing of a pipe that instead connected with the mouth of another Downsider, smashing rotten teeth in a spray of blood and pus.

Frustrated by their inability to bring her down, the anger and hate within their primitive hearts grew more fiery. As it did, Scimidar was transported to an almost ecstatic state of being: reveling in the violent emotions she was absorbing and redirecting back at her attackers.

She was also simultaneously feeling their pain: both from the blows she was delivering and from the litany of sores and diseases that were constant companions of this flotsam of society.

But the pain too was a physiological and emotional sensation she welcomed at such moments as this.

She drove the butt of one tonfa so forcefully into the belly of a Downsider female that the woman spewed the remnants of whatever rancid food had been her dinner.

As the out matched woman toppled to one side, Scimidar brought up both tonfas, crossing them to block the downward arc of a lead pipe being aimed at her head.

The man employing the pipe was large and surprisingly strong; and the force of his swing caused her knees to buckle slightly. The swinging pipe came within an inch of her face before she was able to stop its impetus.

She then began to push back against the pipe, but such was the strength of the Downsider that she was hard-pressed. Worse, being caught in a clench with him had brought her spinning movements to a standstill and left her open to attack from other quarters.

She was so close to the face of the Downsider trying to force her to the floor that she could see the bulging veins in his nose and the yellow cast to his eyes that were symptomatic of a heavy drinker. His rank breath assailed her own nostrils.

And as feared, she now sensed the impending approach of another opponent from behind her. She was unsure if she could break away from the one before the other would be able to club her from the rear.

That's when the first gunshot cracked.

At the sharp and unmistakable sound, the Downsider who was engaging in close combat with Scimidar broke off and backed away from her fearfully. Freed from their clench, Scimidar spun to face the threat she had sensed behind her.

Only there was no threat.

Standing there, stunned expression reflected in nearly lifeless eyes, was Brown Teeth. A wet red flower was blossoming in the center of his chest: and the long knife that he had been poised to thrust at her back now dropped from his limp right hand.

A second shot roared.

Brown Teeth's head jerked back sharply as a lead projectile slapped into his throat. The slug's exit blew out a thick slab of his spinal column, and he toppled heavily over backwards.

Three more shots rang out in rapid succession. A Downsider woman screamed shrilly, as the brains of the man nearest to her seemed to explode from his skull and spray her with bloody gray matter.

A third man groaned heavily and managed to stagger a few steps before the bullet in his belly put him on the floor. Scimidar's eyes narrowed as she saw ropy intestines ooze from the mortal wound.

With that, the battle ended. The few Downsiders still on their feet turned tail and ran. Their screeches of fear and shock remained in the air long after they vanished into the cover of the tunnels.

Scimidar had long since dropped into a low crouch: her eyes warily scanning the darkness from where the gunshots had come. But she sensed no threat; she could detect no imminent danger.

So she allowed herself a moment now to "digest" fully the wealth of emotions and sensations around and within her: the pain and fear that could not mask the lingering hatred of the injured and wounded still laid out on the platform.

Even the hollow oblivion of the dead was grist for her emotional mill.

She found it all to be exhilarating beyond description or explanation.

Her breasts rose and fell as she breathed in and out deeply; her eyes were wide and sparkling. Every nerve in her body tingled. Had Captain Cooke been there to witness her response to this violent mayhem, he might have mistaken it for the same one he had seen when she was gripped by sexual orgasm.

At last she rose fully erect: retracting the tubular shafts of her tonfas and returning the grips to their normal resting places on her outer thighs.

Even as she did so, the figure who had fired the earlier gunshots finally stepped forward out of his place of concealment in the shadows and into the light.

The man was unfamiliar to Scimidar, but so striking in appearance, even at a distance of some twenty feet, that she knew she would never forget him.

He stood two or three inches taller than herself, with the dusky skin and dark eyes of a Latino, set in a face that could be best described as ruggedly handsome.

He appeared to be her age or slightly older. His thick black hair hung partially down over his forehead. On either side of his face, slightly longer, narrow and tightly braided strands dangled.

A thin silver ring pierced the right nostril of his aquiline nose. A delicate silver chain attached to that ring looped back to his right ear, where the other end was hooked to an earring that was shaped like a human skull.

Scimidar's eyes scanned down. The gunman wore a short, waist-length leather jacket whose blackness was flecked with the reflected light from silver studs set in the material. On each hand he wore black leather gloves: each finger of the gloves was cut away to expose his long, thick fingers, and metal studs dotted each knuckle.

His nearly skin tight light gray trousers were tucked into the tops of black boots of the type favored by bikers. Chains circled the low heels of each boot, much like the spurs of an old-time cowboy.

Scimidar's eyes moved back upward, pausing to gaze with undisguised interest and approval at the man's groin. So clinging was the material of his trousers that it not only revealed but highlighted the thickness of what appeared to be a quite formidable penis snaking down the inside of his left leg.

Reluctantly tearing her gaze away from his male member, Scimidar returned her scrutiny to the man's hands.

In them he was holding a rather unusual weapon. In appearance, it looked like a lever-action rifle whose barrel had been cut short, as had its butt. The lever appeared to be much larger than normal. She couldn't know the specifications of the rifle, which in its modified state was only twenty-five inches long and weighed a mere six pounds.

Around the man's slim waist sat a wide belt with extra shells in loops. Attached to the belt and strapped to his right thigh was a customized holster sling to carry the weapon.

The man spoke not a word to Scimidar; but he wore a cocky grin on his face as he casually yet with deliberate care reloaded his rifle with .44 Mag rounds.

Scimidar made no effort to initiate a conversation with this gunman who had unbidden insinuated himself into her personal fight; so the two of them stood less than seven yards apart, simply staring at each other in silence.

The woman was puzzled and slightly disconcerted; though her expression revealed neither. For some inexplicable reason, she was experiencing greater difficulty getting a complete empathic "read" on this unusual man than had ever been the case for her with anyone else.

She could identify and absorb some emotions from him—supreme confidence being the strongest—but only some: and those only in fleeting snatches. She thought he was intrigued with her. She knew she was intrigued with him.

The silence between the two of them stretched on for a full minute before finally, feeling inexplicably drawn to the gunman but also rather frustrated by the barrier around his psyche, Scimidar spun away and leaped from the loading platform. Landing catlike, she set off at a trot down the tracks.

The man's smile broadened as he watched the blonde hunter sprint away.

"So that was Scimidar," he muttered softly, shaking his head.

He had heard of her many times on the streets of which he was a frequent denizen, but never before had he actually laid eyes upon her or seen her in action. He was impressed on both scores by what he had witnessed: by her fighting prowess and by her breathtaking beauty and raw sexuality. He found himself wanting to know more.

He returned his short gun to its holster and sauntered over to more closely examine the corpses cluttering the loading platform.

Kneeling beside the body of the first man he had shot, he pried the dead Downsider's mouth open. The brown teeth, along with other physical features, were enough to convince him he had targeted the right miscreant.

He searched the pockets of Brown Teeth and the others until he found what he expected and wanted: a can of red spray paint. The Downsiders had an inordinate fondness for tagging buildings topside with sprayed graffiti.

After vigorously shaking the can, the gunman walked around the fallen Brown Teeth, spray-painting a circle on the floor all the way around the body. He then laid down a diagonal line that ran from one side of the circle to the other, with the line passing over the Downsider's body.

He then painted a message of his own on the floor below the circled corpse. Stepping back to inspect the words when he was finished, he nodded approvingly. It was a message he felt sure all other Downsiders would understand and take to heart.

It read: *Don't mess with Mother's girls.*

Satisfied that his mission was successfully accomplished, he tossed away the spray can and headed for the stairs that would take him back up to street level.

A few steps up, he stopped and turned back around. He prided himself on possessing keen hearing, but he could detect no sounds coming from the direction in which Scimidar had run. He admired her stealth.

He shrugged. After all, she and her business were of no real concern to him.

# CHAPTER 13

*A* mile away from the subway station where bloody battle had just been waged, Stavros Bolgarus waited impatiently inside an abandoned garage.

The bombing expert had been holed up alone here for more than twenty-four hours, and was growing increasingly jumpy. If not for the fact that his anonymous employer had gotten him out of a situation that had become far too hot for him to handle and had offered him such an enticingly large amount of cash for services not yet specified, he would have vacated these dreary premises hours ago. His only company had been his own shadow, cast in the faint glow of but two sputtering light bulbs.

Growing almost unbearably bored and anxious, he lit up an unfiltered cigarette of a cheap European brand. The floor around him was already littered with scores of his butts.

"Those things will kill you."

The voice speaking to Bolgarus had come from above and his head snapped up nervously to see a black-and-white figure dropping down from a catwalk running below the building's ceiling.

Scimidar's legs bent beneath her, absorbing the impact of her long plunge effortlessly. When she rose upright, her tonfas were already in hand, metal tubes extended.

"Who are you?" Bolgarus said, his voice cracking.

"The girl of your nightmares," she replied, striding toward him.

Bolgarus froze in place, unable to move for fear.

"Don't hurt me," he pleaded. "I'm not armed!"

This was true, oddly enough. The very thought of using personal weapons like guns or knives made the bomber's skin crawl. He was actually squeamish about blood and physically quite the coward.

Hence his preference for explosives. He loved seeing the destruction they rendered; gazing at fiery ruins filled him with near-orgasmic excitement. He also savored the knowledge that he had killed on a massive scale, but always viewed his handiwork from a safe distance away so he did not have to bear direct witness to the fruit of his labor in all its gruesome splendor.

Scimidar winced as she drew closer to this trembling excuse of a man. She had expected and anticipated being assailed by waves of violent emotion coming from him; but instead found herself having to fight against a flood of fear washing over her.

"Oh, God," he moaned, sinking to his knees and throwing his arms over his head. "Please don't hurt me."

Scimidar looked down on him with undisguised contempt. Fear was likely her least favorite of the spectrum of emotions she absorbed from others. Fortunately, she had trained herself to shrug it off so as not to be herself overwhelmed by fear and so rendered ineffectual. In this case, it was also offset, though only slightly, by the rather titillating sense of perversion that also seeped from the bomber's pores.

She shook her head slowly, grievously disappointed by the realization that this particular prey, timid and fearful mouse that he was, had proven to be no real challenge to her at all; nor had he added anything meaningful to her intimate and extensive knowledge of the panoply of human emotions.

She sheathed her left tonfa and reached her hand out for him, only to pull it back sharply to retrieve her weapon as a low, rumbling sound began to fill the garage.

Accompanied by a roar and screeching of many tires, a pack of ten motorcyclists came racing into the building. The floor twitched slightly and the walls bounced back the noise through the nearly empty structure.

Scimidar stepped several paces back away from the cowering and confused Bolgarus, her legs spread and weapons at the ready as the bikers began to circle around the pair of them.

With the worldwide oil shortage and consequential high prices for gasoline (hovering at the moment in the United States at around $10 a gallon), the owning and operating of trucks and automobiles had greatly diminished.

Largely because of this, the motorcycle had enjoyed a resurgence in popularity. Hand in hand with this had come a significant increase in the numbers and membership of outlaw biker gangs.

The average civilian rider settled for the new generation of small and fuel-efficient motorcycles; outlaw bikers demanded more power between their legs.

Scimidar had no doubt that the bikers circling her like vultures, all of whom were sitting astride customized, vintage Harley Davidson V-Rod Destroyers, belonged to just such an outlaw gang.

The machines such as they drove were originally built for drag racing, designed to cover a quarter mile in under ten seconds thanks to their 1,300 cc "Screamin' Eagle" engines.

These machines had never been considered "street legal," nor were they now. But what did outlaws care of such rules as this? After all, one could not abide by rules and regulations and still deserve to be thought of as an "outlaw."

Each Harley now circling the blonde hunter was painted in identical metal-flecked black paint; each rider was dressed in similar black leather.

Like most biker gangs, this one was racially segregated: in this case, whites only. One thing that did seem to set them apart from most gangs was the total absence of any distinctive identifying patches or logos on their jackets.

Scimidar knew well that there were biker gangs that essentially ruled various parts of the city, or at least parts of the criminal activity within the

...THE BIKERS BEGAN TO CIRCLE...

city; but beyond that she knew relatively little about them or their culture. Her own activities had never brought her into direct contact or conflict with any of them.

Until now.

One of the bikers pulled up between her and Bolgarus and came to a stop. The other bikers followed his cue and halted their circling, still keeping Scimidar surrounded.

The biker blocking her path to Bolgarus made loud smooching sounds with his lips as he leered at her.

"C'mon, baby," he said in an oily voice. "Give daddy a kiss."

"She's way too good for the likes o' you, Tony," one of his comrades said, eliciting chuckles from some of the other outlaws.

"I don't know about that," the biker named Tony rejoined. "I hear she's quite the slut."

"Mebbe so," yet another biker said. "But you better be careful. 'Cause I hear she's got a pretty pussy…but it's full o' *teeth*."

All of them, even Tony, laughed heartily at this.

"Maybe we should pull those chopper," Tony then declared. "And see if the tooth fairy comes to visit her."

"If it did—the fuckin' cunt'd prob'ly beat it ta death," another biker snarled.

It seemed clear the bikers knew exactly who Scimidar was. But unlike the disheartened Downsiders, they exhibited no fear of her; indeed, some at least seemed to relish the thought of taking her on, to see if her reputation on the street was deserved.

The outlaw named Tony then stopped talking, stopped smiling, stopped laughing. In response to a slight jerk of his head, the nine other bikers swung off their cycles and began slowly and menacingly to close in around Scimidar.

She had shown no reaction to their crude innuendoes and veiled threats; had spoken not a word to them. But she smiled slightly now, welcoming the flood of testosterone-fueled aggression that gushed out from them and flooded over her, filling her. It completely dispelled all traces of the mewling cowardice she had absorbed from the still cringing Bolgarus.

This, she knew, was going to be fun.

She slowly turned in a tight circle to evaluate her approaching foes, noting with pleasure that none of them was carrying a firearm.

In a seeming contradiction to the ultra-violent times in which they lived, individual ownership of guns was noticeably more rare than in the past. This was not attributable to any surge in morality or lawful attitudes: quite the contrary.

The prime factor at play here was the sheer number of wars and other such armed conflicts being waged around the globe. Arms and munitions makers reaped such enormous profits from supplying these organized and not-so-organized armies—whether they were national, guerilla or private—that they had little interest or incentive in pursuing sales to individuals. So most had stopped doing so.

But since the first troglodyte picked up the first branch or bone and used it to club a foe to death, the world has never known a shortage of weapons. The bikers surrounding Scimidar displayed a wide variety of them: chains, pipes, knives and brass knuckles. They also, of course, greatly outnumbered her.

Neither fact bothered her in the least.

The bikers spread out slightly and then began to close in slowly around her—only to freeze in their tracks as a plaintive, wailing sound suddenly came drifting through the cavernous building. The echoing effect caused by the structure's emptiness added to the eerie quality of the sound.

Scimidar was as puzzled by it as were the outlaws. To her ear, the sound appeared to be coming from a *harmonica*, of all things. She saw a wicked grin then twist the cruel lips of the biker called Tony.

"Is that you, *Gitano*?" he said with a hiss.

Boot heels sounded on the garage's concrete floor, as stepping forward came the Latino man who had injected himself into Scimidar's fight with the Downsiders back at the subway station. Apparently, he was intent on doing so again.

He was holding his odd little rifle in one hand, his harmonica in the other. He now stopped playing the mournful tune, smiling as he slipped the instrument into a pocket of his jacket.

"This ain't yer dance, spic," one of the bikers snarled. "Walk away."

"I think I'd rather stay," the gunman answered, unafraid. It was the first time Scimidar had heard his voice; it was low and deep and spoke of strength.

"Then you'll die...just like the bitch."

"Says the man who brought a knife to a gun fight," Gitano replied easily.

Without further warning, he snapped his short rifle up and fired. The threatening biker flew back as the heavy slug drilled into his chest and tore a ragged chunk out of his heart.

At that, the fight became general.

While the bikers' attention had been focused on Gitano, Scimidar had retracted the metal tubes of her tonfas to leave the steel blades exposed. Before Gitano's first victim hit the floor, choking on his own blood, she had leaped forward and slashed at the neck of a biker who made the mistake of turning his back on her.

The honed steel sliced cleanly through the biker's spine. Like a marionette whose strings had been snipped, his legs buckled under him. Involuntary muscles twitched a time or two before he died.

A fist wrapped in brass knuckles skipped harshly along Scimidar's ribs and she elbowed the attacker in the side of his head. With one tonfa she deflected a lunging knifeman, then kicked fiercely up between his legs.

Off to one side, Gitano crouched and began to rapidly cock and fire his rifle. One bullet caught a biker squarely in the side of his face. The man's lower jaw was ripped away with a savage splintering of bone. His mouth filled with blood as he slapped both hands over his face. Muffled and gurgling cries of pain and fear escaped from between his fingers.

Another biker's body jerked as a slug tugged at his left sleeve. This didn't spare him, but simply twisted him so that the next lead projectile entered below his right ribcage and burst his lung.

Scimidar's sensitive nostrils and eyes stung as gray gun smoke drifted over the scene. She hurtled forward, tonfas whirling, sending a biker scuttling back away from her.

Rather than follow after him, she leaped straight up in the air and spun. The outlaw who had been sneaking up behind her was caught off-guard, unable to defend himself as the blonde smacked him across the side of the head with one foot.

He stood stunned as she landed in a low crouch at his feet and brought her razored blade sliding across his exposed stomach. Flesh and muscle tore, parted and peeled away from the resulting wound as part of the biker's intestine and its contents spilled hotly out onto the floor.

A biker whirling a chain overhead charged toward Gitano. The first bullet to strike him seemed barely to slow him down. Swept up in pain and anger, though, his momentum carried him past Gitano, who easily and nimbly dodged to one side.

Spinning the small rifle with one hand, Gitano pressed its barrel to the back of the biker's head and pulled the trigger. The .44 slug screamed through bone and brain and blew out the front of the biker's face, taking an eye with it.

The magazine of the model of rifle Gitano used only held five shells, and he had just expended the last. With no time to reload in the face of the remaining attackers, he slapped the gun back into its special holster.

His right hand then flashed to the back of his neck and from a sheath beneath the collar of his jacket he extracted a switchblade knife with a double-edged blade that was nearly six inches long.

The nominal leader of this animalistic pack, the outlaw named Tony, had remained seated on his bike as the fighting swirled around him. He looked down with revulsion at Bolgarus, who was still cravenly crouched next to the Harley. With one hand, the bomber was desperately clinging to Tony's pants leg.

The biker was no mental giant, nor did he need to be to see that the tide of battle was definitely turning implacably against his crew. Knowing his first obligation was to retrieve the cowering bomber for his leader, Tony reached down and grabbed Bolgarus by the scruff of his neck.

"C'mon, ya little prick!" he sneered, roughly pulling Bolgarus up to his feet and practically slinging him over the back seat of the Harley.

The acrid smell of smoldering tire rubber rose from the concrete as Tony spun his powerful machine and roared toward the exit from the garage.

Seeing this, Scimidar pushed herself to quickly finish off a biker who was blocking her path. She recognized him as being the outlaw she had earlier kicked in the groin. She ducked under the swinging arc of a lead pipe he had picked up to replace his fallen knife, then plowed her shoulder into the biker.

At the same time, Gitano was warily circling around the final biker, who was armed with brass knuckles worn on both hands. Having shaken off the blow to the head he had received moments ago from Scimidar, the outlaw now fought with less impetuosity.

Seeing an opening, he shot out a short, clipping jab. His metal-encased knuckles caught Gitano on the chin. Staggering back, he stumbled and fell. As he hit the floor, though, he flipped his legs over his body, rolling and coming up to one knee as the biker rushed forward to finish him.

Like a striking adder, Gitano's hand flashed forward, driving the blade of his knife into the biker's inner thigh and then ripping the steel upward.

With a choking sound, the outlaw recoiled. The knife blade had sliced through his femoral artery, and blood sprayed as from a broken water main.

Body quivering, he dropped to one knee before pitching over sideways. He would bleed out in less than a minute.

Not far away, Scimidar's shoulder drove her foe back and spilled him flat on the floor. The pipe clattered from his hands even as Scimidar's right arm brought her tonfa up under his exposed chin. She closed her eyes against a gout of gore as she neatly sliced his neck from ear to ear.

She didn't wait for him to die, but leaped quickly to her feet. Retracting her blades and slapping her tonfas into place, she raced after the biker who was attempting to escape with Bolgarus in tow.

Amazingly, by heading off at an angle, the blonde hunter nearly succeeded in catching up with the roaring bike. Bolgarus was tantalizingly close as she stretched out her right hand in an attempt to wrest him off the Harley.

Her fingertips grazed the cloth of the bomber's jacket but could find no purchase. They did, however, close around part of the bike's backrest and latch on.

Once clear of the building and its adjoining sidewalk, the outlaw rider gunned his bike in a sharp turn to the right out onto the street. The bellowing machine lifted Scimidar off her feet and she was helpless to stop herself from being flipped loose from the bike.

Parallel to the pavement, her body spun like a top; sailing several feet before slamming hard to the street and rolling still more.

She lay where she came to rest for just a moment, panting heavily: then pushed herself up to one knee.

Only to find herself looking directly into the blinding headlights of an oncoming car!

# CHAPTER 14

*R*eacting with lightning impulse, Scimidar sprang upward in an arcing back flip. The now familiar sensation of moving in slow motion overcame her as she saw the speeding auto fly below her, its horn blaring as it missed her by mere inches.

Then real time resumed as she completed the back flip. But she was unable to finish it adequately, and her hands landed awkwardly on the pavement. So as not to risk breaking her wrists, she immediately executed another somersault.

Her landing this time was even more disastrous, made so by a pile of bagged garbage into which she slammed. Entangled in the bags, most of the breath pummeled out of her, she was unable to stop herself from tumbling down a short flight of concrete steps leading to the entrance of a basement apartment.

The impact left her dazed and breathless for seconds that painfully stretched into a full minute and more. Kicking free of the garbage, she made her way back up to the street.

By the time she did so, the biker and Bolgarus were long out of sight. Curious bystanders who had taken cover at the first sounds of gunfire were now dotting the sidewalk. Their mumblings filled the air like the buzzing of bees.

Between the masking cacophony of emotions they were emitting—fear, relief, curiosity, excitement, puzzlement—and the rapidly increasing distance between her and her prey, Scimidar knew she had lost Stavros Bolgarus for now.

She had no doubt that if she could ever manage to get within close proximity of him again, she would be able to detect and recognize his distinctive psychic signature; but there was no way she could successfully pick out his trail from here. It would be like trying to recognize a single footprint inside a shoe factory.

Instead, she chose to return to the garage across the street. There she saw the man she now knew to be called Gitano, calmly walking amidst the fallen bikers, nudging each one with the toe of his boot to insure they were dead. He appeared relaxed and unconcerned on this killing ground, taking the time now to reload his short rifle. He smiled his cocky smile as Scimidar approached.

"There you are," he said. "I was afraid I'd lost you."

"Not lost," she replied. "Just momentarily misplaced."

"I take it your man got away?"

"For now."

"Better luck next time."

Scimidar's eyes moved to the sawed-off rifle he was holding in his right hand, its barrel resting atop his right shoulder. The gunman himself slouched slightly to one side, the thumb of his left hand hooked in his gun belt.

"That's a rather ugly looking piece of hardware you have there," she said, flicking her chin in the direction of the rifle.

"Hey, now," Gitano said defensively, pulling himself more erect. "It's a classic, and very hard to find nowadays.

"And if it was good enough for Steve McQueen, it oughtta be good enough for anybody."

"Who's he?" she said disingenuously. "The man who made it?"

Gitano shook his head and sighed. "Who's Steve McQueen? Really? It's obvious your education is lacking, *chica*."

"I don't think so, Mister...'"

"We haven't been formally introduced, have we?" he said, then bowed courteously at the waist.

"*Gitano Rosa*, at your service."

"'Gypsy Rose,' huh?" she said, smiling warmly. She should do it more often, Gitano thought; it enhanced her already considerable beauty.

"And I'm..."

"I know who you are," he said, matching her smile.

"And this little baby is called a *mare's leg*," he explained, holding out his weapon for her to examine more closely.

"Give it a feel before you judge it too harshly."

To his surprise, this violent lady he had seen kill harshly, effectively and without hesitation recoiled from his rifle as if she was afraid of it.

"What's wrong?" he asked.

"Weapons that kill at a distance repulse me," she answered almost venomously. "They sicken me, almost physically so."

"That's what's so repugnant about an animal like Bolgarus. He's the man I'm after; a terrorist specializing in bombings."

"The little squirrelly guy? He's a bomber?"

"One of the worst. His ugly little toys have killed hundreds, maybe thousands."

"I understand why you'd want him stopped," Gitano said. "But what difference does it make *how* you kill? The victims are just as dead."

"Oh, but there *is* a difference," she defended adamantly. "A big difference. The way I do it, up close, equally matched and feeling my enemy's deepest emotions...it's almost poetic." Her expression and voice grew harder.

"His way...is just slaughter."

Gitano failed to understand fully her distinction, nor did he think he wanted to. Still, he didn't push her further and simply holstered his weapon in its tie-down scabbard.

"Well," he said, "you're just lucky none of these bikers happened to be carrying one of those 'weapons that kill at a distance.' I have no doubt some of them do own guns."

"Probably. But the outcome of the battle would have been the same if they had brought them," the blonde hunter asserted confidently.

Gitano, having seen her in action twice this night, would not have bet she was wrong.

"So, who are these men?" she asked him.

"The hell if I know," he replied, frowning slightly.

"But they obviously knew you," she observed pointedly.

"Hey, they knew you, too," he reminded her. "And you're not the only one with a reputation in this town."

"True."

"I've got a hunch, though," he continued, kneeling down beside one of the slain bikers and tugging up on the right sleeve of the outlaw's leather jacket.

"Take a look at this."

Scimidar knelt beside him, making sure to avoid the fresh, wet blood pooling around the body. On the inside of the biker's exposed wrist she could see a tattoo of a skull and crossbones. Right below the skull, between the two bones, was a Nazi *swastika*.

Gitano quickly checked a few of the other bikers to confirm his suspicion: each bore the identical tattoo on his right wrist.

"They're *Freebooters*," he said grimly.

"I've never heard of them," Scimidar said.

"I expect you don't move in the same social circles," Gitano said dryly. "It's a gang founded and run by one bad-ass motherfucker.

"Maybe you *have* heard of him: an ex-con named *Roger Jolly*."

"Jolly Roger," she said softly.

"One and the same. Some of his playmates in the state pen started transposing his names to mock him.

"They stopped mocking after he shanked a couple of 'em.

"By then, though, he'd kinda taken a shine to the name; he liked being thought of as a pirate. So he took the old sign of the Jolly Roger flag, the skull and crossbones, and made it his personal trademark. Hateful bastard that he is, he thought adding the swastika made for a nice flourish.

"Every member of his gang sports the sign on his right wrist. Jolly had to outdo them, of course, so his tattoo is ten times bigger and planted right in the middle of his chest.

"He's carved out his own little kingdom, right in the heart of Hell's Kitchen. Word is that the size of his gang has grown considerably over the past six months or so."

"I'm thrilled for them," Scimidar said sarcastically. "But big as it might be, it's still just a biker gang, yes?"

"Well, yeah."

"So what would bikers want with an Eastern European explosives expert? A terrorist?"

"I don't know," Gitano admitted. "So far as I know, the 'Booters have always been content to ply the usual biker trades: drugs, prostitution, a little numbers running and a touch of a protection racket.

"What need or use they'd have for a weasel like this Bolgarus, I can't imagine."

As he stopped talking, the gunman took note of the intense way the woman was staring at him, and realized she was suspicious of him as well.

"And what's *your* role in what's transpired tonight, Mr. Rosa?" she asked, giving voice to that suspicion.

"Gitano," he said casually. "Mostly, just right place, right time."

"Purely coincidental?"

He smiled slightly. "Well, I've seldom heard the word 'pure' applied to me—but, yeah. I had my own reason for being down in the subway tonight. In fact, I was there before *you* were."

"Why?"

"That's really none of your business, now, is it, lady?"

"And this was none of yours," she retorted firmly, motioning toward the bodies laid out around them.

"Good point," he admitted, pausing for only a moment before continuing on. "Are you familiar with a place called *The Velvet*?"

"I've heard of it," she said. "It's some sort of sex club, isn't it?"

"Among other things. It's also a bar and a strip joint. It's owned and operated by a woman named Irma Fucher—though most folks call her Mother.

"She's good people…and I do odd jobs for her."

*Extra-legal jobs?* Scimidar wondered.

"A few nights ago, one of the girls who works for Mother was assaulted by a Downsider while she was on her way home. He beat her nearly to death."

"The first man you shot tonight," Scimidar surmised.

Gitano nodded tightly. "Mother wanted to send a clear and unmistakable message that such behavior directed against her and hers would be dealt with swiftly and firmly.

"I was the messenger.

"Before the night's over, word of the man who was killed in retaliation for the attack on Mother's girl will spread all the way through Downside."

"And eventually to Topside, too," Scimidar said.

"Damn straight it will."

"Do you always take the law into your own hands?" she asked.

"What is the law?" he replied rather contemptuously. He spread his arms out to either side.

"Down here, even up there, the law is little more than an urban legend. It may exist for some, but not for most of us. The only law, the only justice we ever see is what we grab for ourselves."

"And the authorities stand by for that?"

"Mostly. As long as the lower classes only kill each other, those you call the authorities usually turn a blind eye. So we make our own laws; we achieve our own brand of justice.

"And that's how you and me came to meet. My target just happened to be a member of the pack you stumbled on at the station."

"That story sounds reasonable enough to be true," she conceded. "But it doesn't explain why you followed me here—to a place and a situation in which you had no stake."

Gitano shrugged and gave her another of his boyish grins. "I'd actually started to leave the station and just go on home."

"But you didn't. Why?"

"I'd heard a lot about you, *chica*; about the kind of things you do—and I figured if I followed you, you'd lead me into something wild.

"I was right."

As Gitano was speaking, Scimidar was straining, trying empathetically to detect any signs of deceit on his part. Incredible as her abilities were in this regard, they were not infallible; it was possible for her to be tricked or misled, especially by pathological liars.

She also had to contend with her continuing difficulty in locking in fully on this man's emotional responses; but her instincts told her he was being mostly honest.

As with many of the men she encountered, he seemed interested in more than one type of "wildness."

But then, she knew well, one needn't be a psychic to detect such desire in a man.

"So, what's our next move?" he asked, breaking her concentration.

"There is no 'our,' Mr. Rosa."

"Gitano."

"Gitano. I appreciate all you've done to help me this evening. But what happens next is really none of your concern."

"The hell it isn't."

"I beg your pardon?"

"Your double-whammies aren't the only thing on the line here, sister.

Like you said, at least some of these 'Booters know who I am."

"Because you're one of them?" she asked sharply.

Gitano sucked in his breath loudly, but said nothing. He held his right arm out toward her and pulled up the sleeve of his jacket. There was no sign of a tattoo.

"The one who called me by name is the one you let get away," he said, making her flinch slightly. "He knows who I am and what I did here.

"That makes me a marked man now…and that's definitely my concern."

"Fine," she said, following a pregnant pause during which she had been forced to accept the logic of his argument.

"We'll partner up on this," she told him grudgingly. "For now."

"Good. So I repeat, what's our next move?"

"I'm not sure," she admitted. As she talked she was walking amidst the bodies of the bikers, holding her arms out over them.

"I'm trying to get a reading on where they came from; but I'm feeling pulled from every direction."

"Probably because the 'Booters have hideouts all over the West Side," Gitano said.

"But I might just know the best place for us to start looking."

# CHAPTER 15

*T*he name of the bar on 10th Avenue was *The Lost Treasure.*

A treasure it wasn't, however: to call it sleazy would have been to elevate it above its station. The dilapidated building that housed it was dark and dirty; in an earlier time, the rat-infested hellhole would probably have been condemned and demolished. It was a magnet for the dregs of society and the activities in which they engaged. Even the liquor was of poor quality; being laced, so it was said, with gunpowder and other additives even more vile.

The Freebooters loved it.

Secretly owned by Roger Jolly, it served as the main headquarters and one of multiple hideouts for him and his gang of outlaw bikers.

At he moment, he was starring in an impromptu performance staged for their amusement.

Atop a scruffy, filthy pool table, a thoroughly inebriated and utterly naked young woman named Kat was squatting on all fours. Kneeling behind her, wearing nothing but a pair of slick, black leather chaps bedecked with silver conchos, a harsh fluorescent bulb overhead serving as his spotlight, was Jolly Roger himself.

With loud, animalistic thrusts he was virtually pounding his erect penis into the girl's moist but raw core. She braced her elbows against the rough felt surface to keep from being pushed off the table.

Around the table, gleefully watching this obscene display—Kat's initiation into their less than exclusive club—were several Freebooters and their old ladies, cheering their undisputed leader on.

Sweat beaded his furrowed brow and his eyes were wide with delight as Jolly looked down in fascination at the sight of his slick cock driving into the girl's willing pussy. He tingled at the sensation of his heavy balls slapping against her thighs as he penetrated her to the root.

Kat grunted and tried to buck her ass back in rhythm with his forward lunges. From time to time she would tilt her head back and open her mouth, the signal for one of the other women to pour more bourbon down her throat.

"Deeper!" she yelled, spraying some of the booze into the faces of the delighted and howling spectators. "Fuck me harder, you bastard!"

Jolly laughed and gladly complied, eliciting a howl from Kat as he grabbed her hips and began to slam even harder into her innermost recesses. Some of the other bikers began to bang the palms of their hands against the felt top of the pool table in cadence with Jolly's savage thrusts.

With a yell that sounded like equal parts pain and pleasure, the biker overlord pulled his cock free of his drunken lover's pussy, sliding it upward between the cheeks of her ass so as to spew his load out and over her back. The outlaws roared their approval at this ostentatious display of their leader's manhood.

Like a bronco buster who had successful completed his ride atop a bucking horse at a rodeo, Jolly hopped from the table and began to strut about, arms held in the air as congratulatory hands slapped him on the back.

Strolling to the front of the pool table, he grabbed Kat by the hair on both sides of her head and pulled it forward to meet his mouth in a kiss that was nearly as bruising as had been his sexual rutting.

The girl's eyes were glazed over from her stuporous condition, but she managed a weak smile. He grinned back at her, and light reflected back in her eyes, shimmering off the solid gold caps that covered all of Jolly's upper front teeth. Then he looked past her and gave a curt nod.

To her surprise and dismay, Kat next felt a fresh pair of rough hands take hold of her hips, and looked over her shoulder to see one of the other bikers had shucked his pants and taken Jolly's place to her rear. Her head rolled back toward Jolly, who eyed her coldly.

"What is this, lover?" she asked with slurred tongue.

"Round Two," he replied.

"No," she groaned, the realization of what was about to happen slicing partly through her inebriation. "I don't want this."

Jolly again kissed her, this time biting down on her lower lip hard enough to draw blood. As he pulled back, he saw tears welling in the young woman's eyes. He liked the look.

"You gotta do it, baby," he told her. "You gotta take every man here." He looked beyond her at his followers. "Maybe even some of the girls!" Loud and rude catcalls from males and females alike greeted this.

"I don't wanna," Kat moaned as the biker kneeling behind her positioned himself.

"And I say you gotta," Jolly replied. "Don't make me look bad in front of the others for bringing you here." The steel in his eyes told her he would not be swayed.

"This is the way it's got to be, Kat. Only then will you be accepted into the family. Only then will you be my girl. You want that, don't you?"

"Uh-huh," she said meekly. "But..." She looked back again, saw that all the bikers were lined up behind the table, eagerly waiting their turn at her.

"Uhhh!"

A sharp, cutting pain caused her to scream and bow her back. The biker behind her had planted the head of his tumescent cock at the entrance to her anus and plunged it into her with a single, ripping thrust that came without either warning or benefit of any lubricant. Kat screamed yet again, while those around the pool table laughed.

"Make him stop!" she begged Jolly, who merely smiled and patted her on the cheek before turning his back and walking away.

One of the other women grabbed Kat's hair and jerked her head back to pour a fresh round of whiskey down her throat. Tears mixed with the liquor.

Yet another of the gang's old ladies stepped up to Jolly, offering him a dingy bar towel. As he used it to wipe the sweat from his brow, the woman reached down and lovingly stroked his flaccid penis. He chuckled as she then thrust the fingers of that hand into her mouth to suck on the remnants of come and pussy juice she had wiped from his member.

After sharing that taste with her by way of a deep kiss, Jolly sidled up to the bar, slapping his hand on its smooth surface. In response, the bartender poured a large shot of tequila (some of the good stuff, not the crap he served others) and slid it over to him. The biker lord downed it in a single deep gulp, then held out the empty glass for a refill. This one he would take time to savor.

He turned his back to the bar, resting both elbows atop it, and settled back to watch the show. Kat had buried her face into the felt covering of the table and was gripping the railing with both hands. The biker who had ravaged her anally had finished and relinquished his spot only after swiping blood off his deflating penis and spreading it across his victim's buttocks. This neither bothered nor deterred the next biker who eagerly took up position behind her.

Jolly grinned evilly. Some biker gangs accepted women as more-or-less equal partners: the Freebooters did not. No woman who was unwilling to submit to his will and that of his men would be welcomed into their ranks. Every woman in the bar had undergone the same inhuman torment as Kat was now receiving; none showed her any pity for what she was enduring.

As a fresh wail of pain rose from Kat, Jolly took a leisurely sip of his drink.

Life was good.

But all the noise of the revelry, save for the lingering moans of Kat, came to a halt as the front door of the tavern was kicked open loudly.

# CHAPTER 16

*B*y the time Gitano Rosa strode over the threshold and into *The Lost Treasure*, he already had his mare's leg rifle in hand, cocked and ready for action.

"A big man like you oughtta know better than to get caught with his pants down and his dick in his hand, Jolly," he sneered.

While it had not bothered the biker king in the least to strut around nearly naked in the presence of his gang, these words from an outsider shamed and enraged Jolly. He pushed away from the bar and flung his glass to the floor, shattering it.

Save for the tinkling of the glass as it skittered across the tiles, the only other sound in the place continued to be the muffled sobs of the girl

Kat, who had at last gained some respite from the ravages of the bikers. The outlaw who had been fucking her had leaped from the table and was hurrying to pull up his pants.

"What the fuck were you thinking, greaser, that you would come in here and disrespect me in my own house?"

"You got something I want, Jolly," Gitano replied, unbowed.

Jolly's upper lip lifted slightly in a sneer, revealing his gold teeth. "We got lot's o' things. Be more specific."

"I want Bolgarus."

"Sounds like a disease that'd make your dick fall off," the biker said, eliciting low, almost crazed giggles from some of his followers.

"He *is* a disease. And I want him."

"Well, that ain't what you're gonna get," Jolly declared.

He scratched idly at the large skull and crossbones tattoo on his chest before turning his back on Gitano and motioning for the bartender to serve him a fresh drink. His head swiveled to look toward his expectant gang members.

"Kill him," he growled.

Gitano dropped into a slight crouch, rifle clenched in both hands. Unlike at the garage, he had observed several bikers here who were in possessions of handguns and he prepared for the worst.

Before shot one could be fired from either side, the large, frosted front window of *The Lost Treasure* virtually exploded inward as Scimidar came physically hurtling through it.

Prepared for this dynamic distraction and taking advantage of it, Gitano opened fire on the momentarily paralyzed bikers. He didn't direct his fire at the easiest and perhaps most viable and vulnerable target—Roger Jolly was clearly unarmed and relatively defenseless—but rather at those who were carrying firearms.

Yet his first shot did not come in his own defense, either. As she was still several feet off the floor, Scimidar saw that one of the more quick-witted of the bikers was drawing a bead on her with a semiautomatic pistol. Before he could pull the trigger on her, though, the side of his head dissolved in a gush of bone, blood and brains. He had been taken out by a shot from Gitano's ugly but efficient rifle.

Hitting the ground running, Scimidar plunged into the midst of the milling bikers to make it more difficult for any to turn a gun on her without hitting one of their own. Still, several shots rang out; sounding as loud as cannons in the rather confined quarters of the tavern.

Her tonfas were in full-bladed mode, and she slashed skillfully to right and left. A biker who reached for a pool cue as a weapon left the stick and his hand on the table as steel sliced cleanly through his wrist. He toppled over, screaming and clutching at his spraying stump.

Gitano heard as much as felt a bullet sizzle through the air past his ear. He rapidly cocked and fired his mare's leg twice and was rewarded by seeing the outlaw who had fired at him drop his own gun to clutch at his belly.

Scimidar winced as a chain struck her blocking right arm and coiled around it, but knew this was better than if it had reached its intended target of her head. She jerked the arm, pulling the chain-wielder closer, then swiveled and drove the blade of her left tonfa into his side just under the ribcage.

One of the biker women landed a punch on Scimidar's right jaw. The blonde hunter countered by smacking the woman with her forearm, around which the chain was still wrapped. Teeth flew from the distaff biker's mouth and she dropped to the floor.

Gitano went over backwards as a thrown bottle clocked him high on his forehead. As he hit the floor, a biker made to leap atop him. A .44 slug from the mare's leg met him, tearing into his throat and flipping him to one side.

Half-naked and still unarmed, Roger Jolly had begun sliding down the length of the bar toward the back of the room. His confidence in his crew's ability to dispose of Gitano and the woman was now beginning to evaporate.

Once clear of the bar, he broke into a full run. Pushing through a swinging door, he fled down a long and narrow hallway that led to the tavern's storage room.

There, oblivious to the chaos ensuing at the front of the bar, Stavros Bolgarus was seated at a small table, hungrily devouring a thick pastrami sandwich he was washing down with a frothy mug of beer. Two armed bikers stood guard behind him.

Their hands snapped up, pistols at the ready, at the sound of the storage room door banging open, relaxing then when they saw it was their leader.

"What's wrong?" Bolgarus asked, his voice muffled by the large bite of sandwich in his mouth.

"We're getting outta here," Jolly replied tersely, grabbing the bomber by the collar and unceremoniously jerking him to his feet.

Bolgarus shoved the remnants of the sandwich into his face and tried vainly to snatch up the beer mug as Jolly began to drag him toward the tavern's back entrance.

The door leading into the storage room again slammed open, and again the two guards rapidly raised their guns. Jolly protectively pushed Bolgarus behind him.

Standing in the doorway was a sight to make them all cringe. Jolly's girl Kat swayed on unsteady legs, down which trickles of blood ran. Her hair stood out in all directions, and her tear-streaked mascara gave her the look of a nightmarish and demented clown.

"Help me, dammit!" she wailed pitiably.

"Oh, fuck," Jolly muttered. "Grab hold of her, Mickey," he directed one of the guards, "and let's get the hell outta here!"

As they fled, the battle continued to rage at the front of the tavern. One of the bikers lunged at Scimidar with a pool cue, holding it like a spear. She nimbly sidestepped him, then slashed the side of his neck, neatly severing the carotid artery.

Another gunshot rang out, and she spun to see an outlaw stagger back and fall through another of the bar's windows. He had been taken out by Gitano, who was now hastily attempting to reload his rifle.

Unseen by him, a Freebooter had come up behind him and was raising his pistol to take a head shot.

Scimidar reared back her right arm, then snapped it forward, flinging her tonfa. Its flight was true, and several inches of cold steel slid between the biker's shoulder blades. He jerked, his fingers reflexively tugging at the trigger of his gun. The slug plowed harmlessly into the floor.

With that, whatever fight remained in the outlaws still standing fled, as did they. Most raced for the door, at least one simply exited by diving through a broken window. At their passage, only Scimidar and Gitano remained standing, alert in case another attack was forthcoming.

When it became clear that none was, Scimidar bolted for the swinging door through which she had seen Roger Jolly dash, racing like a hound on the scent of its prey. Gitano followed as quickly as he was able, hard on her heels.

When he sprang into the rear storage room, he found Scimidar standing just outside its open back door, peering into the night.

"You were right to bring me here," she told Gitano as she stepped back into the room.

She bent and ran one hand over the top of the table where Bolgarus had been dining. Her eyes narrowed and she scowled slightly.

"HELP ME, DAMMIT!"

"He was here, all right," she murmured, staring at the crumbs that were all that remained of the bomber's sandwich. "His stench is still in the room, in the air." She straightened and turned her gaze on Gitano, who moved to stand beside her.

"I have to get back on his trail."

"You might want to rethink that, chica," Gitano said.

"What? No. Why?"

"From what you told me earlier, his trail's probably already going cold. And I'm fresh out of leads for you.

"I knew about this place, sure; it's no big secret to any of us who prowl the streets. And I know the Freebooters have plenty of other places they can go to ground, sprinkled all over this side of the island.

"But even if I knew where those places were—and I don't—Jolly could have taken your boy to any one of 'em. Or to some different location altogether."

"What do you mean?"

"I mean I know the kind of man Jolly is, and the kind of criminal pies he and the 'Booters usually have their fingers in. Like you said, big time terrorism is a little bit out of their league.

"I'm of the mind that Jolly's nothing more than a hired gun, a middle man acting on behalf of an even bigger fish.

"We don't know who that is—or where he is."

"Still…"

"On top of that," Gitano observed, "you've got a more immediate and pressing problem you need to address."

"Such as what?"

"Such as that." Gitano pointed toward the floor, and Scimidar lowered her eyes. Next to her left foot, she saw a small but spreading puddle of *blood*.

"That blood is *yours*, chica," the gunman said. He softly took her left hand and raised her arm.

The cloth of her night suit was ripped and she could see a deep, nasty gash running from her elbow nearly all the way down to her wrist.

She had most likely cut it on a shard of glass when she came smashing through the tavern's front window. Caught up in the heat of battle and its immediate aftermath, she had not noticed it until now.

"It's nothing to worry about," she insisted. She tried to pull her arm away from Gitano, but he refused to relinquish his grip on it.

"I've seen big, strapping men bleed out from nothings like this," he said firmly.  "It needs to be tended to now, as quickly as possible."

"I can deliver you to a hospital emergency room in no time."

"No!" she exclaimed.  She pulled away, this time with force enough to extricate her arm from Gitano's grasp.

"Hospitals and I don't get along," she said softly, letting the injured arm hang limply at her side.

"Being trapped inside a building surrounded by pain and suffering like that…makes me feel like I'm dying, too.  And not in the usual way.  It's… too much.  Even for me."

Gitano nodded.  "I understand."  She thought maybe he did, and was somewhat surprised by that.  He closed his eyes in thought for a moment, and was smiling when he reopened them.

"I know just the place," he told her.

"It's nearby…and it's discrete."

# CHAPTER 17

From an inside pocket of his leather jacket, Gitano removed a bright red kerchief and used it to partially cover the worst of the gash in Scimidar's arm.  Keeping the arm elevated, he then led her back into the saloon.

Leaving her side for just a moment, he knelt beside the body of one of the slain bikers and removed the man's belt.  Looping it around Scimidar's left arm just above the elbow, he drew it tight to restrict the flow of blood to her lower arm.

He rapidly led her from the bar.  There was no sound of police sirens, no sign of anyone coming to investigate the recent rounds of gunfire and breaking glass.  Even if someone had bothered to call the law, a shortage of manpower and a general disinterest in the doings of such neighborhoods as this guaranteed that the police would be in no hurry to dispatch anyone to the scene.

Moving quickly but not roughly, Gitano guided Scimidar along a circuitous route that led mostly southward.  Shortly, upon reaching what she assumed was a specific building on West 37th, Scimidar was quietly ushered into an apartment complex that outwardly appeared no different than any of the many others surrounding it.  By means of a dimly lit stairway, the pair made their way to the building's roof.

Once there, Gitano paused to briefly loosen the makeshift tourniquet from around Scimidar's arm. As he then tightened it again, he sharply scanned her face. Given the natural paleness of her skin, he could tell little from this perfunctory scan.

"We don't have far to go now," he told her. "Do you think you can make it all right?"

"Of course," she assured him. "I'm fine." But though she stubbornly refused to admit further to this man who was still a virtual stranger, she was beginning to feel a bit woozy and dizzy from the loss of blood.

She bit down lightly on her lower lip as she then saw what was apparently to be the next leg of their journey. Gitano had lifted a long board, no more than eighteen inches wide, and extended it out from the roof where they stood until the end of it came to rest atop the next building over, forming a sort of jerry-rigged bridge.

"Come on," he said, hopping up on the board and extending a hand to Scimidar.

She found that by focusing her eyes on him alone, looking neither up nor down, that she was able to stave off vertigo long enough to make the precarious walk to the next apartment.

She breathed a sigh of relief as her feet came to rest firmly on the tar paper of the roof; then frowned as she watched Gitano retrieve the board, walk across the rooftop and repeat the process by extending it over to the next building.

Scimidar was sweating profusely by the time they repeated this harrowing maneuver three more times.

She bent at the waist, hands on her knees, breathing heavily. Her body jerked involuntarily when she felt Gitano's arm circle her waist.

"I'm sorry for all this cloak and dagger stuff," he apologized softly. "But it really is necessary."

She could do nothing more than nod.

"But it's over now," he said. "We're here."

Gitano led her from the roof into the building. There appeared to be but a single apartment occupying its top floor; and he stepped up to its door and began rapping on it in an odd sequence of knocks that Scimidar assumed to be some sort of prearranged code.

In response to the series of knocks came the sound from inside of multiple locks being thrown back. The door then opened to reveal a Hispanic woman of average looks who appeared to be perhaps a few years older than was Gitano.

At the sight of the gunman, a wide and welcoming smile lit up the woman's face. Without saying a word, she threw her arms around Gitano and practically dragged him in out of the hallway.

Seemingly unnoticed, Scimidar followed him, softly closing the front door behind her and also saying nothing.

Squeals of joy rang out, as from a nearby bedroom a little boy and girl came rushing into the room. They playfully threw themselves at Gitano, who responded with hugs and kisses.

Scimidar did her best not to listen to what any of these people were saying to each other, feeling sure that she was intruding on the man's welcome home by his wife and children.

Adding to the mild mayhem, an even older woman, plump and also Hispanic, came bustling in from what appeared to be the kitchen area.

"*Gitanito!*" she exclaimed happily as she threw her arms around the gunman.

"Hello, *Mama*," he said respectfully and lovingly.

By now, Scimidar most definitely felt she didn't belong here, giving her a sense of discomfort that even all the warm emotions she was absorbing from those around her could not dispel, and was contemplating trying to slip quietly out of the apartment.

But then Mama Rosa spied her and rushed over to greet her also, firmly hugging the somewhat embarrassed blonde hunter before slipping a matronly arm around her waist and pulling her reluctantly into the front room.

"Where are the manners I worked so hard to teach you, Gitanito?" Mama gently scolded her son. "You haven't introduced us to your beautiful lady friend."

Gitano grinned sheepishly. "Mama, this is Scimidar." He made a half-hearted wave toward the plump woman. "This is my mother."

"Sit, sit," Mama Rosa commanded, half-pushing Scimidar down into a comfortable easy chair. Bending at the waist, she brushed the hair back from Scimidar's face and stroked her cheek.

"So pretty," she said kindly, then frowned with concern. "But so pale! You need something to eat!"

"Oh, no…" Scimidar began, but Mama Rosa had already spun around and hustled away toward the kitchen.

"Don't bother to fight it," Gitano told Scimidar, shaking his head lightly. "You won't be allowed to leave now until you partake of something."

Scimidar smiled wanly.

"Give me a hand here, Emelita," Gitano said to the woman Scimidar took to be his wife. With his hand cupping the elbow of her injured left arm, he assisted her in rising up from the chair and led her into another room.

"She's been cut pretty badly," he explained to Emelita, after he had again seated Scimidar: this time in a straight-backed chair beside a small table.

"Let me take a look," Emelita said, gingerly removing the kerchief from Scimidar's wound.

Some of the blood had dried to the cloth of the kerchief, and as Emelita slowly pulled it away, the wound began to bleed afresh.

A bottle of rubbing alcohol and a roll of gauze sat atop the table next to the two women. Emelita cut off a swatch of the gauze and folded it over on itself several times. After dousing it thoroughly with the alcohol, she used it to begin cleaning the edges of the wound.

Standing and watching nearby, Gitano silently gazed in admiration at how stoically Scimidar was enduring what had to be considerable pain: none of which was reflected in her face.

"She should be in a hospital," Emelita declared.

"No!" Gitano and Scimidar exclaimed simultaneously.

"She's afraid of hospitals," Gitano explained.

"I'm not *afraid* of them," Scimidar corrected him adamantly, casting a baleful look in his direction. "I just don't like them."

Emelita smiled thinly.

"Whatever. I'll do what I can." She had pulled up a low stool and swiveled a light stand over so she could see better.

"Why don't you go play with the children, Gitano," she said without looking up at the gunman, "while I take care of this."

"Are you sure you don't need me here?"

"We women can take care of it just fine," she replied, glancing up and giving Scimidar a comforting smile. "I'll call you if I need you."

Scimidar twisted her head to watch as Gitano somewhat reluctantly left the room, then looked back at Emelita.

"I want to thank you and your husband for all of your help," she said.

To her astonishment, Emelita threw her head back and began to laugh raucously in response.

"My *husband*?" she roared. "He's not my husband, sweetheart...he's my baby *brother*!"

Still chuckling, she bent back over to more closely examine the edges of Scimidar's wound.

"I would have thought you already knew that," she said softly.

"Why would you think that?"

"Well, the two of you are together…"

"Oh, no!" Scimidar replied, a bit more forcefully than she had intended.

"That is, not in the way you mean, I mean. I mean…you know what I mean."

"Really."

"Really. We just met a couple of hours ago, for God's sake."

"Hmm."

"You don't believe me?"

"No reason not to. But all I know is that Gitanito never brought a woman here before."

Scimidar didn't know how to respond to that, so she said nothing.

Only now did Emelita look back up at her again. The warm smile on the woman's face, the slight twinkle in her eye, for some reason made the blonde hunter feel slightly uncomfortable.

"Mama was right; you *are* beautiful."

Scimidar hung her head and remained silent.

"I can probably stop the bleeding long enough for you to make it to a doctor," Emelita told her.

"I don't like doctors any better than I do hospitals," Scimidar said sternly. "Can't you stitch it up?"

"Probably," Emelita replied, frowning briefly. "But I'm only a nurse, and this is far from being a sterile environment."

"I'll take the chance if you will."

Seeing that Scimidar was deadly serious, Emelita finally shrugged.

"Stay here," she said. "I'll be right back."

True to her word, less than five minutes later she returned, now wearing latex gloves and carrying a small metal tray with various implements and supplies atop it—and a half-full bottle of vodka.

After setting the tray down, Emelita offered the bottle to Scimidar, along with four pills she held nestled in the palm of her other hand.

"Oxycodone and liquor. Not a combination I'd normally prescribe," she said. "But you make do with what you have. In this case, I think they'll do just fine."

Scimidar looked down at the pills and could see they were authentic prescription medication.

"Where does someone who's just a nurse come by drugs like this?"

"Do you really wanna know?"

Scimidar smiled. "Probably not."

"Take as many of them as you think you'll need to…"

Scooping all four pills from Emelita's palm, Scimidar knocked them back and washed them down with a deep gulp of the vodka.

Emelita suspected this was not the first time the blonde had indulged in either. What she couldn't know was that, along with her other abilities, Scimidar had seemingly developed an enormous tolerance for drugs and alcohol. While she could and did become high or intoxicated, on a fairly regular basis, the effects dissipated relatively quickly; she seldom suffered from any sort of next day hangover.

Scimidar looked back up at Emelita and winked. "Add a couple lines of coke to the mix, and we'd have the makings of a good party!"

"That, I'm afraid, I can't help you with."

"Then this will do."

"O-kay," Emelita said slowly. "It should take a few minutes for the 'anesthesia' to kick in."

"That's fine. Meanwhile, can I ask you a question?" Another swig of the vodka.

"Sure," Emelita replied, even as she was starting to prepare her needle and sutures.

"Why does Gitano go to such lengths to keep your location secret?"

"That *is* a bit extreme, isn't it?" the gunman's sister agreed. "But he thinks it's necessary to protect his family; and he'll do anything to achieve that. Only a handful of people are even allowed to know his last name."

She saw Scimidar's right eyebrow arch slightly at that, correctly deducing that she was one of the few who had been so entrusted by her brother.

"I don't criticize him for this, though. I'm too grateful to him for everything he does for us.

"My husband Eduardo, God rest his soul," Emelita said, quickly crossing herself, "left us three years ago. Leukemia.

"There's a little neighborhood clinic not far from here, where I work as a nurse. I love it, but what it pays barely covers rent and groceries for me, the children and Mama.

"Gitanito pays the rest.

"But he makes enemies in his line of work, so he tries to keep our location, even our existence and connection to him, a secret from others."

"So you know what kind of 'work' it is that he does," Scimidar said. Even in her own ear her speech was beginning to sound a little slurred.

"Mama doesn't; but yes, I know. Oh, not from him, I don't. He refuses to talk about it. But I'm from the streets as much as he is. So I hear, I know.

"I just don't tell him I know."

Having just taken another gulp of liquor, Scimidar now put a finger to her lips and made a shushing sound to indicate Emelita's secret was safe with her. Emelita smiled; her patient was nearly anesthetized now.

"And I respect my brother's privacy, too, so I ask him no questions. That's another reason he lets almost no one know about us, or about this apartment. We're a haven for him, one he needs."

"Then I should feel honored," Scimidar quipped, definitely slightly drunk now.

"Yes. You should," Emelita replied seriously.

"Gitanito's a good man, Scimidar. That's why my children adore him. It's why Mama and me love him so much. It's why we would do anything to protect him.

"From any danger."

Scimidar said nothing in reply. There was no need to. The message had been received.

"That should be good enough," Emelita announced, lightly tapping her hand around the edges of Scimidar's wound and getting no reaction.

"This is still gonna hurt, though," she warned, just before tipping the bottle of rubbing alcohol and pouring its contents liberally over the gash.

It did hurt. But other than gritting her teeth and hissing as her arm involuntarily jerked slightly, Scimidar bore it without complaint.

She did take another healthy pull on the vodka bottle before nodding at Emelita to proceed.

Working deliberately but quickly, using needle and thread that had both been soaked in alcohol, Emelita did a nearly expert job of stitching the wound closed.

"You do good work," Scimidar complimented her as she tied off and snipped the sutures.

"I'm afraid you'll still have a scar after it heals," Emelita warned her. If she expected this news to upset her lovely patient, she was mistaken.

"A scar will just give me more character," Scimidar said in a breezy tone. She took one last swig of vodka and then offered the nearly empty bottle to the nurse.

Emelita now accepted it gratefully, tipping the bottle to her lips and draining it. Setting the empty bottle aside, she then reached for her roll of gauze and set in to bandaging Scimidar's arm.

The blonde hunter, still tipsy, only half suppressed a giggle as she and Emelita stepped back into the apartment's front parlor. What had amused her so greatly was the sight of the macho Gitano, down on his hands and knees, docilely giving his little niece and nephew a pony ride.

"Well?' he said, his head snapping up as he caught sight of the two women.

"She'll be fine," Emelita assured him, before bending down and shaking a finger in his face.

"But next time," she admonished with a scowl, "take better care of her."

Scimidar silently took note of how certain Emelita seemed to be that there would *be* a 'next time.'

"Everybody…get in here!"

All eyes turned to see Mama Rosa standing in the doorway of the combination kitchen and dining room, both hands resting on her ample hips. "Supper's on the table!"

"You too, little girl," she ordered, raising her right hand and pointing at Scimidar. "A helping or two of my tamales will put some color back in those pretty cheeks!"

Scimidar looked to Gitano for guidance as to how she should respond. He simply shrugged.

Knowing by this gesture that it would be both pointless and useless to decline Mama's invitation, she headed toward the kitchen.

As she did, she felt tiny fingers wrap around her hand, and looked down at the smiling face of Gitano's niece.

She couldn't remember the last time she had experienced such a feeling of unadulterated happiness and innocence.

She returned the child's smile and allowed herself to be tugged along toward a food-laden table.

Later, and not for the first time, Scimidar found herself placing a hand to her mouth to suppress a belch.

After the others had gone off to bed, most unwillingly, in the case of the children, she and Gitano had retired back onto the roof of the apartment building.

"You didn't like Mama's cooking?" Gitano inquired, as he spied her swallowing down yet another passing of gas.

"I liked it too much!" she corrected. In addition to the homemade tamales, Mama had served chile rellenos, refried beans, rice and corn tortillas. It had taken but little of her gentle yet persistent prodding to convince Scimidar to partake of it all.

Twice.

She sighed contentedly now, having drawn in a lungful of the cool night air. Her eyes seemed to dance in rhythm with the twinkling of the stars.

Gitano, enjoying both the sights and the company, nonetheless at last broke the silence.

"Have you given any more thought to how we can find your bomber?"

She didn't reply immediately. One particular star had taken her fancy, and she hesitated to let it leave her sight.

"You know you've already done far more than was asked or required of you," she finally said.

"We've been over this before."

"And we'll go over it again," she said firmly, now lowering her gaze and turning to face the gunman.

"I still say this is not your affair. You're free to walk away from it; and I urge you to do so."

He could see that her suggestion was earnest and sincere, but he was unswayed.

"I'm in, chica," he said with steel resolve. "And that's that."

She actually growled softly. "Fine. I can't stop you. So what do you suggest we do?"

"I suggest you take your Shimmies home and put them to bed," he declared. "You lost a lot of blood tonight, remember? And it'll take more than Mama's tamales to make up for that. You need to rest and recoup your strength."

"And what will you be doing while I'm just lazing about?"

"I'll be using my connections, my contacts on the street, to try to ferret out where the Freebooters and their new best friend have gone to ground."

"Let me offer you another idea," Scimidar suggested.

"Bolgarus is a bomber, but clearly he didn't smuggle a bomb into the city with him."

"So the bomb was already here, waiting for him," Gitano said.

"Maybe. But the information I got from my sources indicates that he likes to build his own explosive devices, from the ground up."

"I see where you're going, chica. There are a limited number of sources for the types of materials necessary to build a bomb of any real size or power."

"Exactly."

"So I'll focus on pumping for those sources. Till then, go home and be patient, eh? I'll contact you as soon as I get any solid leads."

"All right," she said reluctantly. "I'll wait...but only until sundown tomorrow. You'll need my address."

"I already know where you live," he informed her.

"You do?"

"*Everybody* knows where Scimidar lives," he replied. "That's how they know to avoid it.

"Me, though, I'm different. Because you are so well known on the street, I thought it might be wise to check you out, even before our chance encounter tonight."

The blonde hunter wasn't sure she liked that notion. It still seemed possible to her that this aggravatingly elusive gunman had been spying on her for some nefarious purpose: and that their meeting had been no accident or coincidence at all. But again, she gave no voice to these suspicions.

So instead she jumped to her feet. "Until tomorrow, then."

Spinning on her heels, she set off at a run toward the opposite end of the roof. Upon reaching its edge, and without bothering with the board she and Gitano had used to bridge the gap earlier, she launched herself into the darkness toward the next structure.

Easily crossing the span between buildings, she landed lightly and continued onward, nimbly leaping over alleyways until she was out of sight in the night.

Having anxiously followed her to the edge of his roof, Gitano stood with one foot up on its ledge, leaning on his bent leg and incredulously watching the blonde hunter in motion, shaking his head in wonderment.

This Scimidar was clearly unlike any other woman he had ever met.

And he wasn't sure that was a good thing.

# CHAPTER 18

*I*nside an opulent penthouse suite overlooking Central Park stood a large man whose skin was so black as to be almost purple.

Dressed in nothing save a royal blue, velvet dressing gown, he stood before a wide, floor-to-ceiling window, gazing out over the park. Even at night, with large swatches of it shrouded in shadows, he found it to be a beautiful and soothing sight.

"Sir?" a female voice said respectfully from behind him.

The man known only as *Shadrak* sighed deeply, turning away from the window to face the source of the voice.

It had come from a tall, lithely muscular black woman. Her hair was cut in a short, mannish fashion and she was dressed in a black suit and tie. Even though it was night and indoors, she wore mirrored sunglasses.

"A man named Jolly and another gentleman are downstairs," she announced. "They say you're expecting them."

Shadrak nodded solemnly. "Make sure they're disarmed, then bring them here."

"Yes, sir."

Moments later, this private bodyguard, for such she was, and another who in gender, dress and physical appearance was virtually identical to her ushered in Roger Jolly and Stavros Bolgarus.

The biker overlord fidgeted as Shadrak silently scrutinized him. Jolly bristled at the very thought of working for a nigger; but the amount of money he was being paid made him downright liberal in his attitude toward this powerful man of color.

"We ran into a little trouble," Jolly said by way of prologue.

He then recounted his own version of what had transpired at *The Lost Treasure*. His narrative left out all mention of his state of flat-footed nakedness at the beginning of the violent encounter. Before coming here, he had made sure to detour to one of his other hideouts for a change of clothes. He was now dressed in black boots, leather pants and a leather vest he left unbuttoned to display the tattoo on his chest, of which he was so proud.

As was always the case during their infrequent but sometimes necessary personal meetings, Shadrak inwardly bemoaned the circumstance that he felt compelled him to avail himself of the services of such trash as this.

"And who was it you say that burst in on you and nearly derailed my plans?"

"There were two of 'em. One was a nobody: a greaser hired gun who calls hisself Gitano."

"And the other?"

"She was the really dangerous one. Crazy as a loon, too."

"She?" Shadrak felt his pulse quicken.

"The hunter. The one with the big blades. Scimidar."

At the mention of the woman's name, Shadrak's mouth tightened. Her presence, her intrusion into his carefully planned machinations, disturbed him greatly, but he fought to insure this did not show in either his voice or demeanor. He had hoped to put off any direct confrontations with her, still wanted to do so.

"It seems the man is of no consequence," he said slowly. "As for the woman, forget her as well. For now.

"If the time comes when she needs to be dealt with...I'll do so personally."

"I hate to just let Gitano off the hook," Jolly complained, still seething from the shame the gunman had heaped upon him.

"He means nothing to me," Shadrak replied, never having heard of the man. "So you have my permission to do anything you like with him."

Jolly grinned broadly, flashing his sparkling teeth.

The grin widened further as Shadrak walked over to a large oaken desk and extracted a leather bag from a metal box sitting atop it. The outlaw licked his lips in anticipation as he heard the clinking of what he knew to be gold coins inside the bag.

"For services rendered thus far," Shadrak said, tossing the bag to the biker, who grunted lightly as the bag slammed into his stomach. He held onto it, though, hefting it in his left hand and nodding to his employer.

"You're free to go now, Mr. Jolly. But I want you to remain available at all times. I intend to call on you and your Freebooters again, soon."

"We'll be at your service," Jolly assured him, winking conspiratorially.

"N'Tora, show him the door."

One of the bodyguards motioned for Jolly to follow her. Unsure of what was expected of him, Bolgarus half turned to follow.

"Not you, Mr. Bolgarus," Shadrak said forcefully. "You remain here."

Bolgarus did as he was told, and a silence fell over the room until Roger Jolly and his escort were gone from sight.

"You know why you were brought here?" Shadrak then said.

"I do. Your agent in Istanbul gave me a full briefing when he contracted for my services."

"I trust you have no qualms about obeying my instructions, helping me reach my goal."

"None whatsoever."

"Good. As you know, smuggling you out of Europe was more troublesome than we had originally thought. As a result, time is short in which to fulfill the task I have set for you."

"I'll do everything I can to make up for the lost time, sir," Bolgarus said humbly.

"And I have faith that you will be successful. For now, go with Trevonce," Shadrak commanded, indicating the second guard, who had remained behind.

"She'll show you to the quarters that have been prepared for you. Feel free to indulge in a hot bath.

"Arrangements will be made to have a meal brought to your room. I suggest you turn in early, get a good night's sleep."

"Of course, Mr. Shadrak. Thank you."

"And then tomorrow, Mr. Bolgarus...we'll go shopping."

# CHAPTER 19

*A*fter the bomber Bolgarus had departed from the room, Shadrak again stepped over to the window, enjoying another long look over Central Park.

Having grown up in rank squalor, surrounded every day by bleak concrete and steel, he deeply loved green, open spaces such as the park.

He'd never regretted having *bought* it from the cash-strapped city.

At the press of a button, a silk curtain slid across the window, and he turned and left the room. From there it was but a short walk to one of the penthouse's many bedchambers.

Standing at stiff attention next to the entryway into the room was yet another of his clone-like female bodyguards. Because of her mirrored sunglasses, he couldn't tell if she so much as glanced at him as he opened the door of the chamber and stepped inside. If she had done so, she gave not the slightest indication that she was even aware of his presence, though obviously she was.

As he entered the room she was guarding and closed the door after, Shadrak was confident that she would not disturb him, no matter what sounds might emanate from within.

He stood leaning against the door, a cool smile on his lips as he stared toward the bed that was the only item of furniture in the room. Lying atop it was an attractive young woman, naked.

She was spread-eagled on the bed; her wrists and ankles tied to the bedposts by velvet ropes. She was not resisting her restraints, but rather was enjoying them.

"What took you so long?" she playfully whined. "I was afraid you'd gone off and forgotten me."

"How could I forget?" he said, slowly walking toward her and beginning to loosen the sash of his robe.

"I guarantee you won't forget this," the woman purred, thrusting her hips invitingly up off the bed to more prominently display her pussy. Its lips were open and already glistening with dewy moisture.

She smiled in anticipation as Shadrak allowed his robe to drop to the floor. He was already erect, and while no longer than average, the cut penis that was seemingly growing out of a thicket of pubic hair was nearly as big around as was the bound girl's wrists.

Unlike her, he seemed to be in no hurry. Rather, he teased her, stepping just close enough for her straining tongue to snake out and lightly run across the head of his cock before pulling back away from her.

Smiling, he softly ran one hand through her flowing auburn hair, down her face and neck to her right breast. The woman moaned as he leaned over, took the swelling nipple of her breast into his mouth and bit down on it.

He felt her suck in her breath loudly as his right hand traced down her tummy and into the valley between her legs. His fingers spread and slid deftly along either side of her throbbing clitoris as she squirmed at his touch.

She moaned more deeply as his middle two fingers spread the lips of her pussy and plunged into her steaming hole. They began to move in and out even as his thumb strummed at her engorged clit.

"Oooh," she groaned in disappointment; Shadrak had ceased his manual manipulations just as she had reached the verge of orgasm. But she smiled as he slid his fingers into her mouth. Like a suckling child she licked her own thick juices from his hand.

"Fuck me," she said softly, breathlessly.

"I don't think you really want it," he replied, twisting one of her nipples so sharply she jerked and yelped slightly.

"Please fuck me," she begged, knowing that was the response he wanted. "Please. I can't wait any longer."

Only now did he climb onto the bed, positioning himself between her splayed legs. But the tease had not ended yet. He took his cock in hand and rubbed it up and down along the outside of her pussy lips, occasionally beginning to insert it, only to then pull out. Her back arched as she thrust her hips up in a futile effort to fully ensnare his penis.

Finally, when she thought she could bear it no more, he pushed fully into her in one, long thrust.

"Yesss," she hissed as she felt his heavy balls slap against the cheeks of her ass.

Shadrak dropped his head between his shoulders in order to look down at the point where their bodies now joined; he found the contrast of his black cock against her pale white skin to be aesthetically pleasing.

For long periods of time, the desire for sex would be absent within him: other compulsions drove him more strongly. But when the urge was upon him, he wanted the full measure of its pleasure. He found it now by driving not violently but forcefully into the compliant woman laid out beneath him.

Her entire body began to quake violently and he quickened his own thrusts, driving them both over the edge. He slammed as deeply into her as he could; reveling in the spray of come that filled her pussy to overflowing.

Once both parties had been thus satisfied, her orgasm being important to him only as a sign in his mind of his own expertise and virility, Shadrak lost all interest in the woman. Her body was still jerking lightly as he pulled out of her and slid off the bed.

Rising and again covering himself with his robe, Shadrak smiled as he looked down at the satiated woman. Eyes closed, she squirmed and sighed contentedly. Tying the sash around his middle, he exited the room.

Without deigning to look at the bodyguard still standing next to the door, he said, "You know what to do."

"Yes, sir," she replied, also not looking at him.

"Make sure to dispose of the body properly."

"Yes, sir."

# CHAPTER 20

*T*yler Sinclair frowned as he switched on the security camera in response to a buzz at the mansion's front gate.

"Who is it?" he spoke into the intercom, though he was nearly certain the man standing at the gate was the one Tyler's sister had told him about.

"The name's Gitano," the dusky man confirmed. "Scimidar's expecting me."

When Tyler opened the front door, the two men took a moment to silently eye each other.

"Nice digs you have here," Gitano said at last, pushing past Tyler and stepping into the foyer without being invited.

"We like them," Tyler replied, moving to get out ahead of Gitano. "If you'll just follow me."

Gitano attempted to be unmoved as he gazed about, but found it difficult. "Nice" did not begin to adequately describe the rich surrounding in which he now found himself. He'd never felt more out of his depth, though he strove not to let the foppish fellow accompanying him see this.

As can happen with both human and animal males, the two of them had taken an immediate and intense dislike to each other.

Gitano was ushered into a room where his eyes instantly lit on Scimidar. She was standing in the middle of the chamber, clad in a fresh version of her night suit. He saw a slight, dark-haired woman kneeling beside her, seemingly adjusting the material of the suit along one thigh.

"I was about to head out without you," Scimidar said by way of greeting.

"Don't you know that good things come to those who wait?" he replied breezily. She rolled her eyes.

"You've met my brother, Tyler," she said.

"I've had the pleasure," Gitano said, while pointedly avoiding looking at Sinclair.

Instead, he bent over next to Celeste. Taking her chin in his hand, he lifted her head and greeted her with a disarming smile.

"And who's this pretty little doll?" he asked. Celeste averted her eyes, blushing to the roots of her hair. Scimidar was amused by her reaction to the gunman's charms.

"That would be Celeste," she told Gitano, then assumed a businesslike demeanor.

"I assume you've brought me something."

"You should never show up at a home for the first time without a gift," the gunman said.

"Then I suppose I owe your mother and sister a gift."

"Are you kidding? Appreciating Mama's cooking is the best gift you could give her!"

"Still, I'll see that they receive something more appropriate."

"Suit yourself, chica."

"And you said you brought me something."

"I have. I've been busy: spent most of the day feeling out arms dealers I know. I think I've winnowed our list of possible suspects down to one who traffics solely in the kind of ordinance you say Bolgarus would want and need.

"I thought you might like to come with me to check him out."

"I would." Scimidar delayed long enough to give both Celeste and Tyler a warm kiss. "Don't wait up for me, children."

The two of them, the only family Scimidar had, stood shoulder-to-shoulder, watching as she strode from the room with Gitano.

"I don't trust that man," Tyler said coldly. "No good will come from letting him into her life."

"I think he's cute," Celeste countered, lightly stroking the side of her face where the gunman's fingers had rested. "And mysterious, too. Not a bad combination."

Tyler snorted derisively and stomped away.

Twenty minutes later, Ray Crawford dropped Scimidar and Gitano off at the address Gitano had given him.

No words passed between the two hunters, but almost in unison they stepped back-to-back to scan the street and nearby buildings for any suspicious activity.

Seeing nothing untoward, Gitano led the way down a short flight of concrete steps leading to the basement dwelling and workshop of the arms peddler who was at the top of their list of potential suspects.

Gitano tested the handle of the door and shot Scimidar a warning look when it turned easily in his hand. The two of them stepped clear of the entryway as he pushed the door open. No gunfire greeted them: no noise of any sort.

The place was nearly as dark as it was quiet, though the open door now cast a stream of illumination over it. The pair entered cautiously, with respective weapons in hand.

"We're not alone," Scimidar whispered as they made their way deeper into the building. The front area appeared to be living quarters, so she moved through it quickly, eyes focused on the beaded curtain partitioning it off from the rear of the structure.

They pushed through the curtain, entering an area that resembled a small warehouse or storage facility, with rows of metal shelving. Guided by her empathetic senses, Scimidar moved directly to one aisle, pulling up short as she spied the body of a man sprawled out on the floor.

Dropping to one knee beside him, she rolled the body over. What she saw was a middle-aged man, his hair an entangled nest, his face darkened by a two or three day growth of beard.

"That's him," Gitano said, stepping up close behind Scimidar. "Crocker. He's the arms dealer."

The weapons peddler loudly sucked in air, trying vainly to inflate a

GITANO LED THE WAY DOWN...

lung that had been punctured by a bullet. As his eyes fluttered and his lips struggled to form words, Scimidar leaned in closer, lifting him slightly in hopes of easing his efforts to breathe.

"Empire…" the wounded man appeared to gasp.

His body jerked violently once, then again, before going limp in the blonde hunter's arms.

Even in the faint light, Gitano could see Scimidar shiver. He realized with horror that she must be experiencing Crocker's death along with him, and wondered how she could bear ever to put herself in that position.

Her shoulders hunched as her eyes slid back in their sockets. Her breathing began to wheeze as if she too could not draw in air. Her quivering almost reached the level of convulsions.

That's when Gitano grabbed her by the shoulders and pulled her away from the expired arms monger.

He held her tightly in his arms as her breathing gradually returned to normal. As it did, she raised her head to look into Gitano's eyes. Neither spoke.

Then she pulled away from him.

"I'm all right," she said, shaking her head and arms and shifting back and forth from one foot to the other.

Gitano assumed she was traumatized by her shared-death experience. But the truth was that she had rather enjoyed that moment. It was the emotions she had honed in on from Gitano and from herself that had left her shaken.

"Bolgarus was here," she said at last.

"You can sense him?"

"Yes, but only faintly. Like a lingering breeze: strong enough to identify it as being him, but too weak for me to follow, as I could if I had an object he had been in contact with."

"It's obvious he's been gone for at least an hour, which means our friend on the floor didn't die quickly or easily."

She didn't speak of another fading presence she sensed as well. This one was vaguely and slightly familiar: like a half-forgotten memory. The source of it eluded her.

"We should search this place," she told Gitano. "Maybe we'll be able to figure out what was taken."

"Good idea," Gitano concurred.

The pair made their way up and down the aisles of shelving. All manner of ordinance was displayed there: rifles, pistols, ammunition and explosive devices, and the means to deliver them. But they also saw a few shelves that were bare, with nothing to indicate what they had held.

"Hold it," Scimidar said, as a faint sound came to her ears. "Don't talk, don't move," she told Gitano.

He did as she directed, and now he too detected the noise. He used a finger to motion toward where he thought the sound was originating. He and Scimidar crept around the edge of a row of shelving.

"Good Lord!" she whispered.

Her eyes had fallen upon a small electronic device that was attached by several variably colored wires to blocks of some sort of gelatinous substance. She suspected the device had been activated by the opening of the door when she and Gitano had entered. It had to be some sort of bomb, she knew.

And on its front face was a digital display panel that was rapidly counting down toward zero.

Gitano had also spied the explosive device counting downward, and without need for words he and Scimidar turned and ran from the room.

Past the body of the slain arms dealer they raced and back out through the front door. They were perhaps halfway up the steps leading to the sidewalk when the booby trap detonated.

In a heartbeat, a huge fireball filled the storage room, setting off other explosives. The walls bowed outward and the sheet of flames shot toward the opening of the basement apartment and out into the open air.

Scimidar felt flames licking at her heels as she continued upward. Upon reaching street level, she felt a strong hand latch onto her wrist.

Gitano had grabbed her and next slung her roughly to one side, throwing his own body atop hers.

The pavement bucked under them as the exploding ordinance rocked the entire building. The fireball that had been chasing them erupted skyward in a swirling miasma of heat. Windows on the lower floors of the building exploded outward, raining tiny shards on the street below.

Even before the smoke could clear, before the lingering echoes of the blast could dissipate, Scimidar could feel that Gitano's body had gone limp above her.

Fearing the worst, she quickly slithered out from underneath him. Carefully rolling him over onto his back, she was relieved to see his chest rising and falling. His eyes fluttered open, straining to focus.

"I must be in heaven," he said, looking up at Scimidar's anxious face and flashing his now familiar smile. "'Cause there's no sight that beautiful on earth."

"Do lines like that really work for you?" she asked flippantly, hoping to hide the concern she felt.

"Hardly ever," he replied. He tried to sit up, only to feel his head spin, causing him to drop back to the pavement.

"Let me help you," Scimidar said, putting an arm around him and assisting him in sitting and then standing.

"You're pretty wobbly," she observed. "Maybe I should take you to see Emelita."

He shook his head, grimacing regretfully from the effort. "No need to worry her and Mama. Besides, my place is closer."

"You don't live with them?"

"No. It wouldn't be safe. I have my own private quarters, under *The Velvet*."

"Then let's get you there," she said, placing his left arm over her shoulder and sliding her right arm around his waist.

"I never argue with a pretty woman," Gitano muttered.

"The hell you don't," she retorted.

Moving slowly, she led him away from the smoldering building.

Hidden from her sight by the billowing black smoke rolling out and up from the wreckage, hovering some thirty feet in the air, was a small, mechanical drone.

Being a machine, it gave off no emotional signals that might have alerted the blonde hunter to its presence.

But the camera located in its belly was tightly focused on Scimidar, and the drone slowly followed after her at a safe distance.

# CHAPTER 21

At City Hall, Mayor Dylan Holt was working late, a not unusual practice for the politico, given New York's myriad of problems and demands.

The last item on his schedule for the day was not one he relished. It was to be a private meeting with a constituent whose wealth, influence and past campaign contributions entitled him to such preferential treatment.

Shadrak was not one to forego such perks, either.

The mayor somewhat dreaded this particular parlay. In the last election, despite having earlier supported Holt's political ambitions, Shadrak had unexpectedly run against Holt in the mayor's bid to retain his office.

Holt had won by a comfortable margin, and Shadrak had seemingly accepted defeat gracefully. But something about the man still caused the mayor's hackles to rise. Shadrak was, after all, a man unaccustomed to being denied whatever he wanted.

Still, such was the man's influence, and so great was the city's need for his continuing financial largesse, that Holt made every reasonable effort to accommodate him.

The mayor frowned when the buzzer on his intercom sounded and his secretary announced his guest's arrival.

"Thanks, Sally. Send him in, and then you can call it a night. Say hello to the husband."

Holt rose and stepped from behind his desk as Shadrak showed himself into the office. Holt noted he was wearing his trademark white suit and hefting his elaborate walking stick.

"Come in, sit," the mayor said, gesturing to a chair. "Can I offer you some refreshment?"

"None for me, Mr. Mayor. Thank you."

"Hope you don't mind if I indulge; it's been a long day."

"Not at all."

Walking over to a cabinet set against one wall of the office, Holt rattled two ice cubes into a thick glass before pouring in two fingers of Scotch. He remained with his back to his guest as he took the first sip, savoring the slow burn as the liquor slid down his throat on its way to his stomach.

"I know you're just as busy as I am," he said, finally walking over to take a seat facing Shadrak. "So please, feel free to get right to the point of your visit."

"Thank you; I will," Shadrak replied, leaning back in his chair and crossing one leg over the other.

"Plainly put, I want to have more direct input in regard to the day-to-day running of the city. I feel I'm entitled."

"Really?" Holt responded. The ice cubes in his glass clinked lightly as he swirled it about in small circles. Just the hint of a smile tugged the corners of his mouth upward.

"No offense, Shadrak, but based on the results of the election—I'd say the majority of the voters in New York think otherwise."

Shadrak, iron will keeping his anger in check, waved one hand in a dismissive fashion.

"That's just one of the flaws of democracy," he said haughtily. "It allows such decisions to be made by people too stupid to successfully run their own lives."

Holt frowned slightly. "Let's cut to the chase, shall we, Shadrak? Other than wishing the bedrock of our free society to disappear...what exactly is it you want?"

"For a start, Mr. Mayor," the bold billionaire bluntly declared, "I want to be a participant in the summit meeting you've scheduled for tomorrow night here in City Hall."

Holt was astounded that Shadrak would even know of this planned meeting. "I'm not sure I know what you're talking about," he stammered.

"And I'm sure you do, Dylan."

Holt took another drink before replying. "All right. Fine. Yes, such a meeting is scheduled."

Inwardly, Holt was seething that Shadrak was in possession of this knowledge, as it had not been widely disseminated.

In addition to the mayor, only a select few had been asked to join in the summit: his deputy mayor, the chief of police, the district attorney and the five borough chiefs were among them.

Also attending would be several key members of the CCC, an organization Shadrak had steadfastly refused either to join or support.

The purpose of this gathering was to begin to design a comprehensive plan to attempt to revitalize New York to something at least resembling its former glory, thus fulfilling one of Mayor Holt's campaign pledges.

"May I ask how you learned about the summit?" Holt said at last.

"You can ask," Shadrak replied, an oily smile twisting his lips.

Holt coughed to cover his discomfort, took another sip of his drink, all the time trying to think of a way to phrase his next words as diplomatically as possible.

"I can assure you that no slight was intended, Shadrak," he lied, in the smooth way that comes naturally to all the best politicians.

"Merely an oversight, I'm sure," Shadrak lied equally effortlessly.

"Of course. That being said, however, I hope you understand when I say that I'm afraid you lack the standing to be invited to join us at this late date."

Shadrak simply stared at him uncomfortably.

"Perhaps next time," Holt added lamely.

"Perhaps next time," Shadrak repeated flatly, following a long pause. Unbidden, he rose to his feet and the mayor followed suit.

"Despite this little contretemps," Holt said, "I hope that, as the city moves forward, it can continue to count on your generous support."

"Of course it can," Shadrak assured him, though there was no warmth in the tone of his voice.

To Holt's mild surprise, the billionaire did not make a move toward the door of the office; but instead went to stand before one of its windows, looking out into the night.

"It's a truly lovely sight," he said.

"What's that?" Holt asked, walking over to stand beside Shadrak.

"The Empire State Building," the man in white replied, nodding his head once. From where they stood, the two men could easily see the iconic skyscraper rising up toward the heavens.

"More than any other landmark," Shadrak observed, "I think it symbolizes all that is great about this city of ours."

"I couldn't agree more," the mayor said, smiling fondly.

"It's more than a hundred years old," Shadrak continued.

"But as long as it stands...so does New York."

# CHAPTER 22

*T*he club known far and wide as *The Velvet* stood ten stories tall, with every floor save the top one devoted to unadulterated debauchery, sixteen hours a day, seven days a week.

In truth, a fair amount of such behavior also occurred on that tenth floor. But there it was of at least a slightly more private nature, as the entire floor comprised the personal dwelling of the club's owner: Irma Fucher, better known as Mother Fucher.

Occupying a corner on East 21st Street and Park Avenue, close to Gramercy Park and only a few miles south of Scimidar's residence, it was a favorite destination and playground for the rich, famous and infamous from all over the world. As such, *The Velvet* was guarded accordingly. Searchlights and armed guards protected the roof. At ground level, concrete barriers manned by even more guards blocked access on all sides.

These highly trained and highly paid guards, most of them ex-military, let Gitano and his blonde companion pass through without pause, though: each of them being familiar with him and the favored position he held with their employer.

While still slightly shaky, Gitano had largely recovered from the shock of the explosion in which he had been nearly caught, but Scimidar still kept close watch of him.

Her lingering suspicions of him had now all but dissipated. It was obvious that he had been taken as much by surprise by the booby trap explosive as was she; had he been leading her to her death, he would surely have done so in a way that did not so endanger himself.

But more than this. In that moment when he had grabbed Scimidar's wrist to hurl her to safety, for just that instant and for the first time, she had been able to firmly and unequivocally read his emotions. His concern for her safety was real and strong.

"What precisely is *your* position in this House of Pleasure?" she asked him teasingly, eliciting a wan smile.

"Mother Fucher keeps me on a permanent and very generous retainer to perform special jobs for her," he explained.

"Like the 'job' at the subway station?"

"*Just* like that, chica," he said seriously.

"Among other things, *The Velvet* is known for its discretion. Mother makes sure the police are paid well and often to leave it alone.

"No public scandal has ever come to roost on its doorstep or that of any of its patrons; what happens in *The Velvet* stays within its walls.

"Any attempt to use what goes on here as a tool of extortion or blackmail is dealt with swiftly and most unpleasantly."

"With you as the principal agent of that action," Scimidar surmised.

"You bet your Tartugas. No exception. No quarter. That fact is well known, by every employer and every patron of the club."

Scimidar nodded. Some of this was already known to her. After her first encounter with Gitano she felt the need to do a background check, in an attempt to learn as much about him as he apparently knew about her.

Even with her personal contacts and access to what remained of the once nigh omniscient Internet, she had uncovered nearly nothing about this intriguing gunman and little more about the legendary *Velvet* itself. But it was enough to leave a strong impression.

"Gitano!" a voice made gravelly by gin and tobacco called out loudly, when they had barely crossed the threshold into the club.

Scimidar glanced up and saw a tall, voluptuous woman wearing a long, crimson gown rushing toward them with outstretched arms. Scimidar smiled in appreciation. This had to be Mother Fucher herself, a woman nearly as legendary as the club she had built from scratch and turned into a multi-million dollar enterprise devoted to all things sexual.

Scimidar's discerning eye could see that Mother was a woman who could be described as being of a certain age. Skillful application of make-up and artful plastic surgery combined to give her a far more youthful appearance than that probable actual age.

Mother was boldly curvaceous: what men of another time might have called *zaftig*. She made full use of her most prominent attributes in that her gown did not conceal her enormous breasts so much as serve to display them.

It was so low cut as to fully expose them, scooping underneath to provide support and make them appear even more prominent. Her aureoles were as big around as teacups. Each distended nipple, the size of the last joint of a man's little finger, was pierced by a thin silver loop from which dangled an ostentatiously large diamond.

Obviously fond of her favorite enforcer, she enveloped Gitano in her arms and planted a loud, wet kiss on his lips. Just as obviously returning her affection, Gitano tugged gently and playfully on one of her nipple rings and graced her with his warm smile.

"Mother," he said, throwing one arm around her while using the other to gesture toward his companion, "I'd like you to meet Scimidar."

Scimidar extended a hand, which Mother ignored in favor of throwing her arms around the blonde's neck and kissing her as deeply as she had Gitano. It was not entirely sexual so much as sensual, and Scimidar responded in kind.

Yet Mother was frowning slightly as they pulled apart. "And why is it you've never graced us with your presence before, Miss Scimidar?" she growled in feigned annoyance.

"I guess I was just afraid all this would be too much for me, Mother," Scimidar replied in equally faked innocence.

Mother studied the blonde hunter's face for a moment, then threw her head back and laughed loudly.

"Sweetheart," she said at last, slightly gasping for breath, "if everything I've heard about you is true—you'd have half the people in here chewed up and spit out before midnight!"

Scimidar attempted a coy smile. "Why settle for a snack when the buffet costs no more?"

Mother laughed again, hugged and kissed her again. "But you'll come visit us from now on, won't you?"

Scimidar sighed. Even no farther than she had come into the club, the bursts of sexual excitation erupting from everywhere within its confines was filling her with raw desire.

"I suspect I will," she told Mother, who smiled knowingly at her.

"We won't keep you, Mother," Gitano said. "We were just on our way down to my place."

"Not yet, you're not," the proprietress declared boldly. "Not until we've given this sweet thing the grand tour of all *The Velvet* has to offer!"

Without waiting for a reply, Mother looped her arms around those of Gitano and Scimidar and nearly dragged them into the inner recesses of the club. Sensing the futility of resisting, they meekly followed along.

The ground floor of the club had the appearance of being a fairly typical if high-end strip joint. Three main stages and their attached runways spotlighted the work of several dancers. Three bars and scores of topless waitresses served the beverage needs of customers enjoying the show. Lights flashed in multiple colors and directions, and the loud bass beat of the music was timed to match that of the average human heart.

In the span of only a few minutes, at least four different women—waitresses and strippers—made sure to personally greet Gitano with hugs and kisses, rubbing themselves against him like enchanting and alluring kittens.

Scimidar smiled at what she perceived as being their crude and simplistic attempt at seductive overtures. While Gitano was understandably receptive to these gestures on a purely physical basis, and no doubt felt an egotistical boost from their fawning attention, she sensed he was not as emotionally responsive as his admirers would have liked.

Once again it had become difficult for her to fully read his emotions. She thought she did detect some feelings of affection coming from him; but suspected they were directed at the matronly hostess of *The Velvet* rather than at her nymph-like employees.

Mother led them to a slightly smaller back room. Here the strippers were all male; the patrons here divided about 70/30 between gay men and straight women.

They paused briefly next to a stage upon which gyrated a muscular black dancer. The tiny pouch of his G-string did nothing to conceal or even fully cover his large and semi-erect cock.

Spying Mother, he danced over near her and began to thrust his pelvis toward her. In response, she slid one hand between his legs and up the crack of his ass. She then leaned forward and ran her tongue up his pouched penis. The audience watching this, most of them regulars who knew Mother by sight, went wild, hooting and hollering their approval.

The dancer turned around and thrust his bare butt toward the matron. Laughing, Mother slapped its right cheek soundly before turning from the stage and leading her two charges away.

As they moved back into the main salon, Scimidar noted the row of smaller booths wherein she assumed private dances were being performed. She watched as a small, waif-like blonde led a man in a business suit toward one of the booths. The tent in the front of his trousers spoke to what was to follow inside.

Mother, smiling approvingly at all she saw, escorted her two guests to the center of the facility. Only now did Scimidar notice what had the appearance of a large glass cylinder rising up from the floor and through the ceiling.

As they drew closer to it, she was able to see that this was in fact an *elevator*, set inside a transparent shaft.

"Only two people have access to this," Mother said as she gave Gitano a firm hug. In response to Mother placing her palm against an electronic keypad, the glistening, golden door of the elevator whooshed open for them to enter.

They all stepped into the car's mirrored interior. Mother pressed a button and the elevator slowly rose, allowing them a panoramic view of all that transpired below and around them.

As if she was an enthusiastic real estate agent, Mother stopped the car at each subsequent floor and described the wonders of each level.

The second floor housed an enormous sex shop, dealing in everything from magazines, videos, games, sex toys and novelties to sexy lingerie. Half the space was given over to voyeur booths, for those who liked to watch live sex acts (singles and doubles, straight and gay) being performed for their masturbatory pleasure.

Mother explained that not all the performers inside the booths were professionals. Often, married men who liked to watch their wives being fucked by other men would arrange to put their mates in the booth with one of the young studs in Mother's stable.

Those who patronized the third through fifth floors were those who wanted to participate rather than merely watch. Here, singles could hook up for easy, anonymous sex, for a healthy fee.

Given that the majority of those wishing to avail themselves of this service were solitary men, the slack in available sex partners for them was taken up by prostitutes: male and female freelancers who were being paid for their talents by Mother Fucher (their "pay" being a fair percentage of what she collected from the hefty cover fee charged the single men for their admittance into the club). Again, this service was provided to those of all orientations.

The sixth and seventh floors of *The Velvet* were dedicated to those couples, married or otherwise, who were serious serial swingers. Each of these floors was divided into areas sporting different and occasionally changing design motifs.

At varying times, a certain amount of space would be devoted to the entertainment of devotees of numerous specialties and fetishes: orgies, B&D, S&M, water sports, even faux necrophilia.

"We've even had a few requests for a bestiality chamber," Mother told them. "But there are some lines even *I* won't cross!" With that she again launched into loud laughter.

The top two floors of the club, below the penthouse level, were reserved primarily for the use of high-end call girls: those who in days gone might have been called courtesans. Their quarters too were designed to elicit the feel of various motifs: ancient Rome, the palace of Louis XIV, an Ottoman harem, even a futuristic space station.

Each of the girls allowed to ply their trade here was first meticulously screened: no arrest records, no dependence on drugs or alcohol allowed. Each was also required to possess at minimum a bachelor's degree of college education or the equivalent. It was demanded of all that they be as expert at conversation as they were at "entertaining."

This was because the men and women who patronized them hungered for their company as well as their bodies. That was why they were thoroughly trained in conversational as well as sexual skills. Wide knowledge of current events was a must.

Since their clientele consisted of the elite of society—industrialists, executives, bankers, brokers, celebrities and politicians—the prostitutes' discretion was of especially paramount importance and was demanded of them. No breaches of this policy were tolerated.

As with all other sections of the club, these floors also catered to both genders and all orientations, with a small but skillful cadre of male hookers, both straight and gay.

"Isn't it wonderful? And all mine!" Mother smiled as would a parent at its beloved child.

"I'm so, so proud of *The Velvet*."

Scimidar was most definitely impressed with Mother Fucher's creation.

At every level of the club, she had quite literally been surrounded by and absorbing into herself massive waves of sexual desire and energy; and in so doing had become incredibly aroused herself, as if she was experiencing the passion of hundreds of others within herself.

She shifted her stance slightly, to ease the damp heat building between her thighs.

Much more of this, and she might well orgasm without even having been physically touched.

Her eyes moved to Gitano, to find that he appeared to be largely ignoring the sexual activity going on all around them and was instead focusing his dark eyes on her. She felt an unaccustomed sense of vulnerability, as if he was stripping her of something far more important than her clothing.

It made her slightly uncomfortable, especially since she was continuing to have difficulty reading all his emotional reactions. At the same time, the air of mystery about him was proving to be an attraction she had never experienced with any other man,

The elevator stopped its ascent at that moment, pausing as Mother Fucher dipped a hand into the deep valley between her voluminous breasts and fetched out a distinctively shaped key. She inserted it, twisted and tapped another button. The car then smoothly glided upward, only to stop at the penthouse level where she lived.

With her arms around each, Mother led Gitano and Scimidar out of the elevator.

"Be it ever so humble," she said, as she took them on a brief tour.

A fountain stood in the center of the quarters, with water gushing up and out of a sculpted phallus. Colorful murals on the walls and pieces of statuary all represented couples in a wide variety of sexual positions. In a large cage, peacocks strutted gracefully. A huge canopy bed draped in red and purple satin dominated one wall. The carpeting, white with flecks of gold, was luxuriously soft and thick.

"Humble?" Scimidar said as she gazed around at the gaudy opulence. "Only by Caligula's standards."

Mother burst forth with her loud laugh. "Thank you!" she said. "Decadent Roman madness was just the ambiance I was striving for."

"I'd say you succeeded," Scimidar replied archly.

"Please, sit and enjoy." Mother motioned toward a sofa upholstered in plush crimson satin, before which was a coffee table that consisted of an oval glass top resting atop a sculpture of a naked man on all fours between the legs of a similarly naked woman.

"Have a drink or three with me!"

Scimidar looked to Gitano for a cue as to how she should respond to the invitation.

"Another time, all right, Mother?" he said. "I've had kind of a rough night."

Mother frowned, her brow furrowing with concern. "Oh? Anything I should know about?"

"No," he assured her. "Nothing to worry your pretty head about."

"Oh, such a sweet boy," she said, stroking his left cheek lightly. "I'm disappointed you can't stay, of course; but I understand."

Rising slightly on her toes, she kissed him on the lips; as she did so, her left hand dipped down to give his crotch a playful squeeze. His mouth moved close to her ear.

"I haven't had the chance to tell you before," he whispered, "but your little 'problem' has been taken care of."

"For good?" she asked.

"For good. He'll never lay a hand on another girl."

Mother smiled as she pulled away from him. Gitano knew that Mother would make sure the news concerning the fate of the offending Downsider would be spread. The message it conveyed would be clear to all who heard it.

Mother turned and held her arms out to Scimidar. As they hugged, Mother's hands slid down to cup Scimidar's ass, pulling her close and grinding her groin against the blonde.

An electric tingle went through Scimidar, and she moaned lightly as Mother then kissed her tenderly but deeply.

Just before ending the embrace, Mother whispered to her, "Be good to him."

As she drew back, Mother stroked Scimidar's cheek, smiling warmly at her.

"And you will come visit me again, won't you?"

"I promise, Mother."

"Good. Now go—go!" Mother said, shooing the two of them toward the elevator. "I'm going to stay here for awhile."

As the doors of the elevator closed, Scimidar saw Mother pouring herself a large snifter of brandy. There was a rather wistful look on the older woman's face.

"I like her," Scimidar said as the car began its slow descent. "And I could tell she liked me."

"I'm glad," Gitano said.

"But the affection she feels is tinged with just a bit of jealousy, too."

"What do you mean?"

"I mean she clearly has designs on you: sexual and romantic."

Gitano chuckled and shook his head. "That's crazy, chica. I mean... she's *Mother*, for God's sake!"

Scimidar smiled and similarly shook her head, amused and entertained. So like a man, she thought; he was oblivious to what was to her obvious.

As the elevator neared the ground floor, Gitano extracted from his pants pocket a key Scimidar noted was identical to the one Mother had used earlier. This time, it caused the car to continue on downward past the ground floor to the basement level of the building.

"My private quarters are down here," Gitano explained. "Mother gave the place to me out of gratitude, she said. Part of my payment for my loyalty and my services to her. She won't let me pay rent or even the bills."

"She's a generous woman."

"She is. And a good one."

"And she loves you."

"Not in the way you mean," he said, sounding mildly defensive.

"Of course not."

The elevator doors slid open and Gitano stepped out. When Scimidar didn't immediately follow, he leaned back into the car.

"I'm sorry," he said. "I just assumed you'd like to see my place too while you were here. I didn't think to ask."

"Are you asking now?"

He looked down at his feet and idly scratched the back of his head. When he glanced back up at her, he flashed his beguiling smile.

"To be honest with you, I don't want the night to end just yet. So, yeah; I'm asking. Would you like to join me?"

"I think I would," she replied quickly, smiling and stepping out of the elevator.

# CHAPTER 23

*G*itano held the door for Scimidar as she crossed the threshold leading into his somewhat Spartan living quarters.

A trace of a smile lifted the corners of her mouth as she gazed about her.

Like Gitano himself, the place fairly oozed testosterone.

What little passed for décor had a definite Old Western theme, interesting to her mind, as it came from a man who had probably spent his entire life east of Newark.

Hanging on the walls were Indian blankets, various types of vintage, period piece weapons (doubtless fully functional) and several posters from old time Western motion pictures. Included was one for a film entitled *Tom Horn*, that apparently starred the Steve McQueen person Gitano set so much store in.

A few small statues, Western artifacts and Indian pottery were displayed around the domicile. Scimidar admired the fact that while the dwelling was clearly and totally masculine in tone, it was also very clean and orderly.

A brief tour was all that was needed to take in the entirety of the apartment, ending in a master bedroom that continued the Western theme of the rest of the domicile.

"Are you still feeling the effects of the explosion?" she asked, noticing him rubbing the back of his neck at the base of his skull.

"A little bit," he admitted.

"Maybe I should go," she reluctantly offered, although she wanted to stay and get to know him better. "Let you get to bed and get some rest."

"No." He shook his head. "I'm almost good as new, no lingering pain that a handful of aspirin won't cure. You're more than welcome to stay awhile, if you'd like."

"All right." Maybe she'd let the heightened sensual emotions of *The Velvet's* patrons get the better of her or maybe she was still feeling the effects of their most recent close brush with death or maybe this enigmatic loner simply drew her to him like a magnet.

No matter the reason, she felt hot, damp and needy in his presence. And as she rarely denied herself any of the pleasures of the flesh, she meant to act on those feelings.

Gitano had made it clear from the beginning that Scimidar intrigued, even beguiled him, and the barrier that seemed to drape around him couldn't conceal the arousal that inflamed him as well.

The only question she couldn't yet clearly answer was how long it would take for the two of them to succumb to what she now thought to be the inevitable.

He gave her a warm smile. "Give me a minute to clean up a bit," he said, unzipping his leather jacket and tossing it over the back of a chair. The black T-shirt he wore underneath it hugged every hard plane and angle of his broad chest.

The fact that he felt comfortable stripping down in front of her without feeling any self-consciousness but also no egotism, favorably impressed Scimidar.

He walked in to the adjoining bathroom, not bothering to close the door behind him as he jerked off his T-shirt and flung it into a corner. He filled the sink with water; and briskly washed his hands, face and torso.

Still toweling off as he re-entered the bedroom, he saw that Scimidar had made herself comfortable by taking a seat on the end of his wide bed.

As she expected would be the case, the gunman was muscular and trim, with bulging biceps and hard, flat abs. She quickly noted that his smooth and nearly hairless golden skin was speckled with lighter bits of discoloration she recognized as being small scars from earlier battles in his life.

A small, puckered scar near his left shoulder was clearly the remnant of a bullet wound.

"Care for a drink?" he offered as he tossed his towel back into the bathroom.

"Sure."

"Bourbon all right?"

"That would be fine."

"I take mine on the rocks. You?"

"I'll have the same."

He retreated to the kitchen, returning a few minutes later with two glasses and a bottle. Handing one glass to her, he easily dropped down into a soft leather chair facing her.

He reached into a nearby table drawer and pulled out a small bottle. Shaking three or four pills into his palm, he downed them all at once, taking a sip of bourbon to ease their passage.

"Not bad," Scimidar complimented after taking a swallow of her own drink.

"You can thank Mother for that," he replied. "Before I came to work for her, beer was the only brew I was familiar with."

"The two of you have quite a relationship."

"I suppose."

He shrugged as he held his glass out toward her. "To good booze."

"And good company," she replied, clinking her glass against his.

Gitano stared at his drink a moment before speaking again.

"Can I ask you a question?"

"I suppose," she replied, smiling as she took another drink.

"This has been dancing around in my head for quite a while. Since before I actually met you, and only knew you by reputation.

"Is it true that you're a…what is it…an empath? You feel whatever other people close to you feel?"

"That's right," she said somewhat hesitantly, fairly sure she already knew the question that was about to follow.

"So when you fight people," he continued, "even kill them; do you feel their pain? Feel their dying moments?"

"I do," she replied stiffly. She reached out with her mind, seeking any sign that he was being judgmental of her. She detected no such feeling; but then again he was maddeningly difficult for her to fully read.

Gitano shook his head sadly. "If that's the case…why on earth would you subject yourself to such torment?"

"You think there's something wrong with me?" she asked tightly.

"No," he said firmly. "I don't think there's anything wrong with you. I'm just trying to understand, that's all."

"Really?"

"Really. Why do you do it?"

Her brow knit in thought as she took another slow slip of her bourbon. "It's kind of difficult to put into words."

"Try," he encouraged, smiling. "And I'll try to keep up."

She chuckled lightly, and he felt warmth from the tinkling sound.

"At first," she said, "when I was young and couldn't yet control it at all, it was awful. Like being emotionally haunted by a hundred ghosts in agony, all at once.

"But with time and training, I learned to distance myself from them, a little. When I did, I began to realize just how many layers of every emotion there are: an entire, wonderful quilt.

"We label emotions as if they were absolutes: love, hate, joy, sorrow. But did you know that there are at least a dozen different kinds of hate?"

"No."

"Most people don't. I haven't yet counted how many types of love there are. But I feel them all, understand them all to an extent. To be able to do that is wonderful, a gift beyond imagining."

"Even the negative emotions?"

"Even those. Because each emotion, each layer of each emotion, shows me things I never knew existed. Gives me insights that made me realize that each of us is an entire universe."

"Still sounds like it could be too much."

"It could be. Every day of my life I risk being overwhelmed in a universe of emotional universes."

"And how do you handle the deaths? And how close you come to dying yourself?"

She drained her drink and fixed him with a piercing gaze. She was entering territory she seldom breached with others, not even Celeste. Yet she still felt herself wanting to open up to this man she barely knew. Despite her difficulty in reading him, her instincts told her she could trust him, just as she trusted her instincts to guide her true.

"That all boils down to one awful but simple truth, Gitano. No one feels more alive than someone who's almost died does."

He raised his eyebrows in astonishment at her answer.

She smiled at his reaction, then leaned toward him and shook her now empty glass, rattling the ice cubes.

"And if you'll be kind enough to give me a refill," she said, "I'll tell you something I've never told anyone else."

# CHAPTER 24

Scimidar took a deep sip of her drink, relishing the taste.

"So?" Gitano urged impatiently. "What's this deep, dark secret?"

"You won't believe me if I tell you," she teased with a glint in her eyes.

"Of course I will. You've never lied to me yet, have you?" he joked in return.

"Not yet, no."

"So?" he again prompted. "Is it the secret of life and death?"

"You're half right."

"Which half?"

"Death."

"Now we're getting somewhere!" he said with relish. "What about it?"

"It's simple, really." She held her glass up to the light, studying its contents.

"You see, I'm the only living person on earth who knows what really lies beyond the grave," she said in a matter-of-fact voice.

"You're joking, right?"

"You don't believe me?" she asked, cocking her head to one side.

"I don't know. I'm not sure exactly what you mean."

"Let me explain." She leaned toward him. "Everyone, of course, knows precisely what life is. They experience it and therefore don't need to have it described or explained to them.

"A few of them, only a handful, really, have partaken in traumatic events usually called 'near death' experiences.

"Usually, these are people whose hearts have stopped beating due to injury or illness. People who had technically 'died' for as long as several minutes and had then been resuscitated.

"More often than not, these fortunate souls then try with varying degrees of success to tell others what they experienced during that period of un-life: the bright lights, the faces of passed love ones, the sense of well-being and so forth."

He nodded in agreement. "I've read about such things."

"But what they know, what they describe, really *is* only 'near' death," Scimidar insisted.

"You see, once actual, total death occurs...there is no coming back. What happens after that is the speculation on which philosophies and religions are built.

"But speculation is all that it is or ever will be. Because no one who has ever experienced true death has ever returned to tell what it's like on the other side.

"No one but me."

Gitano took a drink from his glass. "That's a little deep for a poor cowboy like me, chica, but I'd like to know more."

She smiled, knowing he was smarter than he was letting on.

"There is," she told him, "a very brief moment beyond the point reached by those who have a near death encounter.

"After that moment—beyond the point of no return, when full death sets in—the consciousness of anyone in death's grip drifts into an irrevocable oblivion."

He gestured toward her with his glass. "Go on. I'm listening."

"What, if anything, exists beyond that—heaven, hell, nothing, a different plane of existence—will forever remain known only to the truly dead with any certainty.

"But in that first, fleeting moment of true, full death, just enough of a person's consciousness remains to register what death feels like.

"It's just a whisper; but if I'm close enough to the person who's dying, I'm able to feel and comprehend this as well."

"...NO ONE HAS EVER EXPERIENCED TRUE DEATH..."

"That's got to be a hell of a thing to feel." He narrowed his eyes as he looked intently at her. "Isn't it horrible?"

"Oh, no. It's exhilarating!" The strange glisten he saw in her eyes made Gitano squirm.

"I've experienced that moment often enough to feel sure that there are even more layers, more levels of death. Just as there are with life and emotions." She hesitated, looking off into the distance as if in a dream.

"Someday," she concluded, her eyes seeming to gaze at something no one else could see, "I hope to solve that mystery as well…short of doing so by actually dying myself."

"But if you follow the dying to that point from which they never return," Gitano pressed, "aren't you afraid that someday you won't come back either?"

"Of course I am," she said. To his dismay he could tell that this thought excited her.

Gitano was astounded by all he had heard, but he felt instinctively that this bizarre, baffling and disturbingly alluring woman was neither deceitful nor delusional in what she was saying to him.

She did indeed know the face of death.

Without thinking or even realizing he was doing it, he reverently crossed himself.

"So tell me," he finally managed to say, "what's the long sleep like?"

"That's the thing," she said somewhat pensively. "True death can probably never be adequately explained, it has to be experienced.

"But if you're lucky, I may whisper one of its more comprehensible secrets in your ear someday."

Almost dazed, nearly overwhelmed by what she had already imparted to him, Gitano rose from his chair and refilled their glasses to give him time to think.

"Just so I got this straight," he finally said. "You not only 'read' other people's emotions, you also experience those emotions as if they were your own?"

"That's right," she confirmed.

"And you have no control over this?"

"Some. Sometimes. But not always. And not entirely."

He whistled softly. "*Santa Maria.* I just realized…that guided tour you took through *The Velvet* must have left you hot as a pistol!"

"Even more than it did you," she said seductively, running one foot gently up the inside of his left leg.

Gitano frowned slightly at this realization that she was experiencing his own arousal, but then decided he liked the thought and smiled at her.

"To new experiences," he toasted, lightly tapping her glass with his own.

The two of them gazed intently at each other while slowly draining their drinks, as the heat built between them. He quickly stood up, accepted her empty glass and set it along with his own atop the table beside his chair.

She smiled suggestively up at him as he approached her. He held out both hands, and when she took them he tugged her up from the bed.

As she rose, she moved to wrap her legs tightly, almost painfully around his waist. He released her hands to wrap his corded arms around her, even as her arms circled around his neck. He kissed her, long and hard, groaning with his rising lust.

He teased and tormented her plump mouth, tasting and nibbling her until he slid between her full, parted lips. As their tongues entwined, she moaned as she wrapped herself tighter around him.

Excitement building, he suddenly spun and pressed her against the wall next to the bed for leverage. She moaned again, letting him know she wanted him as much as he wanted her.

He broke their kiss only to nip and lick down the curve of her neck. Her head rolled to one side and she inhaled sharply as his teeth lightly sank into the flesh at the base of her throat.

Scimidar shivered with excitement. She had been on the brink of orgasm for some time already, barely able to hold it in check. The feel of Gitano's steely erection pressing firmly against her hot center, coupled with the sexual tension she still carried from her trip through the sex club was all it took to push Scimidar into what she knew was going to be only the first of several climaxes.

As she ground against him, bringing fresh waves of pleasure, she dug her fingernails deeply into the sleek muscles of his bare back.

Gitano turned them away from the wall, carried her back to his bed and gently laid her down on his soft gray sheets. He stroked her lustrous blonde hair as they kissed tenderly yet urgently

Unable to wait a moment longer, he quickly stood up, took a step back and shed the rest of his clothing.

With an urgency that matched his, Scimidar sat up and peeled the clingy night suit from her body.

She tossed it, along with her kevlar undergarment and wrappings, aside and fell back onto the bed with limbs akimbo in invitation. He stepped between her parted legs and took a long moment to gaze at her physical beauty, just as she looked at him.

His eyes narrowed slightly as they homed in on one small patch of skin near Scimidar's right ribcage. Left revealed by the removal of her kevlar was a purpled bruise.

"My God," he murmured, frowning with concern. "You weren't just cut during our fight with the Freebooters. You were *shot*, weren't you?"

Her left hand flashed across her body to cover the blemish in her otherwise nearly flawless skin.

"It's nothing," she assured him. "I can barely feel it."

The expression on her face told him he had surmised correctly. Doubtless, her kevlar coverlet had deflected the path of the bullet that had struck her, keeping it from penetrating her flesh. But it had clearly caused damage: which she had not bothered to share with him.

Like his own body, there were several signs of other, older wounds dotting Scimidar's flesh, barely noticeable except under close scrutiny. His admiration of her toughness grew even stronger. As did his desire.

"Please don't make me wait," she said. Refusing to speak further of her injuries, Scimidar instead invited him into the bed by extending her arms out to him.

"Never." He lowered his body between her legs, cradled her face with his hands and pressed another kiss to her hot, swollen lips.

She embraced him and rolled so as to put herself on top. She kissed and licked a path down the center of his flat belly as she slipped her left hand between his legs to cup his heavy balls and squeeze them. With her right hand, she lifted his throbbing cock up off his belly before peeling back the foreskin to unleash its bulbous head.

She looked up at him coquettishly, licking her lips, then ran her tongue several times around the ridge of his penis before taking the entire cap into her mouth.

He groaned with escalating need as he bucked up in an effort to drive more of his cock into the warmth of her mouth, but her grip thwarted his efforts.

"Patience," she said wickedly, letting the dick head pop out of her mouth and giving his aching balls a tighter squeeze.

He nodded, but he didn't mean it. He wanted everything and he wanted it now.

She lowered her head, placed her tongue on the base of his cock and licked her way upward. When she reached the pulsing head, she took in half his length this time, doing her best to drive him out of his mind.

He groaned louder as he placed one hand lightly atop her head, curling strands of her hair around his fingers as she began to rise up and down. And still it wasn't enough.

"Turn around," he urged her.

Lifting her mouth off his cock, she happily nodded in acceptance of his invitation. She crawled up and, turning her back to him, swung a leg over him so that her knees were on either side of his head. She then resumed going down on him.

Gitano slid his hands along the silkiness of Scimidar's back, caressing her ass and tugging its firm cheeks apart to more fully display the plump lips of her pussy. Pulling her down closer, he lapped up her dewy moisture with his tongue.

She tasted as delicious as fresh rain. He licked lightly around her erect clit before taking the tiny bud entirely into his mouth. He began to alternately suck on it and circle it with his tongue.

When he felt her entire body stiffen in the depths of arousal, he obliged her burning need by pushing her over the edge into complete ecstasy.

Relishing the taste and feel of her, he continued to work his tongue and lips until he felt her shiver and come yet again.

He was both impressed and a bit envious of how easily and often Scimidar appeared capable of reaching climax. He realized that her empathetic nature must make sex incredibly pleasurable for her.

At this moment, she was doubtless still feeding off the massive sexual energy permeating *The Velvet*; but in any sexual encounter she would benefit from her ability to combine the pleasures of her own sexual arousal and that of her partner.

He knew now that the whispers of her virtually insatiable sexual appetites must be true.

He was glad to be feeding that appetite—and taking his own pleasure from it.

Scimidar was once again focusing on Gitano's cock: diving so deeply down on it that she took nearly its entire impressive length into her throat.

He rode the sensation, focusing on his pleasure, until she slid one hand between his legs and into the valley between his ass cheeks. He jerked with surprise when she slipped a finger into his puckered anus, but did not resist the intrusion. Indeed, as her digit pistoned in and out expertly and the friction of her moist lips on his straining cock grew more intense, his balls began to swell with the need to spill their load.

"Stop!" he groaned, knowing he couldn't last more than a moment longer.

Scimidar raised her head and looked back at him in surprise. "Why?"

He smiled as he slowly slid a thumb between her lower lips. "I want to be in here."

She nodded, eyes twinkling with understanding as she rose onto her knees beside him.

He wrapped her in his arms and kissed her deeply before she lay down on her back and spread her legs wide for him. She reached up and caressed his cock before she guided his long length to its target.

"Mmm," she moaned, as he pushed as gently as possible into her soft, hot depths until his balls came to rest snugly against the firm swells of her buttocks.

He remained unmoving for a moment, savoring the sensation that her pussy was the mold in which his rock hard cock had been forged, so perfectly did they fit together.

He pulled back slowly and then began to rhythmically lunge in and out of her body. After only a few strokes, Scimidar's hands slapped against the sheets, clawing at the cotton as another climax ripped through her. She moaned louder as he continued to thrust into her, building her toward another release.

Their lovemaking became fiercely passionate, almost violent. As Gitano felt the dam of his own passion about to burst, he increased the speed and depth of his thrusts.

Sensing that instant mere seconds before he would reach the point of no return and erupt within her, Scimidar wrapped her legs tightly around his waist, locking them at the ankles.

Her arms flew to his neck and she lifted herself up off the bed. Responding quickly to her bodily prompting, Gitano rocked onto his knees so that she was now sitting atop his aching cock. He cupped her ass, assisting as she bounced up and down, driving him to the threshold of desire.

That was the moment when she placed her lips to his ear and whispered one of the secrets of the dead.

"*Aaaah!*" he fairly screamed, eyes widening as he found himself in the throes of the most powerful and gut-wrenching orgasm he had ever known.

Scimidar straightened, arched her spine and threw her head back; also screaming in ecstasy as she was washed overboard in the sensory tidal wave of two extraordinary climaxes: her own and his. The orgasmic explosion that started in her belly roared to every other part of her body.

His body jerking slightly, Gitano slowly and gently lowered her to the bed, pulled out of her warm depths and lay down beside her.

Both were breathing heavily, both were bathed in a fine sheen of perspiration. Neither could have said how long they lay that way in silence, letting their respiration and heart rates return to normal, happily soaking in the afterglow.

"Le petit morte," Scimidar finally said softly, almost wistfully.

"What?"

"'The little death.' That's what the French call orgasm."

"Believe me," Gitano said with a smile, "there was nothing 'little' about what just happened to us!"

She chuckled warmly as she nestled closer to him.

"Let me ask you," he said a few moments later. "Would I be right in saying that during lovemaking you experience your partner's pleasure as well as your own?"

"Pretty much, yes."

She rolled fully onto her side, propping her head up with one hand to look at his reaction.

He frowned thoughtfully. "So, even if the guy you were with was the lousiest lover on the planet—you'd get pleasure just by tapping into his release."

She threw her head back and laughed gently, then softly stroked his cheek as his frown deepened.

"It's so funny," she said, looking into his piercing eyes, "what a little boy even the most masculine of men can be when it comes to their insecurity about the size of their sex organs and the quality of their lovemaking."

He started to protest, but he forgot all about it when she placed a hot kiss against his lips and traced a path with her soft fingers down the middle of his belly. Despite having recently spent himself, he found he was quickly responding to her experienced touch.

Scimidar followed her fingers with her lips, pausing to look back up at him and smile.

"I assure you," she said playfully, "you're not the least bit lacking in either department."

He let his head sink back onto his pillow, closing his eyes and smiling contentedly as her plump lips again enveloped his rising cock.

# CHAPTER 25

*M*other Fucher sipped at a cup of strong Irish coffee, the only "breakfast" of which she ever partook. She stood behind one of the bars on the ground floor of her now empty club, poring over a small stack of invoices.

A deep whirring sound drew her attention to her private elevator, and she saw its car rise from below the floor. Its door slid open and the car discharged Gitano and Scimidar, who strolled into the main salon.

Mother smiled wistfully, noting that the blonde hunter was wearing the same attire from the previous night. She assumed it was an amorous and late night spent in the bowels of *The Velvet* that accounted for the pair not making an appearance until well after noon.

That was partially, maybe even mostly correct, but the exhaustion both succumbed to as a result of their harrowing fights and injuries also played a hand in their lassitude.

"Don't take another step," Mother admonished. "You're going to sit and have breakfast, the both of you."

"I'll have what you're having, Mother," Gitano jested.

"Like hell you will," she rejoined. "You'll have *real* food." Using an intercom system that connected to the kitchen at the back of the club, the matron ordered two helpings of eggs, bacon and toast.

Mother stood over them, approvingly watching as they dived into the food set before them. A few minutes into their repast, a guard from outside the club's front entrance walked into the salon, pausing several feet away from their table.

"What is it, Lonnie?" Mother asked.

"There's a girl outside," the guard replied. "She looks pretty rough. Says she wants to see Gitano."

"This girl have a name?" Gitano inquired, dropping his slice of toast back down on the plate.

"She says she just goes by Kat. With a 'K'."

Gitano's brow furrowed. "Doesn't ring any bells. Did you pat her down?"

"She's clean."

Gitano looked at Scimidar, who shrugged. "Go ahead and bring her in, Lonnie."

"Will do."

The guard returned in under a minute, escorting the young woman. Scimidar grimaced as she looked at the face of the nervous and frightened girl, who was sporting both a blackened left eye and a cracked and swollen lip. Neither Scimidar nor Gitano immediately recognized her.

"What can I do for you, Kat?" Gitano asked her.

"I can tell you don't remember me," she began, her battered mouth straining to form the words. "But I was at *The Lost Treasure* the other night.

"I'm Roger Jolly's girlfriend."

Gitano and Scimidar straightened in their chairs, both now very interested in what this bedraggled girl had to say.

"I'm glad you're here, too," she told Scimidar, turning her gaze toward the blonde. "I really wanted to talk to both of you."

"What happened to you?" Scimidar asked. The marks on Kat's formerly pretty face where clearly of recent origin. Scimidar could feel the lingering pain of them within herself.

Kat's hand went toward her swollen eye, from which a tear began to well.

"It was Roger," she said. "I've never seen him so angry. It was because of what you two did at his tavern, in front of his people. Even the next day, all he could seem to think about, talk about, was how you'd humiliated him.

"He was like a volcano building up to an eruption. I tried to calm him down. You know," without even thinking, she ran a hand over the curve of her hip, "soothe him somehow."

She paused, her swollen lips trembling. "But that just seemed to make him even angrier." Her gaze hardened.

"So he decided to take his frustrations out on me."

Scimidar gazed at her intently. "Then what happened?"

"At first I was just afraid; you know, that he might do something even worse.

"Then I got mad." Her teeth clenched. "He had no call to do this to me. No right."

"So you decided to escape," Gitano said.

"Oh, I decided to do a lot more than that," Kat replied, now sounding almost smug as she straightened and threw back her shoulders.

"I'm gonna tell you what his plans are."

Scimidar and Gitano exchanged glances, their interest clearly piqued.

"What sort of plans?" Scimidar prompted.

"It's big," Kat asserted. "Really big. Right now, he's gathering every one of the Freebooters all together in one spot. Within the next few hours, before midnight, he means to launch an attack."

"An attack on what?" Mother Fucher asked, then looked rather sheepishly at Gitano, who merely smiled at her. Like him, the matron was totally caught up in the girl's tale.

"The Empire State Building," Kat said grimly and without further encouragement.

On hearing those words, both Gitano and Scimidar thought back on the last word uttered by the dying arms dealer the previous day.

*"Empire."*

"What exactly does Jolly mean to do, Kat?" Scimidar questioned.

"I only heard parts of his plan. But near as I can tell, he means to set off some kind of big-ass *bomb* right inside the building's lobby!"

"Damn," Gitano whistled softly.

"Yeah," Kat said breathlessly. "I got the sense that it might even be powerful enough to bring the whole damned skyscraper down on itself."

"To what end?" Scimidar asked. When Kat gave her an uncomprehending stare, she rephrased the question.

"Why does Jolly want to blow up the Empire State Building?"

"Oh." The girl shrugged. "I don't know; I didn't hear that part and I was anxious to get the hell out of there.

"But I can tell you what I think. I think it's nothing but the first shot in a war he means to start."

"A war against whom?"

"The K-Town Tigers, to start with."

Scimidar's eyes slid toward Gitano. "They're the ruling gang in Korea Town," he told her.

"The Empire State's right on the border between their territory and the Freebooters."

"And the Freebooters are looking to spread out," Kat added. "Claim even more turf for themselves.

"And they're not just wanting to squash rival gangs, either. The way Roger said it to the others was that this was just a grand gesture, meant to put the whole city on notice that the Freebooters plan to run the whole damned town someday."

"I never thought Jolly was that ambitious," Gitano muttered. "Or that crazy."

"You need to tell us where he is right now," Scimidar said sternly, fixing her eyes on Kat's face.

"He could be anywhere," the bruised girl replied, stammering slightly. "He might be where I last saw him, or he could be in any one of a dozen other locations."

"Then you need to tell us all those locations," Scimidar pressed.

"I've probably told you too much already." Kat's eyes began to cast about nervously, growing fear evident in her features. "If Roger finds out what I've done—he'll kill me without batting an eye!"

"Why don't you sit down, child," Mother Fucher said, reaching out to give the errant girl a supporting hand.

Without warning, Kat grabbed the solicitous matron and roughly shoved her toward Scimidar and Gitano.

Mother heavily hit the table where they sat, sprawling across it, tipping it and them over in a tangle. Taking advantage of the momentary confusion, Kat bolted for the door leading out of the club.

Gitano's first impulse was to look after the stunned Mother Fucher. Taking her right hand in his and placing his arm around her waist, he carefully pulled her up to her feet.

"Are you all right, Mother? Did she hurt you?"

The matron waved a hand. "Only my pride, sweetheart."

"Then let's go after that twisted little bitch!" he barked to Scimidar, who seemed both unruffled and unconcerned.

"There's no need to rush," she told him, laying a calming hand on his arm.

"I've latched onto the girl's psychic scent—and will remain so as long as we don't let her get too large a lead on us."

"You think she does know where Jolly is, and will head back to him?"

"Don't you?"

"Hell, yes."

"Before we get on the trail, though, there's someone I need to contact. His name's Jefferson Cooke."

"The police captain?"

"You know him?"

Gitano grinned. "I know of him. In my line of work, it pays to be aware of men like him." He winked at her.

"And women like you."

One side of Scimidar's mouth curled upward. "Cooke needs to know about this. Whether the threat's real or not, he'll have to take it seriously; and he'll need time to prepare."

Mention of preparations prompted her to check her own weapons.

Holding them tightly, she tested their triggering mechanism, activating the tubular metal shafts, then retracting them to expose the twin blades.

As she gave both tonfas a few whirling spins to insure that they were still in balance, she saw Gitano draw his shortened rifled and check its load.

Mother Fucher's eyes widened at the sight of both, but she said nothing.

"I assume," Scimidar said wearily, "that at this late date it would do me no good to ask you to stay out of this, for your own safety?"

"No good at all," he confirmed. "Where you go, I go, chica." He snapped the mare's leg back into is scabbard and smiled broadly.

"I'll even provide the *wheels!*"

# CHAPTER 26

*T*imes Square had again fallen upon hard times. Some decades earlier, it had become somewhat squalid, occupied by a plethora of low class strip joints, porno theaters and adult bookstores. Hookers hawked their wares more or less openly.

Then came a massive rehabilitation. The sex trade had been largely swept away, replaced by lights and neon signs that evoked images of the Las Vegas strip, minus the gambling parlors.

One wag declared he preferred the squalor.

Most of the lights were extinguished now; vanished along with the businesses they so loudly advertised. The jeweled ball had not dropped there on New Year's Eve for nearly ten years and there was little else there to draw any crowds.

The streets immediately around it were equally blighted. One area just to the west of the square had briefly enjoyed renewed life as a small industrial park. But it too was now abandoned and dark, or so it seemed.

The sun had sunk below the concrete horizon by the time Gitano and Scimidar pulled up across the street from the park; and here they still sat.

The two of them were fittingly astride a motorcycle. It was a vehicle that Gitano had virtually built himself, after having started by obtaining the chassis of a classic Harley Davidson Electra Glide. All else had come from the gunman's own hand.

The baffling girl named Kat had led them on a merry chase after leaving *The Velvet*. For several hours she had drifted back and forth and up and down the island in what seemed to have been an obvious and somewhat clumsy attempt to shake off anyone who might be trying to follow her.

She had no idea that Scimidar had no more trouble following this meandering route than she would have had Kat simply traveled in a straight line.

Since entering the industrial park nearly an hour earlier, Kat had not resumed her flight, leading her trackers to assume that she and they had reached their final destination.

"We need to get in there," Scimidar said at last.

"Agreed," Gitano replied. "I'll lead the way."

"Oh?" she said sharply, one eyebrow arching. "Why is that?"

Before responding, Gitano drew his sawed-off rifle and cocked it. "Because you can bet dollars to donuts that there's a whole slew of cocksuckers in there packing guns. You know: those deliverers of long range death you despise so much?

"Good as you are with those pig-stickers of yours, they do you no good until you get up close and personal.

"Since whichever of us is out in front is the one most likely to draw fire first, it stands to reason that person ought to be able to return their fire. That means me.

"Unless you want to borrow this," he concluded, holding the mare's leg out toward her.

As he knew she would, Scimidar recoiled. Her face contorted in disgust before settling into a look of anger.

"You lead the way," she said through clenched teeth.

Faster than she could move to deflect, Gitano's head lunged forward and he planted a light kiss on her lips before laughing lightly and turning away to lope in a low crouch toward the open gate leading into the industrial park. After taking a deep, cleansing breath and slowly exhaling it, Scimidar followed.

Within no more than a minute, they spied flickering arcs of light coming from deep inside the complex, accompanied by the sounds of heavy equipment. Staying in the shadows, they followed the two to their mutual source.

Taking up positions behind the cover of a dumpster, they cautiously peered around its corners to spy on what was transpiring.

A large crew of men was working diligently. The job they were performing was not one that was natural to them, as their garb indicated they were members of Roger Jolly's outlaw biker gang.

Like ants on a dirt mound, they were scurrying about and focusing their attentions around a large tanker truck.

As Scimidar and Gitano looked on, a front loader was guided to one side of the tanker. Using what appeared to be a sort of improvised funnel, the crew was in the process of partially filling the tanker with thousands and thousands of small, metal ball bearings.

"Look at the underside of the tanker," Gitano whispered.

He pointed out that the Freebooters had apparently already strengthened the truck's suspension with heavy gauge steel springs to aid in carrying an oversized load such as this.

As they continued to watch, a smaller, squatter type of tank truck pulled alongside its larger counterpart, taking the place of the front loader as it finished depositing its scoops of ball bearings.

A flexible hose running from the small tanker was then fitted to the opening of the larger vehicle. From the smell that was lifted on the breeze and carried to their hiding place, Scimidar and Gitano could discern that some sort of fuel or accelerant was now being pumped atop the load of ball bearings.

Moments after the pumping process was finished and the smaller tanker had driven away, a familiar figure came walking out of a nearby building.

It was the mercenary bomb builder, Stavros Bolgarus. Close behind him walked two burly Freebooters, carrying a large chest between them.

From inside the chest, Bolgarus began to remove small electronic packages, one at a time: each the size of a large brick.

Carefully and methodically, but with practiced dexterity, Bolgarus began to attach these packages to various spots along the outer hull of the large truck's tank.

"My God," Scimidar gasped. "Do you see what he's doing?"

"Yeah," Gitano replied grimly. "He's essentially transforming that tanker into the world's largest *fragmentation grenade!*"

The implications were frighteningly obvious to both of them. The number and type of bombs being attached to the tanker were doubtless sufficient in and of themselves to do tremendous damage. But when detonated at the chosen target site, the hundreds of gallons of fuel it would ignite would enhance the force of the bombs' blast by perhaps as much as tenfold.

The explosion would also send the ball bearings now floating inside the tanker screaming out in all directions, round darts capable of tearing through concrete as well as any human flesh unfortunate enough to be within its trajectory.

"Something doesn't seem…right about this," Gitano growled.

"What do you mean?"

"It seems to me that all of this had to have been planned and at least partially prepared well before now."

"Yes? And?"

"But no matter how good he is, that Bolgarus guy must have had to work continuously, almost around the clock to have that many bombs assembled by now."

Scimidar saw where he was leading. "Which would seem to indicate there's something time sensitive about either the hour or the location of the site they mean to attack."

Before either of them could speculate further, a red beam of laser light flashed down at them from above, coming so close to hitting the pair that it actually sliced the chain connecting Gitano's nose and ear rings.

Spinning, the duo looked up to see a small drone hovering in the air behind them. They had no idea that this was the same remotely controlled device that had been surreptitiously following them since the previous evening.

But they could tell, from the increasing volume of the humming sound it was emitting and the red glow building in intensity inside a portal built into its near side—that the drone was preparing to open fire again!

# CHAPTER 27

"**R**un!" Scimidar shouted, the need for stealth now having vanished in that flash of deadly red light.

Both she and Gitano paused for an instant, though, just long enough to see the hovering drone joined by three other such flying death dispensers. Then the duo sprinted away from the dumpster before all four of the drones opened fire on them.

Man and woman ran in zigzagging routes to stay clear of the sizzling beams nipping at their heels.

What they would not realize until it was too late was that the drones were not actually trying to hit them with the lasers—but rather were using the threat of them to *herd* the two humans in a pre-programmed direction.

With the flashing lights melting the pavement all around them, the duo ducked into a narrow pathway, perhaps twenty feet wide, running between the backs of two buildings.

As they neared the far end of the pathway they heard a sudden, loud clanking sound. Accompanying the noise, a fifteen feet high chain link *fence* mounted on tracks slid from the end of one building to the other, effectively cutting off their escape.

So near to it were they when they skidded to a halt that they could hear the humming sound, see the random sparks that told them the fence was electrified.

Neither needed any prompting to turn and run back the way they had come. As they feared, though, they barely made it halfway before a similar chain link barrier had slid across the opposite end of the pathway. They were now effectively boxed in, the only windows in the two buildings on either side of them being set well above their reach.

Anticipating the laser-firing drones posed the more immediate threat, they cast their eyes upward. The four robotic devices were hovering menacingly overhead, but had ceased their barrage. Knowing they were useless for the moment, Scimidar retracted the blades of her tonfas and attached the butts to the outer legs of her night suit.

"I'd say you two are good and royally *screwed*," a taunting outlaw called out to them.

As Scimidar and Gitano stood and watched helplessly, a small group of Freebooters approached from the other side of the fence, coming from the direction from which they had retreated.

Leading this pack was Roger Jolly. Walking proudly beside him, with his left arm around her waist, was the battered Kat.

Two other Freebooters accompanied them. Each of these bikers was holding in hand the leashes of three snarling Doberman Pinscher dogs. As the six beasts drew near, they struggled to break loose and attack the pair standing on the far side of the fence.

The glow from a nearby pole light danced from the mouths of the Dobermans as their lips peeled back to reveal that their canine teeth had been removed and replaced with sharpened steel prosthetics.

"No matter how big a fish is," Jolly said, "it just can't resist biting at the right kind of bait."

Next to him, Kat smiled smugly despite her very real injuries.

"How brave was my little girl here," Jolly bragged. Kat's grin broadened as he pulled her tight and kissed her swollen lips hard enough to make her wince.

"She took a real beating so the story I sent her to feed you would be more believable," he said, turning his gaze to Scimidar.

"And obviously our little trick worked!" he crowed.

The biker overlord's expression changed almost imperceptibly, eyes narrowing, as he unexpectedly saw Scimidar also smiling slightly.

"You poor, deluded little girl," she said, directing her comments to Kat. "It's stupid you are, not brave, to subject yourself to an animal like Jolly."

"Shut your mouth, bitch!" Jolly snarled.

"Or you'll do what, you pompous asshole?" Scimidar replied defiantly.

"Were you both too ignorant to realize that I wouldn't be completely taken in by either Kat or her story?

"I'm an *empath*, remember? So I knew she was being deceptive—but also being partially truthful." She focused her gaze on the girl.

"Don't you see, Kat? You took that degrading beating for nothing. I would have followed after you no matter what."

"Don't listen to her, baby," Jolly retorted, hugging his girlfriend tighter. "She's just blowing smoke up your ass to try to cover the fact that the high-and-mighty Scimidar got tricked into falling into our trap." But Scimidar noted with satisfaction that the smile on Kat's lips was now more strained. Her gaze then shifted back to the biker.

"Jolly, you don't have the brains to lure a drowning man to a lifeboat."

"And yet you rushed headlong into the lion's den anyway," a deep voice boomed from above.

"How sadly typical of you, child."

The sound of the voice was familiar to Scimidar, though as of an echo coming back but faintly and hauntingly from a mountain canyon. It was with some trepidation that she lifted her eyes to discover its source.

She gasped as her gaze honed in on the imposing figure of a black man, dressed all in white and standing alone on a small landing protruding from the upper floor of one of the buildings between which she was enclosed.

"Shadrak!" she whispered, so softly that only Gitano could hear her.

Even after all these years an enveloping sense of terror swept over Scimidar as she recognized the man who must not only be her captor but the architect of the murderous plot she had stumbled upon.

It took all the self-control she could muster to fight her palpable fear in his mere presence. It helped that she could draw courage from her companion, who possessed no such irrational dread of the man in white.

He simply didn't know enough yet to fear Shadrak. She did.

"Would it surprise you," Shadrak said, speaking down to her, "to learn that I have kept myself apprised about your progress and your life ever since that day we met oh so briefly?"

"Nothing about you would surprise me," Scimidar replied.

"Oh, I bet it would," he said with a sparkle in his eye, "though much has happened since that day. Even then, I saw great potential within you."

He shook his head, frowning.

"But instead of achieving that potential...time and time again you proved to be a great disappointment to me."

"I'm so sorry I let you down," she responded, her voice dripping with acrid sarcasm.

"It's yourself you let down, girl." He sounded rather tired.

"More than most, you had shown me you had a true spark of greatness within you.

"But rather than nurturing that spark and fanning it into full flame by growing and refining your capabilities—you've mostly wasted your time, talents, energy and money on frivolity and self-indulgence.

"Now, you're nothing more than a female version of Peter Pan," he said coldly. "Just a little girl playing dress-up, wearing a silly costume."

"It's not a costume," Scimidar hissed. Shadrak ignored her.

"A little girl who never grew up to be a woman."

"Is that why you lured me here?" she said defiantly, her natural courage now diminishing the primal fear she had of the man. "To deliver a lecture on my shortcomings?"

"Believe it or not," he said after a long pause, "I brought you here to save your life."

"That's most generous."

"I think so. After you nearly allowed yourself to be killed by the little package my colleague Bolgarus left behind at Crocker's explosives emporium, it was clear you couldn't be counted on to save yourself."

"And just how do you intend to save me now?"

"By offering you employment."

"What?" Scimidar was clearly taken aback by this.

"As you said, I'm most generous. Come to work for me, following orders...and you'll live. It really is that simple."

"So is this," the blonde hunter replied, raising her right fist and extending the middle finger.

"How crude," Shadrak said, his frown deepening. "And how predictable. I expected your reply would be negative, just not so obscene."

Turning his head toward the Freebooters, Shadrak made a short sweeping motion with one hand.

"SHADRAK!"

In response, Roger Jolly walked over to a small control panel attached to one of the nearby light poles, where he threw a switch. As he did, the fencing closest to him powered down and began to slide open.

Once it retracted a few feet, Jolly's two henchmen released the Doberman Pinschers. Once they crossed to the other side, Jolly again flipped the switch on the control panel, closing the fence and once more electrifying its links.

Scimidar and Gitano tensed for an attack, but the six dogs merely stood their ground, snarling but not charging.

"All you have to do to save yourselves," Shadrak said from above, "is remain standing still for the next hour."

"The dogs as well as the drones have been finely programmed. So long as you do not move, neither will attack you. At the end of the hour, the fences will open and both beasts and machines will retreat.

"What happens now is up to you."

Leaning forward on his ubiquitous walking stick, Shadrak looked down on the entrapped pair with an almost sympathetic expression.

"This is an act of mercy," he said, his gaze focused on Scimidar. "One that Mr. Jolly staunchly opposes." The biker lord barked out a sneering laugh.

"But I grant it to you anyway," Shadrak continued, "out of respect for the potential that still exists within you and that may yet one day prove useful to us both." He sighed heavily.

"Don't make me regret it, child."

"And don't ever set foot in Freebooter territory again," Jolly could not resist adding. "You or the greaser."

"Someday this greaser's gonna slit you from gullet to gut," Gitano growled.

Jolly spread his arms and thrust his pelvis forward. "You're welcome to try any time you like, beaner."

"That's enough, Mr. Jolly," Shadrak said, irritation evident in his voice. "May I remind you we have far more important business to which we must attend?

"I'm off to the Empire State Building," he told Scimidar. "I hope we never meet this way again."

"That's not entirely true, is it?" Scimidar responded. Shadrak was slightly disconcerted to see the shadow of a smile on her full lips.

"What you just said about the Empire State, I mean. You're like that stupid little girl of Jolly's—being just truthful enough to cover a bigger lie."

Even though some distance separated her from him, Scimidar was clearly picking up empathetic vibrations from Shadrak. Only she was cognizant of how uncomfortable her observation had made him, for outwardly he continued to appear perfectly calm and in control.

Gitano, though, decided to play off his partner's probing. "I don't suppose you'd care to tell us what your real master plan is, would you, big guy?" he asked flippantly.

"Really, young man?" Shadrak replied, looking slightly insulted. "Do I look like the melodramatic villain of some cheap spy thriller?"

"Well...yeah. You kinda *do*."

Shadrak blinked a time or two. Then he threw his head back and laughed loudly and deeply before turning and leaving the landing.

# CHAPTER 28

*T*hrough the electrified fencing, Scimidar and Gitano could see a convoy of sorts pulling away from the industrial park a few minutes later.

In the lead was a sleek limousine into which they had seen Shadrak and the bomber Bolgarus enter.

A short distance behind the limo rolled the tanker truck bomb. Bringing up the rear was a large, long phalanx of Freebooters on their motorcycles, with the lead cycle being driven by Roger Jolly. A rather unhappy looking Kat sat behind him, her arms around his waist, her face pressed against his back.

Standing perfectly still as they had been instructed, Scimidar and Gitano silently watched as the convoy rolled out through the front gates of the compound.

Only then, and without turning her head, did Scimidar speak softly to her companion.

"Gitano...can you take out the drones if I handle the dogs?"

She didn't have to see him to know he was smiling. "I was hoping you'd say that, chica."

Her arms already being at her sides, Scimidar very slowly reached for her waiting tonfas. Pulling them free, she flexed her hands in the manner designed to extend their steel blades.

At the sound of the metallic zing as the blades shot into place, and the motion of them snaking out from the handles of the tonfas, the snarling Doberman Pinschers leaped to the attack.

"Now!" Scimidar shouted, springing forward to meet them. Just as quickly, Gitano snapped his sawed-off rifle up in both hands and took aim.

The charging dogs were taken off guard when their intended prey raced right into the midst of the pack rather than fleeing as would be expected.

They fell over each other as they strove to change direction. A tonfa slashed down, severing one dog's spinal column just behind its thick neck. Crippled, it fell limply to the ground.

Gitano opened fire. His first shot cleanly struck the nearest hovering drone, penetrating its outer shell far enough to destroy its inner workings and send it crashing to the pavement.

His second and third shots missed their targets, that were now whizzing around at the speed of hummingbirds, their deadly laser beams flicking out in short but potentially lethal bursts.

A Doberman's steel-enhanced teeth clamped down on Scimidar's left forearm. Before it could exert sufficient pressure to snap the bone, though, the blonde hunter drove the point of her right tonfa into the beast's skull. Its jaws relaxed and it dropped heavily.

Scimidar leaped straight up as another beast pounced toward her. As it passed beneath her bent legs, the woman was seized by her familiar sense of time and motion slowing down.

Yet another Doberman was leaping toward her. She crossed her arms before her, then snapped them apart as the canine drew near, its fangs bared.

As her blades crossed paths, each sliced cleanly across the Doberman's throat. Nearly severed from its neck, the head lolled grotesquely to one side while the body of the beast flew past Scimidar and flopped on the concrete.

Scimidar landed lightly and spun to face the remainder of the carnivorous pack. Realizing their prey had "teeth" as sharp as their own, the three dogs now stalked more cautiously toward her.

Gitano again fired at the drones. His next shot caromed off the side of its target, denting it and momentarily sending it off course, but not disabling it. His following shot was another clean hit, causing one of the drones to spit sparks and emit smoke before crashing into the wall of one of the buildings to either side of the combatants.

Gitano's weapon was now empty, however, and he had no choice but to stand still long enough to reload.

The three Doberman's split apart as they approached Scimidar, the end two moving to the sides while the middle dog went into a crouch and leaped forward.

A crackle of energy lancing through the air caused Scimidar to jerk to one side and start to fall back. Time slowed again and she was able to see a beam of laser light flash past her, able to smell her own burning strands of hair as the beam swept through her tresses, missing the smooth flesh of her face by less than an inch.

With only this slight resistance to its passage, the laser continued on—stopping only when it burrowed into the head of the pouncing Doberman. The dog's skull exploded as its brain boiled and expanded violently.

"Dammit, Gitano!" Scimidar yelled. "You've got to keep those drones off me!"

"I'm on it!" the gunman loudly assured her as he finished reloading the mare's leg.

The drone that had just fired at Scimidar swirled in Gitano's direction as the man pulled the trigger of his weapon. It was another direct hit, one that sent the drone into a fatal tailspin.

Another Doberman leaped toward Scimidar, who nimbly sidestepped it even while slashing at its momentarily exposed underbelly. With a loud ripping sound, the animal's entrails burst from its body.

Scimidar spun quickly, only to be struck in the chest by the forepaws of the last surviving attack dog. She felt herself going down under its weight.

In the air, only one drone remained, the one Gitano had damaged earlier. But its weaponry was still fully functional and it now fired a sustained burst at the gunman.

A cry of pain was torn from Gitano's lips as he felt a searing pain in his left side. The sizzling laser beam passed completely through him, striking the concrete beyond him and leaving a small, smoldering crater.

Gitano spun and fell to one knee. Electronically sensing that its prey was wounded, the drone swept in for the kill.

Fighting agony that made his eyes water, Gitano snapped the butt of his rifle up, braced it against his hip and fired his remaining four shots with lightning rapidity. Two of the shots were direct hits.

Trailing smoke, the crippled drone went into a dive, barely missing the crouching gunman before plowing into the pavement.

Gitano pushed himself back up on his feet, only to stumble drunkenly sideways before falling heavily to the ground.

Scimidar did not resist the last Doberman's momentum, but rather went with it as she fell over backwards.

Striking the pavement with her back, she used her arms and legs to flip the Doberman through the air. Helpless to stop itself, the beast slammed into the electrified fence, dying horribly in a cloud of sizzling hair and flesh as thousands of volts ripped through its flailing body.

As Scimidar rose back to her feet, she saw Gitano still prone on the ground. She retracted her blades and slapped her tonfas into their resting-places on her thighs even as she ran toward the fallen gunman.

"Are you hurt?" she nearly demanded as she took hold of Gitano's left arm to help him up.

"Huh? No. I don't have a scratch on me," he assured her. "I just tripped over my own feet and took a dive."

Still "high" from a violent rush of adrenaline, and given her inexplicable inability to read Gitano as well or as easily as she could most others, Scimidar did not catch his lie.

"Then come on," she urged. "We've got to go after the Freebooters!"

"Just let me reload," he said, doing just that as he also willed himself to move past the pain radiating from his side.

As the gunman followed after Scimidar, moving toward the fence that still held them captive, Gitano passed the Doberman whose spine had been severed. The dog was not dead but was whimpering pitiably as it tried in vain to move its unresponsive limbs.

Gitano cocked his rifle and mercifully put a bullet into the beast's brain.

Scimidar swiveled at the sound of the gunshot, but upon realizing its meaning, turned her attention back to the electrified fence.

"We still have a problem here," she said, "unless we want to wait out the hour until it deactivates itself."

"Maybe I can speed up the process," Gitano offered. Again cocking his rifle, he fired between the links of the fence, placing two slugs into the control box Roger Jolly had used earlier to shut off the electricity and open the fencing.

A shower of sparks spit out of the damaged box and a moment later the ominous humming sound coming from the fence quieted.

Still leery, Gitano tapped the fence with the palm of his left hand, withdrawing it quickly. Receiving no shock, he holstered his rifle, grabbed hold of the fence with both hands and slid it back far enough for him and Scimidar to slither through.

They quickly jogged across the street to where Gitano's Electra Glide was parked and mounted the bike.

"Hold onto your Marimbas, chica," he told her. "I'm gonna open her all the way up!"

Unseen by the woman, he had been pressing his right hand against the laser wound in his left side. As he pulled the hand away, he saw that his palm was slick with blood.

He was determined to ignore the implications as he cranked the throttle on his bike and roared away into the night.

# CHAPTER 29

Scimidar frowned as Gitano braked his motorcycle to a halt.

They had been streaming south on Broadway at full speed and were just beginning to gain on the brutal brigade of bikers racing ahead of them.

"What are you doing?" she snapped.

"They're splitting up!" he replied, jerking his head forward.

Scimidar leaned to the side to get a better view and realized Gitano was right. Ahead, where Broadway crossed 6th Avenue, the main body of the outlaws was turning left onto 34th Street, in the route that would take them to the Empire State Building.

But Shadrak's limousine, the tanker truck and a small band of the bikers with Roger Jolly at its head were continuing straight on, due south.

"Which way do we go?" Gitano asked.

The blonde hunter pondered their options.

"My senses told me that both Kat and Shadrak were only being *partially* truthful whenever they talked about the attack on the Empire State."

"Yeah, which means what?"

"Which means they could indeed be planning to carry out such a maneuver—but only as some sort of spectacular *diversion*.

"It would draw attention and manpower to it, while a second and even more horrible plan—one we don't know about—is put into motion."

"What about your police friend?" Gitano asked.

Scimidar nodded. "We have to assume that Captain Cooke has had time to prepare a welcome for the Freebooters at the Empire State.

"It's Shadrak we have to be most concerned about. And right now, we're the only two people who know at all about this second move he's making toward some other target."

She drew her arms tighter around Gitano's waist, failing to notice that he flinched slightly as she did so.

"We follow the bomb," she said firmly.

"There's never a dull moment with you, is there, chica?" Gitano said with a chuckle, before again opening the throttle on his bike.

At that very moment, in a corridor outside the large conference room on the second floor of City Hall, Mayor Dylan Holt stood alone at a window, looking out over the night skyline of his hometown.

It saddened him no end that the metropolis that used to never sleep was now not nearly so brightly lit in the gloom as it always was back when he was a boy growing up here.

Back before the whole world had rapidly descended into hell.

"Mr. Mayor?"

Holt turned his head to the side at the soft sound of his press secretary Jeffrey Sasser's voice.

"The last attendee you invited to our summit has arrived," the young man informed him. "They're all waiting for you inside."

"Thank you, Jeff," the mayor replied, but did not immediately turn away from the window.

"Take a look out there," he said to his aide, pointing. A few blocks away, he had noticed what appeared to be an unusual number of vehicle headlights bunched rather closely together.

"Is there some sort of parade or procession going on that I'm not aware of?" he asked Sasser.

"Not that I know of, sir," the press secretary replied, quickly thumbing through his scheduling notebook.

Holt smiled as he turned away from the window. "Maybe it's a sign, Jeff. A sign that this old girl of ours is already starting to come back to life. That would be wonderful," he said earnestly.

"She's been dead for too long."

# CHAPTER 30

*C*omfortably ensconced in the back seat of his limousine, the man called Shadrak poured a glass of chilled champagne for himself and another for his pet terrorist Stavros Bolgarus.

"To success," he said, clinking his glass against that of the bomber.

"To success," Bolgarus echoed before taking a sip of the champagne.

Shadrak smiled lightly while staring intently at the mercenary. "You have no idea to what I refer, do you? Nor do you care."

Bolgarus shrugged. "In my business, I've learned that, beyond completing the terms of a contract, it is often best *not* to know too much."

"Very wise," Shadrak replied, sipping at his drink. "But I'm feeling... almost exuberant at the moment. I'd like to tell you what you're about to be a part of. It may change history."

"Then by all means do so," Bolgarus said. At his feet rested a briefcase bulging with money: payment for his services. But until he was safely out of New York and on his way to another country, he thought it well to indulge his current employer in any way he could.

"Right about now," Shadrak began, "a summit meeting is being called to order inside City Hall. Every man and woman of authority in the city will be there.

"Everybody but me." Bolgarus heard the bitterness in Shadrak's voice.

"So we're going to drive that beautiful bomb on wheels of yours straight into the building's front lobby," the man in white continued, growing enthused, "and kill every last one of them!

"Besides the immediate death and destruction it should cause all around it when it is detonated, it should effectively implode the structure—bringing down most of the building and snuffing out the lives of all those unfortunate enough to be inside at the time of the explosion." He paused to drain his glass and refill it.

"In one fell swoop, I will eliminate the entire hierarchy of all of New York City's governing bodies. Chaos will follow, of course, resulting in an enormous power vacuum."

"Into which you mean to step," Bolgarus said.

"Into which I *will* step," Shadrak asserted.

"Sounds like a feasible plan, Mr. Shadrak," Bolgarus said, though in truth it sounded to him more like a crazy pipe dream.

"One thought comes to mind, though," the bomber boldly ventured. "Won't there be extremely tight security surrounding such a gathering?"

"Not so much as you'd think, no," Shadrak declared. "That's part of the beauty of my plan. Even under ordinary circumstances, shortages of funding and officers would make for a marginal cordon around the building.

"But I've injected *extraordinary* circumstances into the equation. That's why I sent that tattooed cow of a girl to tell Scimidar about the planned attack on the Empire State Building."

"That wasn't done simply to lure the hellcat into your arms?"

"Hardly. That was merely a bonus. I knew that whether Scimidar fully believed what the girl told her or not, she would feel she had no choice but to alert the authorities as to the *possibility* that such an attack was imminent.

"By now, I would be willing to wager that virtually every able-bodied police officer on the island is gathered around the Empire State—leaving Mayor Holt's summit naked and exposed.

"And the forthcoming attack on the Empire State is sure to eliminate at least a portion of the city's police force, rendering it less capable of interfering when I move in."

"Then, the Freebooters…?" Bolgarus asked.

"Little more than decoys," Shadrak gloated. "Completely expendable. Cannon fodder, to facilitate the success of my larger endeavor.

"I expect most of them will die tonight…but not until they've served my purpose."

"Does that Jolly creature know this?"

"Of course not. Before the dust settles, he'll be eliminated, too. The remnants of his gang will doubtless be happy to serve as the core of a new police force under my personal command."

His hired bomber looked pensive as he sipped at his champagne. "Is it really necessary to take such drastic measures to achieve your goal?"

"Absolutely," Shadrak replied with the conviction of a zealot or a madman. "I tried it their way, and it did me no good. They were too stupid to appreciate what I offered.

"That was a mistake I won't repeat. You don't *ask* sheep to go where you want. You turn the dogs loose on them and drive them where they need to go."

Bolgarus nodded. "True enough. But isn't it likely the Federal authorities will contest your claim on being the Good Shepherd?"

Shadrak snorted derisively. "They can barely keep the lights turned on. They have bigger concerns than a few dead politicians in New York." He took a drink and smiled.

"Plus, I have enough powerful people in my pocket to insure that no one makes a move against me until it is too late."

"You appear to have prepared for every contingency, sir," Bolgarus said, smiling slyly.

"And would I be correct in assuming that your ambitions won't end with the acquisition of this city alone?"

Shadrak drained his glass before responding.

"Ambition should never end, Mr. Bolgarus."

"I think I know where they're going!" Scimidar, less than three blocks behind Shadrak's limousine, shouted into Gitano's ear as they raced along astride his growling Electra Glide. They had passed Washington Square Park and were now crossing Canal Street.

"City Hall," she said, pointing ahead. They were now within sight of the center of city government.

Because of the extra-legal but semi-official status she enjoyed, Scimidar was privy to insider information denied to most others. So it was that she knew about the summit Mayor Holt had convened for that night. With that knowledge, it took no great leap of logic to discern what Shadrak was planning to do with his tanker bomb.

"We've got to stop that truck!" she urged her companion.

In response, Gitano steered his bike off the street and up onto the sidewalk, killing his headlight and riding in the shadows to avoid being seen by the Freebooters they trailed.

There was a time when such a maneuver would have surely been homicidal and possibly suicidal. Pedestrian traffic in the troubled city now, though, was far sparser.

The move was still not without danger as, virtually in the dark, Gitano ratcheted the throttle up to full speed. Scimidar marveled at the skill with which he handled the bike and was thrilled as the two of them boldly flung themselves into the face of death.

When he at last drew near to the rear of the pack of Freebooters, Gitano swung back onto the street and switched his headlight on again. Gunning the Electra Glide's engine, he roared straight through the middle of the cluster of bikers, zooming past them before most could recognize whom it was.

Seconds later, at the head of the pack, Roger Jolly grimaced as the glare from a headlight suddenly lanced into his side view mirror.

He turned his head as the trailing bike that had nearly blinded him by turning on its high beams drew parallel to him. Astounded, he snarled, revealing his gold teeth.

Beside him, Gitano flashed the biker lord a casual grin, then revved his engine once more so as to leap out ahead of the pack.

Before Jolly or any of the other Freebooters could react to the presence of their enemy, a bright light unexpectedly erupted, filling the entire night sky, turning it nearly as bright as high noon.

Gitano and Scimidar each threw a hand up to shade their eyes from the intense glare.

"Santa Maria!" Gitano cursed as a massive, thundering ball of flame came hurtling down from above, headed straight toward them.

Scimidar remembered back to her conversation with Captain Cooke two days earlier. He had told her that a defunct communications satellite had dropped from its decaying orbit and was expected to make landfall somewhere nearby soon.

With a sinking feeling in her gut, she realized that soon was now—and the somewhere was here!

# CHAPTER 31

*T*railing fire and metal debris, the plummeting satellite seemed to be diving diagonally right down the middle of 6th Avenue.

With no other viable option available, Gitano and Scimidar crouched low over their bike and continued straight on their path as twenty tons of twisted and scorched metal howled its way toward them. In its death throes it spewed electrical discharges in every direction.

So close overhead did the blazing ball of useless technology hurtle that the pair of them found it difficult to breathe as the very air around them became superheated.

Roger Jolly and the nearest ranks of bikers following him also escaped being enveloped in the flames.

The rest of the Freebooters were not so fortunate.

The screaming inferno plowed savagely into the middle of the pack. The cries of the dead could not be heard as motorcycles and their riders were torn to burning shreds and sent flying in all directions. Parts of bodies were inseparable from parts of machines.

The initial impact caused cars on the street to jump up off the pavement and then go flying end over end sideways. The gas tanks of some ruptured and exploded in smaller spouts of fire. Drivers and passengers were thrown from these spinning autos and slammed into walls and pavement, leaving bloody smears. Others were simply crushed by the metal shells around them collapsing inward.

Windows exploded inward. Scores of people were injured or killed, cut to ribbons by jagged shards of glass.

An ear-piercing, groaning sound accompanied the satellite as it slid along, digging a deep furrow in the street. Instruments inside its charred shell blew apart from the heat and force of impact, killing still more bystanders.

Before the crushed and shattered orbital craft fully came to rest, it had left behind a path of destruction the length of five football fields.

Several blocks away, standing in front of the Empire State Building, Captain Jefferson Cooke had seen the fireballs, heard the explosions and correctly deduced the source of both.

It would have to fall to the Fire Department and other emergency servers to respond to this disaster, he knew. He had a far more pressing concern of his own now, for he had just spotted the small army of Freebooters rolling in formation toward his position.

Most of the precious few police officers Captain Cooke had at his disposal had been stationed in a perimeter around all four sides of this iconic skyscraper. In full riot gear, these men and women now hunkered down behind the cover of parked cars.

Cooke had also placed as many sharpshooters as he could spare inside the buildings on either side of all the main streets leading to the Empire State's location, in hope of thus catching the bikers in a three-way crossfire.

When Cooke had received the tip from Scimidar regarding such an attack by the outlaw gang, he had immediately gone to his superiors with that information. Despite his personal dislike for the woman, Cooke knew Scimidar would not have informed him of this threat unless she felt there was a high probability of its veracity.

His superiors had decided, and Captain Cooke had concurred with their decision, that it was best not to alert the civilian authorities just yet. Time was too short and the likelihood of the news leaking prematurely was too great. Discretion was their best hope of not only thwarting the threat but also eliminating it.

The process of evacuating the entire Empire State Building in just a few hours had been much easier than would have been the case in the city's glory days. The skyscraper's available office space was less than half occupied.

Yet its symbolic status had remained undiminished and it maintained its value as a tourist attraction second only to the Statue of Liberty. Its regular occupants had been shuttled to another building, sequestered so as to keep panic from spreading and from tipping off the bikers determined to attack it. Unsuspecting tourists had been likewise politely but forcefully detained.

The police plan had proceeded admirably, and the officers, all armed with high-powered automatic rifles, waited resolutely as the Freebooters rode into the trap. No shots were to be fired yet, as Captain Cooke had ordered, until he signaled them to open fire by discharging his own weapon.

Unlike the other officers, he was armed only with his service pistol. He had only reluctantly allowed his lieutenants to talk him into replacing his suit coat with a bulletproof vest.

A radio check with his men stationed at other points around the building seemed to confirm that his was the only position facing imminent threat. Still, he ordered them all to maintain their current positions and remain vigilant.

While he stood, presenting a tempting target, the rest of Cooke's officers stayed crouched down out of sight as the outlaw bikers streamed closer.

With smooth ease, he drew his weapon from its holster clipped to his belt, holding it at his side. He didn't want to start this deadly dance until the Freebooters were past his hidden snipers. He meant to see every one of the bikers taken down, as a signal to all that this city did not belong to the lawless.

He didn't move as the first bullets began to zip around and near him as Freebooters opened fire wildly. He chose his own target, a large rider whose bristly hair had been shaved into a sort of Mohawk style. Only now did Cooke raise his pistol, gripping it in both hands as he extended it forward and caressed the trigger.

His shot splattered right in the middle of Mohawk's forehead, lifting him and flipping him backward off his bike.

At that, the officers who had been anxiously watching Cooke rose up in unison and began to lay down a withering fire.

The deployed sharpshooters began to expertly pick off the outlaws at the rear of the roaring band. One biker, gravely wounded, swerved and jumped the curb. His body was thrown from the cycle and smashed through the nearest window.

There was no panic in the bikers, though, and they bravely rode on with guns blazing, many of them yelping gleefully. From the corners of his eyes, Captain Cooke saw some of his own officers going down. He tried not to think of it, but to concentrate instead on taking out as many of the enemy as possible.

His ears rang from the din of battle, harsh sounds contained and amplified by the surrounding buildings. The rumble of the bikes, the screeching of metal as some crashed or slid along the pavement. The rattle of weapons firing. The almost maniacal cries of the bikers now being drowned out by the screams of the wounded and dying.

Death, Cooke thought, should not be so loud.

He stopped shooting only long enough to eject his emptied ammo clip and slap a fresh one into its place.

He'd only fired a few additional rounds when his luck finally ran out. A bullet tore into his exposed left shoulder, spinning him and slamming him to the sidewalk.

He could still hear the sounds of guns, knew the battle was not ended. He strove to rise, only to fall back heavily to the concrete. Somewhere, he heard another man scream.

Roger Jolly threw his head back and screamed.

He flew into a killing rage as he saw Gitano and his blonde bitch zoom past him. In the instant, all else was dispelled from his mind: Shadrak's grand master plan, the gun battle he knew was probably already swirling around the Empire State Building. All he knew or cared about now was that he needed to kill Gitano.

He savagely twisted the throttle of his bike, sending it leaping ahead of the rest of the pack, racing after Gitano. He had completely forgotten about the girl sitting behind him, now clinging to him for dear life as he pushed his bike to dangerously high speed.

"Slow down!" Kat wailed, terror twisting her heart. The biker lord ignored her.

"Let me off!" she screamed hysterically, pounding on Jolly's back with one small and ineffectual fist.

He obliged her.

Jolly snapped his head back viciously, butting Kat in the face. Stunned, her nose broken and spraying blood, the girl went limp and slid off the back of the bike.

The doomed girl's body bounced along the pavement—and right into the path of one of the other bikers still following in Jolly's wake. There was no way he could stop or swerve.

The motorcycle, its driver and Kat all flipped into the air in a tangled mass. When they slammed back down to the street, it was too late for both man and woman.

With her final, labored breath, Kat cursed the soul of Roger Jolly.

Gitano, meanwhile, was slowly gaining on the tanker truck and its explosive load.

"I've got to get inside it," Scimidar declared.

Her words were nearly lost in the whine of a bullet screaming past her head. She looked over her shoulder to see Roger Jolly gaining on them, now firing a pistol as he came.

Her mind racing ferociously, Scimidar placed her mouth close to Gitano's right ear and spoke firmly to him.

"Are you sure?" he replied warily.

"Just do it!" she shouted.

Obliging, Gitano revved his bike's engine to the max, drawing closer still to the rear end of the tanker.

He then abruptly jammed on the Electra Glide's front brake, leaning forward as he did so. The dual action caused the bike to nearly stand on its nose while its rear end flipped up.

As it did, Scimidar released her grip on Gitano and his bike—and was sent flying forward through the air!

# CHAPTER 32

**S**cimidar grunted in pain, the breath exploding from her lungs, as she slammed hard into the rear of the speeding truck. Dark spots danced before her eyes as she began to topple backwards and she desperately lunged one arm forward.

She managed to latch her right hand onto one of the rungs of the attached metal ladder that ran up the back end of the truck's large tank. Her fall stopped, though she spun, slapping again into the body of the tank. She bounced back and grabbed purchase with her free hand and her feet, securing her hold on the ladder.

Seeing that Scimidar was "safely" aboard the careening tanker, Gitano expertly righted his bike and spun it around so as to face the Freebooters he knew were oncoming. Rather than continue to flee from them, he decided to make a stand and fight.

Choosing such rearguard action would protect Scimidar's flank, but he knew it would also at least momentarily leave her alone to deal with the death trap upon which she was now a passenger. Whatever he was to do now, he must do quickly so as to be able to rejoin her.

Like a cavalryman of old might have done with his horse, Gitano laid his bike down on its side and threw himself flat behind its shelter as the pursuing bikers bore down on him.

Unlike on the night at the *Lost Treasure*, this time he did not hesitate to make his closest and therefore first target Roger Jolly, who was still out ahead of his pack. Taking careful aim, Gitano opened fire, levering and shooting quickly but smoothly.

None of his first shots struck the biker overlord, but one bullet did puncture the front tire of Jolly's Harley Destroyer. Given the high rate of speed at which the bike was traveling, the flattening of his tire caused the gleaming machine to buck violently, shaking so hard that the controlling handlebars were torn from Jolly's grasp.

The cycle swerved, skipped up off the street and flipped onto its side. Sparks flew as it went into a skid across the pavement. With one leg pinned beneath its weight, a struggling Jolly was carried along with it, being painfully dragged and bounced along the concrete.

At the back of the racing tanker truck, Scimidar sagged with one arm looped through a rung of the ladder to which she clung. Her body ached from the force of her impact and subsequent efforts, and air still resisted filling her lungs.

Refusing to let pain be her master and knowing time must be short, she willed herself to climb the ladder to the top of the vehicle's tank. Balanced precariously atop it, she made her way forward even as the currents of passing air tried to pluck her from her perch.

Inside the cab of the truck, behind its steering wheel, was the vehicle's sole occupant: one of Shadrak's female, clone-like personal guards. The stony-faced woman was under no illusion as to what was to be her fate tonight. When asking for volunteers for this mission, Shadrak had plainly told the women that whomever undertook this particular job would surely die in the process.

So fanatical were those this demagogue had surrounded himself with, so blind in their loyalty, that every one of them had stepped forward without hesitation to volunteer for this "honor."

In truth, Shadrak had not only bought their loyalty by paying them handsomely but had also earned it by virtue of being equally and fiercely loyal to them. He was also generous in many other ways, including continuing to financially support the families of any woman who died in his service.

The kamikaze driver's head jerked upward as she heard a loud thud at the top of the cab. Above her, Scimidar had just dropped down from the tanker she was hauling.

Just as Scimidar flattened herself atop the cab, a bullet ripped upward through its roof, missing her by inches. She rolled as more slugs tore through the thin metal.

One leg came down on nothing but open space as she reached the edge of the roof. She desperately threw herself back in the direction from which she had come, clinging to the edges of the cab and slinging herself toward its rear.

The driver of the tanker had to cease firing for a moment in order to use both hands to steer around a car that was foolishly pulling out from an intersecting street.

Scimidar took advantage of the lull to slither to the left side of the cab. Leaning over and holding one of her tonfas, she flexed her hand on its grip. The telescoping metal tube inside the handle shot out forcefully, shattering the driver's side window.

The impassive guard at the wheel threw her left arm up to protect her face from the flying glass. The pistol dropped from her right hand, which was needed to steer.

Retracting her tonfa weapon and slapping it back into its resting-place, Scimidar swung down and slung open the door of the cab. A hand shot out and pushed against her face, attempting to shove her off the truck.

Scimidar swung her left arm, slapping the driver's hand away. Her left fist then jabbed forward, punching the other woman in the side of the head.

The blonde grabbed the collar of the driver's jacket and jerked, even while swinging her own body in an arc. The driver's mirrored glasses flew off as she was dragged from behind the wheel, allowing Scimidar to see fear there as the woman fell to the pavement below. She screamed horribly as she was dragged beneath the relentless rolling tanker and was crushed by its massive tires.

The tanker bounced and jerked sideways as it rolled over the woman and Scimidar again felt herself being nearly thrown clear of the truck. Her feet slipped from their toehold and only the strength of her arms kept her from falling and possibly suffering the same fate as had the driver.

With no one behind the wheel, the truck swerved to the left, toward a light pole and a row of parked cars. Instants away from being crushed or ripped off the side of the tanker, Scimidar threw herself into the cab.

She twisted the steering wheel hard. She thus avoided a head-on collision, but the open door of the tanker struck the light pole. The door was torn from the cab of the truck and the pole was severed. A spray of electrical sparks flooded the cab of the truck, sizzling where they struck the exposed skin of Scimidar's face.

The truck slid and bounced along the line of parked cars, eliciting a shower of sparks. Scimidar fought with the tanker's wildly rotating steering wheel, managing to tame it and pull back into the center of the street.

When she pressed her right foot against the brake pedal, however, she found that it offered no resistance as she pushed it flat to the floor. Unknown to her, the hurtling body of the driver who had been run over by the tanker had torn free the vehicle's brake lines.

There was no way to stop this hurtling bomb!

# CHAPTER 33

*G*itano took cold, careful aim.

His selected target was Roger Jolly, who was struggling to pull his bruised body from beneath the wreckage of his crashed motorcycle. Gitano started to squeeze the trigger of the mare's leg with a feathery touch.

At that instant, a shot fired by one of the other Freebooters scorched along Gitano's right forehead, causing him to jerk as he fired his own weapon. Thrown off its trajectory, his slug missed Jolly and instead burrowed into the gas tank of the trapped biker's cycle.

The metal on metal impact caused a spark that ignited the fuel within. A small fireball erupted from the ruptured tank, enveloping both man and machine.

Gitano grimaced at the thought of the horrible fate he had accidentally visited upon Jolly. But he had no time for further reflection as the few remaining Freebooters bore down on him.

Bullets spanged around him as he fired his rifle repeatedly, pausing only when there was the need to reload. A slug suddenly tore through the meaty part of his upper right arm, flipping him over.

Lying on his back, he saw a Harley come flying over his own bike. As it sailed past, Gitano triggered his gun twice. The Freebooter was thrown to one side as his bike continued on without him.

Rolling back onto his stomach, knowing his gun was now empty, Gitano reached to his belt for fresh rounds, only to find none remaining.

He cautiously raised his head high enough to peek over the top of his flattened bike. There appeared to be only one Freebooter remaining. This outlaw had apparently also run out of ammunition, for as he gunned his

...PUNCHING THE...WOMAN IN THE SIDE OF THE HEAD.

cycle forward he was menacingly twirling a length of chain in his left hand.

Jumping to his feet, Gitano flipped his sawed-off rifle and grabbed it by its barrel. His teeth clenched and he groaned softly as the gun metal, heated by repeated firing, seared the palms of his hands. Ignoring the pain, he wielded the weapon like a baseball bat.

He stood his ground as the Freebooter raced straight toward him. At the last possible instant, Gitano skipped to his left, pivoted and swung the mare's leg. The stock of the gun caught the outlaw biker flush in the face, crushing his skull like a melon and sending him flying off the back end of the cycle.

The force of the blow sent waves of agony ripping up Gitano's arms, dropping him to his knees. He stared down at what remained of his prized rifle. Most of its stock was gone, and the weapon was surely damaged beyond repair. He numbly let it fall to the pavement, just glad that he had dispatched the last of his opponents.

Then he heard peals of cackling, almost crazed *laughter*.

Turning slowly he saw, to his utter amazement, Roger Jolly on his feet, walking stiffly toward him.

The deranged, giggling biker was literally on fire, as flames continued to flicker on his scorched clothing. Smoke rose and swirled from what remained of the tangle of hair atop his head. Despite this, the wild cast of his eyes and the wicked looking knife he clutched in his hand spoke of his intent to take Gitano into hell with him.

His own eyes narrowed to mere slits as the object of his hatred pulled his switchblade from its pouch at the back of his neck. Flicking it open, Gitano launched himself toward the staggering Jolly.

He slammed into the biker and the two of them toppled together to the street. Hands locked on wrists as they began to roll back and forth. Locked tightly in each other's grip as they were, Gitano found it unavoidable that the flames lapping at his foe burned his own hands and arms as well.

They exacted an even heavier toll on the biker lord, though, as Gitano felt the hand gripping his wrist begin to weaken in strength.

He jerked his arm free and rammed the point of his knife blade into Jolly's side. Gitano rolled so he was atop the biker, withdrawing his blade only to plunge it into his foe's belly. Jolly's arms flopped to the side and his legs twitched weakly as the life began to drain from him.

His mouth quivered as Gitano leaned near his face and smiled.

"I just want you to know something, Jolly. When you die—I mean to pluck out every one of those Goddamned gold teeth of yours and then piss on your fucking corpse!"

A choking sound was all the biker could manage before his eyes rolled up into their sockets and he left life behind him.

Gasping for air, burned and bleeding from both his gunshot wound and the hole sliced by the laser drone, Gitano pushed himself to his feet and drunkenly made his way to his bike.

He had to reach Scimidar.

His leaden feet caught on the front wheel of his cycle and he fell heavily face first back to the concrete.

He was not sure he would ever rise again.

Back aboard the tanker bomb, the object of Gitano's concern found that even though she was not applying any gas to the truck it was not slowing down but continuing on at a steady and unwavering speed.

Still ahead of her was Shadrak's limousine, and he was turned anxiously in his seat, having witnessed what had transpired behind him.

"Damn her!" he hissed, swiveling toward Bolgarus. "That little witch may just figure out a way to stop the truck.

"Can you detonate the bombs attached to it from here, Bolgarus?"

The mercenary gulped loudly. "As you know, sir, your driver was supposed to trigger the bombs after she crashed into the lobby of City Hall."

"Don't tell me what I already know, damn you!" Shadrak snarled, grabbing Bolgarus and pulling him close. "Can you detonate them?"

Bolgarus's fear and phobia about physical violence made his stomach revolt against him.

"Yes, sir," he stammered. "Yes, sir, I can."

"Then do it!"

"But if we blow it up now," the bomber protested weakly, "your plan will be ruined."

"My plan is already dead. That woman has seen to that." He again glared back through his rear window.

"It's only a matter of time before she finds a way to stop the truck safely. Before she can do that—I want it and her blown to hell!"

Bolgarus nodded and plunged his hand into the briefcase carrying his money. From it he extracted a small black box, not much bigger than a cigarette pack.

"This will override the detonator switch inside the truck," Bolgarus explained. "There will also be a fifteen second delay between the time I issue the electronic command and the actual detonation of the devises attached to its tank.

"If we hurry, that should give us time to get safely outside the blast area."

"You heard the man, N'Tora," Shadrak said to the woman driving the limousine. She nodded silently before pressing her right foot hard against the accelerator. The powerful car leapt forward quickly.

"Now get on with it, Bolgarus!" Shadrak snapped.

"Yes, sir." The mercenary punched in a six-digit code and then pressed a recessed button on the small control device.

Inside the cab of the tanker truck, Scimidar heard a loud beeping noise. A device attached to her right on the dashboard lit up and digital numbers appeared on a small display screen.

When she saw the numbers begin to count down toward zero, she recognized that the device and its purpose were identical to the one that she had seen in the sub-basement hideout of the arms dealer named Crocker.

She was sitting inside a massive bomb that was about to explode!

# CHAPTER 34

s the hurtling tanker truck neared Reade Street, Scimidar cast her eyes frantically about, her mind awhirl in search of an idea that might divert disaster.

Her best and possibly only hope appeared to one side ahead, in the form of the gaping entrance to a subway tunnel. Since it was well past nightfall, she knew there would be no commuters inside the station proper.

Though the tanker's brakes had been disabled and its speed preset, the steering still appeared to work normally, so Scimidar jerked the wheel and set the tanker on a course straight toward the opening into the subway.

The timer on the detonator was down to six seconds when she leaped out of the gaping hole where the door of the truck had been. She hit the street in such a way that she was able to roll, come up onto her feet and take off running.

She knew that the body of the tanker was too wide to fit entirely into the subway entrance. She also remembered that it was filled with hundreds, if not thousands of ball bearings that would momentarily fill the air like deadly miniature missiles.

As the fuel-laden truck caromed down the steps of the subway tunnel before lodging at an awkward angle in its entryway, Scimidar slid over the hood of a car parked across the street. She crouched low behind the wheel closest to the engine block where she would enjoy the greatest measure of protection.

She had barely done so when the tanker exploded.

Because of the quick action she had taken, a significant portion of the blast force, the flames and the ball bearings were diverted downward into the subway.

Upon hearing the initial crash of the tanker as it rammed into the tunnel entry, a band of Downsiders who had been congregated on the loading platform below rushed forward to investigate this disruptive intrusion upon what they considered to be their exclusive domain.

They became the first victims of the blast.

A blazing fireball enveloped those closest to the point of the detonation. Their internal organs melted before they had time to scream. The bodies of those coming behind them were torn to bloody shreds by the deadly barrage of ball bearings. The tiled walls of the station became a grotesque Jackson Pollack mural, painted in blood and guts.

A few of the Downsiders would miraculously survive, though horribly scarred or devoid of limbs. In the days to come, as details of the explosion became more widely disseminated, it would become accepted lore among their kind that this had been a deliberate attack orchestrated against them.

Consequently, their hatred for Toppers in general, and Scimidar in particular, would grow and intensify.

But the surface and those who crawled upon it did not escape the full force of the blast, either. The street buckled and cracked. Shock waves shattered windows. Ball bearings delivered injury and death.

Even in these hard times, the streets of New York were never completely deserted; there were small numbers of cars on the streets, pedestrians on the sidewalks. At least one auto was lifted and thrown through the front of a building. Half a dozen passersby were killed or maimed by the blast or the shrapnel-like ball bearings.

The engine block of the car behind which Scimidar sheltered stopped most of the destructive force, though she saw ball bearings tear through other parts of the vehicle and slam into the pavement near her. She threw her arms over her head to protect it from flying pieces of glass from the car and the nearest building.

Her ears ringing painfully, she rose to her feet and surveyed the carnage. Wails of pain assaulted her and her stomach twisted into an aching knot as she began to empathetically feel the pain of all those who were victims of the explosion.

Like an ancient Valkyrie dispatched to a battlefield to harvest the souls of the fallen warriors and escort them to Valhalla, she stood in the grasp of oblivion. Multiple impressions of the dead and dying victims' last conscious thoughts poured into her in an emotional maelstrom that threatened to overload her mind and her heart. She was driven to her knees and began to sob softly.

Overwhelmed by both the beauty and the horror of it all.

# CHAPTER 35

*A*t City Hall, Mayor Dylan Holt gaped in anguish, staring out a window. The nearby explosion and its resulting fireball had been clearly heard and seen from the site of his summit, and what he had expected to be a hopeful triumph in the instant turned to dust in his mouth.

Jeffrey Sasser and other aides were quickly but unflappably evacuating the conference room, directing the summit participants toward an emergency exit tunnel that in turn led to a large, bombproof safe room below ground level.

Holt was the last to leave, and then only at the urgent insistence of Sasser. The mayor took one last look out the window before joining the others, wondering inwardly what horrible, fresh wound had now been inflicted on his beloved city.

At the Empire State Building, Captain Jefferson Cooke was back on his feet. Though the left sleeve of his shirt was soaked in his own blood, he stubbornly shook off any efforts to direct him to the aid station he had ordered to be set up in the lobby of the skyscraper in anticipation of casualties that appeared certain to run up into the scores.

He stepped out stoically to assess the aftermath of the fight. Most of the outlaw bikers were now merely corpses littering the street and the sidewalks. It would be a long time, if ever, before the Freebooters would represent any viable sort of threat again.

A few had managed to escape with their lives, the rest were being handcuffed and prepared for transport to One Police Plaza. All were doubtless looking at long prison terms.

Cooke had also seen and heard the explosion that has occurred a few blocks to the south and found his steps turning in that direction, only to pull up short when he felt something tugging at the cuff of his slacks. He looked down to see a mortally wounded Freebooter trying the raise himself up by pulling on the cop's leg.

Scowling, Cooke put a bullet through the biker's brain.

The officer then again turned his attention toward the area of the explosion, where even in the dark of night a thick black cloud could be seen billowing up into the air. Every instinct he possessed screamed out for him to investigate the cause of the blast and to render aid.

But logic and duty told him that at the moment he had neither the time nor the manpower to spare. After all, it was not Freebooters alone who had suffered casualties in the recent gun battle.

Bodies uniformed in blue also dotted the scene. Those survivors who were not herding prisoners were needed for crowd control and providing emergency care for the wounded. Cooke knew that first and foremost he had to remain onsite and look to the welfare of his own officers.

The veteran cop's mind was also already racing ahead to see what all this meant to the near future. Given the city's severe shortage of funds, it would certainly be months, perhaps even years before the losses to the police ranks could be adequately replaced. That in turn meant New York would likely become even wilder and more lawless, if such a thing were possible.

The Citizens Crime Committee would probably attempt to insert itself even more deeply into the affairs of the police department. That in turn would likely mean even more reliance upon freelance agents such as Scimidar.

That thought, Cooke hated most of all.

Back near Ground Zero, the object of Cooke's loathing stepped out from behind the car where she had taken refuge, her emotions quickly coming again under her own control.

Seeing the debris and chaos around her, knowing the even greater damage that must have occurred below ground, Scimidar had no doubt her greatest fear would have been realized had the tanker bomb reached its intended target.

A nearby movement caught her eye and she turned to see an automobile rolling very slowly toward her. As it drew close before coming to a stop, she saw that it appeared to be largely undamaged save for a hole smashed in its front windshield.

Her brow furrowed as, through the hole and the spider web of cracks radiating from it, she was able to see the middle-aged man who was the driver of the vehicle. It seemed a hurtling ball bearing had struck the man head-on, blowing out the back of his skull.

Averting her gaze in the opposite direction, she could in the distance faintly make out the glow from the taillights of another car heading away from the scene of the explosion.

That served to remind her that the two men most directly responsible for turning the street of New York into a charnel house—Shadrak and Bolgarus—were still alive and certainly even now making their escape.

Stepping quickly to the adjacent car's driver's door, she opened it and gently dragged the body of the driver out. As she did so, her stomach twisted in revulsion. She didn't like to touch the fully dead, for she felt nothing from them but a cold, empty void that she found to be terribly disconcerting.

Not for the first time, she momentarily flashed onto a recurring nightmare that frequently haunted her sleep. In it, she was locked inside a morgue, where she had no emotions save her own to sustain her. Eventually, even those deserted her, driven out by the total emptiness of death. The results did not kill her, but did drive her mad.

Still, she managed now to handle the slain driver's lifeless body respectfully. She dragged it off the street and onto the sidewalk, where she laid the man out with his arms folded over his chest.

She then took a seat behind the steering wheel of his still-running car, ignoring the blood on its headrest. She didn't like to drive, but she did know how, and did so now as she set out in pursuit of Shadrak's limousine.

Inside that elegant escape vehicle, Shadrak was attempting to calm the rattled nerves of his hired bomber.

"None of this was your fault, Mr. Bolgarus," he said soothingly. "The full payment is yours to keep, and I will make all the necessary arrangements to get you safely out of the country."

"Thank you, sir," Bolgarus replied absently. "But what about you? Won't the authorities be after you as well?"

"Don't you worry about me or my future," Shadrak replied calmly, patting the bomber on the arm. "This is not the end of my endeavors, but merely a momentary setback.

"I've already lined up a dozen credible witnesses who will swear I was in Cuba tonight. Coupled with my not inconsiderable wealth and influence, no one should be able to tie me to this messy little affair.

"The only two possible witnesses against me are Scimidar and her dusky new boy toy, and both of them should be easy to impugn in the eyes of the law.

"That's if either of them is even still alive."

"I think at least one of them may be, sir," N'Tora said from the front seat. The bodyguard/driver pointed to her rear view mirror, in which could be seen a pair of headlights coming from behind them and closing fast.

"We're being followed."

The limousine had just started over the Brooklyn Bridge.

"Stop the car, N'Tora."

"Yes, sir."

"What?" Bolgarus whined. "Why stop now?"

Shadrak ignored him as he opened his door. "Wait here for my return," he ordered his driver. "I'm fairly certain who our pursuer is—and I'd like to deal with her personally for having derailed my lovely plan."

"No!" Bolgarus pled, grabbing at the sleeve of Shadrak's jacket. "This is insane! We can still get away if we just keep going!"

His entreaties were cut off sharply when Shadrak backhanded him across the mouth.

"Do as you're told, Bolgarus," Shadrak commanded as the cowardly bomber cowered against the far door.

"If he tries to leave, N'Tora," he ordered his driver, "kill him."

The impassive woman nodded in silent acknowledgment.

With his ornate walking stick in hand, Shadrak began to stride resolutely back in the direction from which his car had come. Scimidar, behind the wheel of her commandeered car, had barely pulled onto the metal expanse when she saw the man in white captured in the beams of her headlights.

She had expected he and his co-conspirators would turn off either north or south down the FDR Expressway, but was determined to follow wherever he went. She now stopped, exited the car and walked forward to meet him.

As she drew within twenty feet of him, Shadrak raised his cane high in both hands, holding it horizontal to the ground.

"I suppose we both knew in our hearts that it would have to come down to this sooner or later, child," he said. His voice sounded almost sad.

Assuming from his stance that the only weapon he intended to use against her was his walking stick, Scimidar drew her tonfas and held them up in front of her. With a flex of her fingers, the tubular steel shafts sprang upward into sight.

As she resumed walking toward her foe, though, she saw Shadrak twist the shaft of the cane up near its handle—and unsheathe a long and ornately decorated steel sword blade hidden within it.

He tossed away the hollow shaft of the cane and made a few slashing passes through the air with his damascene sword, smiling confidently.

In unspoken response, Scimidar crossed her arms in front of her. With a subtly different flex of her fingers, she caused the metal tubes to retreat back into their housing inside the tonfas, leaving the glistening steel blades exposed and signaling that this would be a fight to the death.

Now it was her turn to smile.

# CHAPTER 36

*W*ith a bloodthirsty yell, Scimidar leaped forward.

Taken somewhat off-guard by the suddenness and savagery of her attack, Shadrak allowed himself to be driven back.

Watching from the back seat of the limousine and seeing Shadrak retreat before the blonde hunter, Bolgarus the bomber grew even more frantic and afraid.

"Get me out of here!" he demanded of the driver. "This is his fight, not mine. I want no part of it!"

The woman N'Tora, turned in her seat to watch the battle, said nothing to the mercenary, merely fixing him with a look of complete and utter contempt before returning her gaze to the struggle being waged nearby.

It seemed clear that the fight excited the woman, emotionally and possibly even sexually. The very thought sickened Bolgarus.

Desperate to escape, he grabbed the neck of the champagne bottle from which he and Shadrak had been drinking and which was resting on the seat beside him. Before N'Tora could notice or react to what he was doing, Bolgarus swung the bottle and struck her in the face.

The woman's head snapped back, blood spurting from her nostrils, and she slumped over against the steering wheel.

Bolgarus clambered out of the back seat, snatched open the driver's door, grabbed the dazed N'Tora's coat collar and roughly dragged her out of the car. After callously slinging her to the pavement, he hopped back into the limo and drove away.

Behind him, dizzy and bleeding but still conscious, N'Tora managed to rise up on trembling legs. From the shoulder holster worn beneath her jacket, she drew her .45 caliber pistol. Shaking her head to dispel the cobwebs, spreading her legs for balance, she fired several shots at the fleeing automobile.

The limousine's rear window shattered and one bullet struck home, burrowing into Bolgarus' back just inches below his neck.

Jerking convulsively, he released his grip on the steering wheel. The slug had not killed him instantly, so he was fully aware as the limousine swerved out of control and headed toward the guardrail of the bridge.

He knew he should do something to save himself, but his mind had quickly grown sluggish and his limbs refused to obey his commands to move. A stench filled the car, a smell he realized came from his bowels involuntarily voiding.

He tried to scream, but no sound emerged from his throat as the limo flew off the bridge. Its impact with the unyielding waters below finished the job the bullet had begun.

Stavros Bolgarus would build no more bombs.

Back on the bridge, the woman N'Tora's thoughts had already left him and returned to her master. She moved toward the end of the bridge where he was locked in combat with the blonde hunter.

Should the unthinkable happen—should Shadrak lose the fight or even appear close to losing—N'Tora meant to kill Scimidar.

After taking only a few steps in their direction, though, her brain began to reel from the effect of the blow to the head she had received. N'Tora fell to her knees, gun dropping from her hand, then pitched forward unconscious.

Neither Scimidar nor Shadrak took note of this. Every thought, every ounce of energy was devoted to their struggle.

Scimidar lunged at her foe with one blade. He nimbly sidestepped and brought the pommel of his sword down on the back of her neck. She rolled with the blow, arching her back and crossing her blades to stop an overhand slash of Shadrak's blade.

She leaped up, swinging both blades and again pushing him back even as he rapidly parried her instruments of death. He thrust his own blade and Scimidar hissed as it slid along her left cheek, drawing blood. So close were they now that she was able to pop the butt of one tonfa into the man's ribcage. Grunting, he staggered back several steps.

A sadistic grin twisted Shadrak's features and he whipped his sword back and forth in the air.

"You should know," he declared, "that I don't intend to stop with killing you.

"I'll see to it that everyone you love dies as well. And I'll finish by burning your fine old house to the ground."

His bravado wavered slightly when the woman smiled back at him.

"I know you're trying to anger me," she said, "in hope that I'll let that anger guide my attacks and give you the advantage. But you forget that I feel all your emotions as well as my own.

"And the strongest emotion I'm feeling within you right now...is *fear.*"

With an inchoate scream, Scimidar again sprang forward, both blades flashing. Shadrak managed to deflect them, but the fury of her attack again drove him back.

He continued to retreat until he slammed into the guardrail of the bridge and could back away from her no farther. He tried to counterattack, but Scimidar expertly parried his thrusts and swings, surrendering no ground. Shadrak lunged forward. Even as she parried his blade, Scimidar pirouetted, spinning in a full circle.

And then plunged both of her blades into his abdomen.

Shadrak's sword dropped and his hands fiercely gripped at the railing. Pushing her blades deeper into his belly, Scimidar drew closer, until her face was close to his.

"To die will be an awfully big adventure," she said, smiling wickedly. Even in his state of shock and pain, Shadrak recognized the line.

It was from *Peter Pan.*

Next, to the man's amazed and stunned horror, Scimidar leaned in closer still and kissed him lightly on his trembling lips.

A gagging cough issued from his throat as she then shoved him away from her. As she did so, her twin blades pulled free from Shadrak's body, which flipped over the railing and toppled toward the river below.

Scimidar leaned over the guardrail, eyes wide, breasts heaving. The excitement of the battle, the thrill of the killing thrust had left her in a nearly ecstatic state of being. She raised one of her tonfas and gazed at it with glassy eyes, almost mesmerized by the sight of Shadrak's dark blood slowly flowing down the shining blade.

As if not fully conscious of her own actions, she slowly drew the blade closer to her face. The black viscosity of Shadrak's life essence fascinated her.

Her tongue reached out and slid up the flat of the blade, collecting some of the blood and transporting it to her waiting lips. Eyes closed, she moaned softly.

At the sound of a gasping noise her head and body spun around, tensed for further combat. Standing a few feet away, numbly staring at her, was Gitano.

He had a rather stricken look on his face, seemingly sickened and repulsed by what he had just witnessed. Scimidar wasn't really sure what he was feeling; again his emotions proved to be strangely, maddeningly difficult for her to read.

The whole time he stood staring at her he said not a word, nor did she.

Shaking his head slowly, he at last turned away from her and walked haltingly toward his waiting motorcycle. Boarding it, he gunned the engine so as to spin the bike around, then roared away into the night.

Left standing alone, Scimidar was frozen in place. Her entire body then jerked and she took a few steps forward, meaning to follow after Gitano. But then she stopped, realizing it would be pointless. The strength draining from her, she dropped to one knee.

As she did so, she spied a dark stain on the pavement: one caused by freshly spilled blood. She dipped a fingertip in it and raised it to her lips, tasting the scarlet liquid. She knew that it belonged to neither her nor Shadrak.

It had to have come from Gitano.

# CHAPTER 37

*T*hree days had passed.

As the evening shaded the canyons of the city, Gitano Rosa, astride his Electra Glide, pulled up to the private exterior entrance to his quarters below *The Velvet*.

He didn't want to enter his home through the nightclub itself, as was his customary practice. He was simply not in the mood for the girls and their playful clinging, or even for Mother Fucher's solicitous petting.

Unseen by him, Mother was watching his arrival from the window of her ground floor private office. As she took a slow drag on one of the strong Turkish cigarettes she favored, her heart went out to this young man who had become so dear to her. She knew there was nothing he would allow her to do for him now. He wouldn't even tell her what was bothering him so.

But she was certain it had something to do with that strange, compelling woman. Scimidar.

Entering the bedroom of his quarters, Gitano did not bother to turn on the light; the faint glow given off by a small lamp in the living room provided all the illumination he needed or wanted. He carelessly tossed his leather jacket aside and peeled off his shirt.

Self-applied bandages covered a variety of wounds and abrasions on his torso. He scowled as he looked down and saw blood seepage evident in the gauze pad covering the worst of his injuries: the laser burn in his side.

Gitano hadn't wanted his sister Emelita or his mother to know how badly he had been injured, so he had tended to it and his other badges of pain himself. Poorly.

The off-key wail made by someone blowing from one end to the other of a harmonica suddenly assaulted his ears. Reacting instinctively, he spun around in a crouch. His right hand slapped his thigh; only then did he remember his shattered mare's leg no longer rested there.

He relaxed, though not completely, when a familiar figure separated itself from the shadows in a far corner of the room and into the light. Scimidar had the look of a penitent on her face and was holding both hands behind her back.

She was not in her dark night suit now, but rather was wearing an extremely short and rather diaphanous off-white dress. So sheer was the garment that even in the dim light Gitano could see that she was wearing tiny panties but no other undergarments.

Her firms breasts jiggled but slightly as she moved and her nipples pressed for release against the light material covering them. Against his will, Gitano felt himself physically responding to the sight of her, to the memory of their fierce lovemaking.

"Do you think you could teach me to play the harmonica?" she asked sheepishly.

"I doubt it," he replied gruffly. "It sounds like you're tone deaf."

Scimidar bit down on her pouting lower lip, and Gitano found even this small gesture to be strangely arousing.

As for her, it was greatly bothersome that she was again having such a difficult time reading his true feelings. Especially now, when she wanted to do so desperately.

"I brought you something," she said, sliding a short, rectangular mahogany box from behind her back and holding it out to him as a peace offering. She had no choice but to take the initiative and follow her own instincts in trying to reach out to this striking man who had so quickly come to mean more to her than she liked to admit even to herself.

"It's a new mare's leg rifle," she told him. "I found what was left of the old one on the street where you left it. It was beyond repair, so I replaced it."

"You didn't have to do that."

"I wanted to."

"Suit yourself," Gitano growled.

The harshness of his response cut Scimidar to the quick. She was sadly certain that when he had witnessed the sadistic joy she had taken in dispatching Shadrak, the perverse pleasure she had derived from taking his blood into her mouth, Gitano had been so repelled that he would never allow her to reenter the circle of his life.

She set the mahogany box down on a chair and took a tentative step toward him, still hoping against hope. Her eyes widened as they lit for the first time upon the ugly wound in his side.

"You're hurt!" she gasped breathlessly.

Gitano stared at her intently. He wasn't sure if she was speaking only of his physical wound. As always, he found himself confused in the presence of this lovely, deadly woman, less certain. He didn't much like that feeling.

"I can see you didn't make it through that night unscathed, either, chica," he said. Up close, he could now see that she had used make-up to disguise the discoloration of a cut on her left cheek. He suspected there were other wounds he couldn't see.

"Pain disappears," she said softly. "Only memory lingers."

She stepped closer and laid her hands on Gitano's chest. At her touch, both man and woman felt an electric tingle course through them. With little resistance he allowed her to push him back until he dropped down to sit on the edge of the bed they had shared on that night that now seemed impossibly long ago.

Kneeling down before him, Scimidar gently peeled back the gauze patch from the wound in Gitano's side, gasping at how horrible it looked.

"You haven't taken care of this properly," she scolded mildly.

"I did the best I could."

She rose and walked into the adjoining bathroom, returning a few minutes later with a pan of warm, soapy water and a variety of antiseptics and fresh bandaging. It spoke volumes to her about the lifestyle of this unusual man that he found it necessary to keep such quantities of medicinal material on hand.

Neither of them spoke as she gently bathed the wound in his side. Neither of them knew what to say. He winced slightly as she placed an antiseptic-soaked gauze bandage over the wound and wrapped his torso.

She continued on, nursing his various lesser injuries, including the twin holes marking the passage of a bullet completely through his right shoulder. The last injury to which she applied antiseptic was on his forehead.

With her face close to his, they stared deeply into each other's eyes for long moments. Hers moistened slightly.

Scimidar sank down to one knee and laid her head in the man's lap.

"I'm not going to change, Gitanito," she said sadly.

"I know that," he replied with resignation. "Just like I know any man who's crazy enough to stay near you has a good chance of having his wings burned off."

"I understand," she said, her voice so low and soft it was barely a whisper.

"Does that mean I'll never see you again?"

"Are you kidding?" he declared to her surprise. He gently took Scimidar's face in his rough hands as she looked up to see he was smiling.

"Sweetheart...I've always wanted to know what it would feel like to fly into the sun!"

# EPILOGUE

**I**nside a small private hospital in upstate New York, a woman strode toward a specially reserved room.

N'Tora had mostly recovered from the injuries she had sustained the night she had driven Shadrak to his fateful battle with Scimidar. Her eyes were blackened and her broken nose bandaged, but she was otherwise in fighting shape once more.

As she walked down the sterile, antiseptic corridor, her mind flashed back to the moment when she had regained consciousness on the Brooklyn Bridge—just in time to see her master topple over the guardrail.

She had made no effort to attack Scimidar or attempt to stop her from leaving the scene. Even in her dazed and weakened state N'Tora knew this would have been an exercise in futility, probably resulting in her own death.

Instead, she had used what remaining energy she had to rush down to the nearest pier on the East River below. At gunpoint, she had forced the aged captain of a small boat to take her out onto the river.

By use of a small searchlight, she had at last found Shadrak's body floating face up in the cold waters. The man's penchant for wearing white clothing had helped make the search in the dark much easier.

To N'Tora's delight, when she fished him out of the river and onto the deck of the boat she had discovered he was still breathing, if barely. Contacting other members of his core group of elite bodyguards, she had supervised his transport to this small but state of the art facility, which Shadrak himself had funded and owned.

As N'Tora now approached his personal wing of the hospital, she noted with satisfaction that two other bodyguards were on duty as ordered. The two women, each a near clone of herself, were standing alert and vigilant on either side of the door. N'Tora nodded sharply to them before entering the quiet room.

Inside, a doctor and two nurses were efficiently attending to their patient. Shadrak lay abed, swathed in bandages and attached by tubes and wires to an IV bag and various monitoring devices.

N'Tora stopped just inside the door, waiting stoically and patiently as the caregivers went about their duties. Finally, the nurses turned to depart, with the doctor following not far behind them. He stopped as he drew closer to N'Tora.

"Mr. Shadrak must not be disturbed or upset," the physician instructed her. "He needs all the rest he can get." He swiveled his head, looking back at his possibly moribund patient.

"Given the severity of his wounds, the subsequent loss of blood, the broken bones and internal injuries he's sustained—it's a miracle the man's alive at all. He must have the constitution of an ox and the will of a martyr."

N'Tora made no reply, save to nod her head in acknowledgment of the doctor's admonishment. The man shivered involuntarily as he looked at the sphinx-like visage of the woman whose eyes were hidden behind mirrored sunglasses. He then pushed his way out of the room.

In truth, N'Tora had no intent but to stand guard over her employer. But a few minutes after the physician left, she was looking on in surprise as the heavily sedated Shadrak laboriously lifted his right hand and motioned her forward with two fingers.

Quickly stepping close to his bed, N'Tora saw Shadrak's lips moving weakly as he attempted to speak. She bent forward, placing one ear close to his mouth.

"She...was right. Scimidar was...right," the billionaire moaned, the effort clearly taking most of his strength.

"Someday...I'll kill her."

## -THE END-

# LUCK BE A LADY

*M*any years ago, someone asked me if the character *Scimidar* represented what I pictured as being my ideal woman. My succinct, yet artfully and delicately eloquent response went something like this:

"Oh, *hell* no! That bitch is *crazy!*"

Most people don't know this, but in her very earliest incarnation, Scimidar was not even *human*.

At least not a human from this planet.

One of my earliest comic book characters to ever see print (albeit only once, in a back-up story in an obscure one-shot comic entitled *Elite Presents*) was an American Indian named *Deathbringer*.

He was envisioned as being the central character in a science fiction series that might be simply described as "Gunsmoke in Space," in that Deathbringer was one of a small but elite band of galactic "marshals."

That of course meant that there would have to be *other* peace officers who served on the same police force. One of these was to have been a rather wild and tempestuous woman from a jungle planet; a woman sporting an equally wild mane of blonde hair and possessed of empathic abilities that made her a sort of psychic bloodhound.

I called her *Scimidar*.

The name had and has no special meaning or significance. I simply wanted her to have an exotic sounding sobriquet. For no apparent reason the word "scimitar"—the distinctively curved sword wielded by many a hero in Arabic tales—popped into my mind. I simply traded the "t" for a "d," otherwise kept the pronunciation the same—and my girl had her name.

And from that moment till today, she has also seemingly had a life of her own. Somehow, as Arthur Conan Doyle was to Sherlock Holmes, I don't feel that I am so much her creator as I am merely the chronicler of her life and adventures.

It was Malibu Comics that first asked me to produce a comic book series featuring Scimidar, at a time now more than three decades past.

Oddly, the other proposed sci-fi series that initially spawned her never again saw the light of day. Don't feel too badly for Deathbringer, though. I didn't give up on the idea of writing the story of a Native American hero. Changing the genre to one of a purely fantasy milieu and giving him a slight name change, I created *Deathwalker*—in my first prose novel published by Airship 27.

I had made changes in Scimidar as well. She was no longer an alien, and her stories would be set on an only mildly science fictional and slightly dystopian Earth in what would then be considered the "near-future" time of *2005*!

Besides the fact that it was one of the relatively few comics to spotlight a woman as its central character, the book also almost instantly became a bit notorious by also being among the first (aside from the venerable Undergrounds) to be intended for Adults Only.

The series got off to a slightly shaky start, but the ship seemed to immediately right itself once the appropriate artist was brought onboard. His name was (and of course still is) *Rob Davis*, and the two of us proved to be simpatico personally and professionally from the first page we ever co-produced. As Rob himself described the process, he and I always had a great *synergy* together—with each pushing the other to produce his best work.

The character and the series (and I and Rob personally, and Malibu for publishing it) received more than its fair share of criticism, primarily but not exclusively regarding the sexual aspects of the stories. We always just ignored the uproar and told the stories we (and Scimidar) wanted to be told.

Nor was the lady ever an archetypal, noble-hearted heroine. She could be self-absorbed, violent, haughty and cruel. That's precisely what made writing her so appealing to me, though; to take a rather unlikable character and make it so interesting and absorbing that the reader would overlook all the flaws and still be drawn into caring about the character and her fate.

Apparently we did *something* right, because Scimidar continued to roll successfully through a total of seven different mini-series over the next decade before finally coming to a halt in the wake of the massive comics bust of the mid-1990s.

From time to time in the years that followed, fans and friends would ask if there was a chance of me bringing the character back to life—either in comic book form or possibly as a work of prose. But the time just never seemed right, and I was more or less content to move on to other creative endeavors, so I resisted any such urge.

Among those endeavors was an ongoing and extremely satisfying creative relationship with Airship 27 and its intrepid leader *Ron Fortier*, himself a talented veteran of the comics scene. This move also reunited me with old comrade Rob Davis, Airship 27 Art Director.

See where this is going?

It was fate.

Ron asked me to consider writing a Scimidar novel—and this time it *did* seem right. You hold the results in your hands.

What we've produced is not just the next issue of the old Scimidar comics. While old-time readers will be comfortable within its pages, first time readers will find a new experience that will be equally accessible to them.

It includes something that never appeared in any of the dozens of issues of the original series: an "origin story" of sorts, revealing details of the enigmatic lady's early years that have never before been explored or illuminated.

We're all proud of the work we've done and hope you'll agree.

Sometimes…you *can* go home again.

*R.A. Jones*
*March 4, 2017*

# ABOUT OUR CREATORS

*AUTHOR –*

**R. A. JONES** is a native of Oklahoma (originally Indian Territory) where he still resides. R. A. has been a freelance writer and editor for the past thirty years.

His credits include newspaper and magazine columns, articles and short stories. He has been a movie reviewer and commentator in newspapers and on radio. He assisted actor Gary Lockwood (Star Trek; 2001: A Space Odyssey) in the writing of Lockwood's autobiography, *2001 Memories: An Actor's Odyssey*. With Michael Vance, R. A. co-wrote the syndicated comic book and comic strip review column *Suspended Animation* for five years.

The readers of *Comic Buyer's Guide* magazine voted him "Favorite Writer About Comics" in 1985, and in 2006 he was inducted into the Oklahoma Cartoonists Collection Hall of Fame.

He has scripted more than 100 different issues of various comic book titles in his career. Among the more noteworthy are Wolverine and Captain America for Marvel Comics; *Harlan Ellison's Dream Corridor* for Dark Horse Comics; and Star Trek: Deep Space Nine for Malibu Comics. He also co-wrote, for Image Comics, *Bulletproof Monk*, which served as the basis for the 2003 movie of the same title.

His comic book stories, "Cold Hard Facts" and "Three On A Match" which originally appeared in the magazine *Metal Hurlant*, were short films in France.

His novels include *Deathwalker*, *Global Star* (written with Michael Vance and Mel Fox), *The Equation* (co-written with Michael Vance), *The Steel Ring*, a superhero book based on characters from one of the earliest publishers of comic books, Centaur. He also wrote the Western thriller, *Gun Glory* and the sequel; *Comanche Blood*.

*INTERIOR ILLUSTRATIONS—*

**ROB DAVIS** - began his professional art career doing illustrations for role-playing games in the late 1980's. Not long after he began lettering and inking, then penciling comics for a number of small black and white comics publishers—most notably for Eternity Comics, which eventually became Malibu Comics in the 1990's, on their book SCIMIDAR with writer R.A. Jones. Branching out to other black and white publishers and eventually working at both DC and Marvel Rob worked on likeness intensive comics like TV adaptations of QUANTUM LEAP and STAR TREK's many incarnations mostly on the DEEP SPACE NINE comics for Malibu. At Marvel he worked on the Saturday morning cartoon adaptation PIRATES OF DARK WATER. After the comics industry implosion in the late 1990's Rob picked up work on video games, advertising illustration and T-shirt design as well as some small press comics like ROBYN OF SHERWOOD for Caliber. Rob continues to do the odd self-published comic book as well as publisher and designer for his small-press production REDBUD STUDIO COMICS. Rob is Art Director, Designer and Illustrator for the New Pulp production outfit AIRSHIP 27 partnered with writer/editor Ron Fortier. Rob is the recipient of the PULP FACTORY AWARD for "Best Interior Illustrations" in 2010 and 2014 for his work on SHERLOCK HOLMES: CONSULTING DETECTIVE and has been nominated for the same award every year since its inception. He works and lives in central Missouri with his wife and two children.

*COVER ARTIST –*

**TED HAMMOND** - is a Canadian artist who has been creating amazing art for over twenty years. His work has appeared in magazines, ads, books and graphic novels just to name a few. Go to (www.tedhammond.com) to contact him and check out more of his work!

**HE RODE A GUNFIGHTER'S TRAIL**

R.A. Jones

R.A. Jones

# HIS NAME WAS MANKILLER

Young Jason Mankiller never believed his surname was an omen of his future until the Civil War broke out and he joined the Union Army. Fate took him to the fields of Gettysburg. By the time the battle ended, he was sitting atop a small rise surrounded by the bodies of dozens of Confederate troopers. Days later, while drunk, his fellow soldiers had tears of blood tattooed onto his face. From that day forward, the Man Who Cried Blood's reputation spread far and wide.

Ten years later, Jason Mankiller is in Ft. Rogers, Texas, hoping to find a job and bury his past. But the blood tattoo won't let him escape the gunfighter's trail. Writer R.A. Jones delivers an old fashioned western adventure in the grand tradition of Max Brand and Louis L'Amour. Here are pioneering men and women facing the birth of a new American destiny that will demand their blood, sweat, tears and sacrifice. For Jason Mankiller, that promise of a better life will be claimed at the end of a smoking gun.

## PULP FICTION FOR A NEW GENERATION!